To Erna,

Handwritten signature

Fields of Gold Beneath Prairie Skies

Canadian Historical Brides
Book 6 - Saskatchewan

By Suzanne de Montigny

Print ISBN 978-1-77362-531-7
Amazon Print ISBN 978-1-77362-532-4

Books We Love
A quality publisher of genre fiction.
Airdrie Alberta

Library and Archives Canada Cataloguing
in Publication

De Montigny, Suzanne, 1960-, author
    Fields of gold beneath prairie skies /
by Suzanne de Montigny.

(Canadian historical brides ; book 6)
Issued in print and electronic formats.
    ISBN   978-1-77362-531-7   (softcover).--
ISBN 978-1-77362-530-0 (PDF).
    --ISBN 978-1-77362-528-7 (EPUB).--ISBN
978-1-77362-529-4 (Kindle)

    I. Title. II. Series: Canadian historical
brides; bk. 6

    PS8607.E2356F54 2017 C813'.6
        C2017-905281-0
            C2017-905282-9

Dedication

Books We Love dedicates the Canadian Historical Brides series to the immigrants, male and female, who left their homes and families, crossed oceans, and endured unimaginable hardships in order to settle the Canadian wilderness and build new lives in a rough and untamed country.

Acknowledgements

A huge thank you to the following people: To my father, Pol de Montigny for writing his memoirs from which much of my story was taken. To Tim Novak of the Regina archives for aiding me in locating the old homestead near Masefield, Saskatchewan. To Sheila Corneillie and Debbie Simpson for their help in finding my baby aunts' grave. To Yolande Chambers, Georgette Evans, Denis de Montigny, Lilian Ring, George de Montigny, and Lucille Leray for sharing their stories of growing up on the prairies during the Great Depression. To Louise Lupien and Guy Ferland for the information on Dr. Onil Lupien and for their help in finding my great grandfather's home in Ponteix via Face Time. Also to Suzanne Lupien, Onil's daughter for sharing photos with me on a spontaneous visit to her retirement home while in Ponteix. To my writer's group for their endless patience, catching all those little mistakes—Kathleen Schmitt, Rod Baker, Edye Hanen, Douglas Aitken, and Ceil De Young. And to my Beta readers—Stuart West, Madeleine McLaughlin, Joan Donaldson-Yarmey, Darlene Foster, and Louise de Montigny. And finally, to my editor—Kathy Fischer-Brown—for her numerous suggestions that helped me make the book the best it could be.

Funded by the Government of Canada

Fields of Gold Beneath Prairie Skies

Canadian Historical Brides
Book 6 - Saskatchewan

By Suzanne de Montigny

Part I – The Journey

Chapter One
The Soldiers

The shrill whistle blasted, startling Lea. She threw an anxious glance at the train she would board in a few moments, the train that would take her to Canada, thousands of miles from the painful memories that haunted her of the Great War. How could she remain in Belgium after all that had happened, after what she'd seen—so much death and destruction. She wanted a new life, far, far away.

She faced her family for the last time. Tears streamed from *Maman's* eyes.

"I'll never see you again." Maman's words were barely audible through her sobs.

Lea forced down the lump in her throat. "I promise I'll come back to Belgium. It's *not* the last time."

"But you'll be so far away across an entire ocean. And what if there are still Germans waiting in their U-boats? Your ship could be sunk." She burst into a fresh round of tears.

"*Non*, Maman. The armistice has been signed. It's safe now. Besides, I have to go. Napoleon's waiting for me."

"But you haven't known him very long, and you're only eighteen."

Uncertainty at her mother's words threatened her resolve. It was true, the courtship had been short, but hadn't there been many furlough brides, their faces glowing with bliss as they devoted their lives to men they'd only known for a few weeks? At least she'd given him time to make his decision.

Lea's sisters clutched handkerchiefs in their hands while her brothers stared at the ground. Mathilde blew her nose and wiped wet, teary eyes. "Do you really have to go?" she sobbed as they hugged.

Lea nodded. "You know I do. But I promise I'll write."

"As will I."

"And you'll let me know when you find a beau, won't you?" asked Lea.

"If there are any left after the Great War." Mathilde let out a sad laugh.

Lea reached a hand to one of her brothers and kissed both his cheeks. "Good-bye, François."

"Take care," he said, his voice rasping as he attempted to squeeze her fingers with his hand permanently damaged in the war.

"And Camille." She turned to her other brother.

Camille's eyes blinked rapidly. "Keep safe."

"I will."

Then Lea turned to Palma whose eyes blazed with conviction.

"Be strong," Palma whispered in her ear. "I'd come too if I could. I so envy you."

Lea flinched with surprise at her sister's spirit. "Then perhaps you could join us in the new country someday."

Palma's eyes grew distant as though she imagined the possibilities. "You never know. I just may."

The whistle gave its final warning.

Lea lifted the leather suitcase and the bagged lunch Maman had packed and hurried to the locomotive that would take her away from all she'd ever known.

"*Au revoir*," she cried, waving one last time before gripping the railing and climbing the stairs.

The train chugged a slow, rhythmic pulse, steam hissing into the air. The huffing grew faster, the stench of burning coal stinging her nostrils.

Lea stepped into the crowded car, slipping past the other passengers as she dragged her bag to an empty seat.

A man stood up and smiled. "May I help you with that?"

Before she could answer, he hoisted her suitcase up into the rack overhead.

"*Merci, monsieur,*" she mumbled, avoiding unnecessary eye contact as she sat down.

The man nodded, then made himself comfortable on the seat opposite her.

Lea ignored him. It wouldn't be right to engage in conversation with a strange man when she'd soon be married.

Her lips curved up in a private smile as she remembered how she met Napoleon.

It had been a miserable week. The rain had inundated them every day, a ceaseless downpour of cold drops that drenched the streets. Lea had ventured into town a few blocks away, picking her way around large puddles to buy *baguettes* from the *boulangerie*. By the time she arrived in the shop fragrant with pastries and fresh bread, her wet feet squeaked inside her shoes

"Terrible weather, isn't it?" asked the *boulanger.*

"I don't think I've ever seen it rain so much." Lea pulled the hood off her head, irritated the raindrops had spattered her glasses. She removed them, wiping the lenses with a corner of her dress.

"What'll it be today? The usual?"

"*Oui, s'il vous plaît.*"

The boulanger reached over and handed her the two baguettes that would feed her family that night.

Lea gave him the Belgian francs and then hurried home. But by the time she got to the front door, the tips of both baguettes that poked from the collar of her coat were soggy and her shoes covered in mud. She was careful to slip them off since Maman would surely have a fit if even the tiniest bit of muck was trailed in. Ironically, the floor was already sullied. But by whom? Lea heard a familiar voice and groaned. Madame Gagnon, the town gossip had dropped by.

"I couldn't believe my eyes," said Madame Gagnon. "Madame Lambert spent a whole half hour talking to Monsieur Duprés. It was outrageous! If his wife knew, she'd surely divorce him."

Maman let out a helpless breath. "It could be they were discussing business, or maybe even—"

"But what would you expect from such a family?" Madame Gagnon continued as though Maman hadn't spoken. "After all, their daughter ran off with a soldier that she'd only known for a week."

"But there have been many furlough brides. And what harm is there in giving a man something to hope for or to dream of? We have to—"

"But so quickly after breaking it off with her old beau? I tell you, the women in that family are nothing but tramps."

Maman flashed Lea a desperate look.

"I have a mind to tell her husband about their meeting."

"Oh, no, I wouldn't do that if I were you—" Maman said.

"After all, that's what I'd expect if my Jean-Pierre were so unfaithful to me."

Maman's eyes pleaded with Lea. "But they weren't being unfaithful. They were just talk—"

"Well, of course they were being unfaithful," insisted Madame Gagnon.

Lea stood up. "Well, would you look at that!" she said, her voice loud. "It's stopped raining. Perhaps Madame Gagnon would like to take advantage of the change in weather and head home *now* before it starts again."

Madame Gagnon gave her a disparaging look as though she'd been truly insulted, then huffed. "Well, I suppose it's time to prepare supper for my husband."

Maman jumped up from her chair and showed her to the door. "And I'm sure he'll appreciate it. You have a good evening, all right?"

"Yes, likewise."

As soon as the door closed, Maman heaved a sigh of relief. "That woman! She never stops talking. And look at the mud she's brought in. As though I have time to be washing the floor every time she comes to toss her gossip at us. Lea, be a dear and clean it up for me while I start supper."

Lea gave a reluctant nod and fetched the bucket from the back room, filling it with warm water and soap. Grabbing a rag, she knelt on the floor and began wiping away the grime. She had nearly completed the task when a knock sounded at the door. Lea glanced up, pushing aside a lock of thick, dark hair from her face.

"Who could that be now?" said Maman, her brows knitted with irritation. "I do hope it's not Madame Duprés again. Mathilde, stir the onions while I answer the door."

"Oui, Maman," Mathilde said as she took the wooden spoon from her mother.

When Maman flung the door open, two young men stood in the doorway wearing khaki uniforms with knickers that trailed down to high knee socks. They held their helmets in hand, a show of respect.

"Good evening," said one of the men in a strong Québecois accent. "My name is Private Tremblay. I'm a Canadian soldier with the forty-sixth battalion."

"My goodness, you're completely drenched," said Maman. "Please come in."

The men stepped over the sill of the door, looking relieved.

"Thank you," Private Tremblay replied. "We apologize for the intrusion, but our camp is flooded, and our superiors have sent us to find other lodgings. Would it be possible to spare some beds for wet soldiers tonight?"

Lea cast curious glances at the men. The larger of the two had black wet hair slicked back from his forehead—a handsome fellow, really. But it was the other who caught her fancy. A slight man, not much taller than her five feet two, he had dark hair and a little half-mustache—the kind that many men sported nowadays—and the kindest, brown eyes she'd ever seen. *The mark of a good soul.*

As though he felt her gaze on him, he turned and stared at her. Lea blushed. She'd seen that look enough times though she was only seventeen—admiration. Shyness made her turn away.

"Well," Maman replied. "Perhaps my girls could give up their beds tonight for the men who are risking their lives to save Europe from the Germans."

"Oui," Mathilde said, "we can certainly do our share to help the Allies. Lea?" She glanced down at her younger sister. "What do you think?"

Lea regarded the man with the gentle eyes whose gaze was still fixed on her. "Yes, I think we can. We can sleep on the floor of Palma's room."

"Then it's done," said Maman.

The two men nodded, smiling. "Thank you, *Mesdemoiselles.* We'll come back later after we've found places for the other members of our battalion."

"I wish you luck," said Maman, "and if you get here soon enough, there'll be a hot supper for you both."

"Thank you," they each said in turn before trudging off into the streets.

When they returned several hours later, Maman had saved a portion of the stew and biscuits for each soldier to warm his insides. They devoured the meal as though they'd been starved, then settled into comfortable chairs by the hearth where they recounted stories of their home.

Lea listened with fascination as they spoke of their homeland—Canada, the land of promise, a country untouched by the Great War, a nation far from the threat of the Germans.

"I'm from Quebec City," said Jacques, the taller of the two men. "That's where General Wolf beat Montcalm on the *Plaines d'Abraham*. But you'd never know there'd been a war between France and England because everyone there speaks French. It's said the English may have won the battle, but they sure didn't defeat the heart of our people." He leaned back in his chair, his eyes dreamy. "It's such a beautiful place, much like Bretagne, only wilder. I'm so looking forward to going back."

"And me," said Napoleon. "I'm originally from *Trois Rivières*, a town farther up the *St-Laurent* but my father and I, and my two brothers moved out to the new province, Saskatchewan, to get a homestead."

"A homestead?" asked Lea, not recognizing the foreign word. "What's that?"

"It's a plot of land the government gives away for nearly free—a hundred and sixty acres. All you have to do is pay ten dollars and apply. Then, if you clear it, cultivate it, and build a house and barn, it's yours."

"Seems like a good deal to me," said Lea's father, smoking his pipe as he listened, relaxing after a day in the coalmine.

"*Mon père*," Napoleon explained, "already has his homestead and my brothers too, near a town called Wide View. I helped *Papa* clear most of the land, and it's just a matter of time before I apply for mine after this war is over."

Lea found it charming the way Napoleon crowded his words together in the old style of French from the time of Louis XIV.

"It's a beautiful place, Saskatchewan," continued Napoleon. "Miles and miles of flat land as far as the eye can see, and golden fields of wheat. And the skies are like scenes from Heaven—castles, cathedrals, angels, even animals. I've never seen skies like that except in the prairies."

Engrossed by his words, Lea imagined the images in her mind—like postcards she'd seen of France—gentle, rolling hills of pale yellow…or at least that's how it was before the Great War.

"The only thing you'll need now," said Lea's father with a slight smirk, "is a wife."

Napoleon's eyes darted to Lea.

"Papa, really," said Lea.

"Well, it's true. Every good farmer needs one."

Maman rose. "It's getting late. I think it's time we retired for the night."

Lea led the men up the stairs to her room. A small thrill filled her when Napoleon's eyes met hers again.

"Thank you for offering us your room," he said, his admiring gaze unwavering.

Lea felt her face warm. "*Ce n'est pas de quoi.*"

"I do hope we'll have time to speak some more in the morning."

Lea's heart leapt. Offering a reticent smile and a nod, she hurried away, her stomach fluttering.

Chapter Two
The Unwelcome Visitors

Lea had dozed off despite the jolting movement of the train. When she awoke, they were nearing the port town of Ostende where she'd board the boat to Dover, one step closer to her fiancé and her new life. She sat up straight, blinking through sleepy eyes, her brain still in a daze.

The Flemish town had survived attacks by the Germans, with much of the Flemish architecture still standing. She eyed the structures with curiosity—tall thin buildings with false façades, a hook jutting out near the top, undoubtedly used for hoisting furniture from the streets below. So Dutch in flavour. But it wasn't the architecture that fascinated her so much as the damage done to the port by the German bombing. Wreckages of ships still lay in the grey harbour of what had once been a beautiful resort town. How different from the postcards of the stunning beach and hotels her aunt had sent years before. Lea had dreamed of spending a holiday bathing in Ostend's warm waters as waves lapped along the shore; yet here the town lay, grey and abysmal, a reminder of what the Germans had done. She looked away, only too glad to be leaving.

When the train pulled into the station, the man who sat across from her stood up and lowered Lea's suitcase for her, his smile a bit too friendly.

"Merci," she replied, then grabbed the handle and hoisted it up before he could offer her more assistance.

"I can carry it for you if it's too heavy," he said, trailing behind her.

Lea glanced back over her shoulder. "It's okay, monsieur. I thank you for your kindness, but it's not *that* heavy."

She descended the stairs of the train and gazed about at the destruction—the crumpled buildings, the broken roads—until she spied what appeared to be a semblance of normalcy, a dock still intact, a ferry that seemed operational. She walked toward it, uncertain. When she got closer, confusion gripped her, and she swung about. Was this the right place? She'd never been too far from home before except to help fallen soldiers on the field after a battle. She shook away the memories of injured men with opened wounds and bloodied heads. Someone tapped her on the shoulder. It was the man from the train.

"Madame, let me help you, please. You look lost, and I speak the language here."

Lea gave another look about, then gave in. "All right."

"Where is it you want to go?"

"I need to catch the ferry to Dover."

"It's over there." He pointed to another dock.

They walked in silence for a spell.

"What are you going to do in Dover?" he finally asked.

"I'm going to Canada…to get married," she said, her words intended to keep the man in his place.

"Ah, another furlough bride then?"

"Well, not exactly. Perhaps more of a post-war bride."

"And a beautiful bride you'll make." He gave her arm a flirtatious squeeze.

Lea feigned ignorance of the gesture.

Together they walked to the station where he ordered her ticket in Flemish. She handed the money to the agent behind the counter, then turned, and thanked the man.

He accompanied her to the gangplank, then tipped his hat, wishing her luck in her new life before stepping away.

"Thank you," Lea called out, half-relieved, yet slightly disappointed he was leaving. It'd been fun to have a gentleman pay attention to her once she realized he had no ill intentions.

For a moment she questioned her decision to leave Belgium. After all, there were still other men left that one could marry. Hadn't this gentleman just proven that? And how well did she know her little Napoleon? She shook her head. No, she'd made her promise, and the money had been sent for her. She had to go through with it. If only Mathilde had been there.

Perhaps this man would have been a match for her.

By the time she boarded the ferry to Dover, Lea's stomach rumbled. She'd run out of the bread and cheese Maman had packed for her. Carrying her suitcase, she made her way to the small cafeteria on the ferry and ordered tomato soup—small fare for the hunger that consumed her, but with the few bills she possessed, her money had to last all the way across the Atlantic Ocean and to the city named Regina where she'd meet her husband-to-be.

"Regina," she whispered, recalling it had been named after Queen Victoria. *A new city, a new province. Far from all the madness.*

She sipped on the salty soup, and chewed the hard, crusty bread that accompanied it. Thinking of the man who'd helped her, her mind drifted back to the days that followed the soldiers' stay.

"I've never been so itchy in my whole life!" Mathilde had cried, scratching her armpits.

"Did you eat mussels again?" asked Palma.

"No, this is different," said Mathilde. "These are more like bug bites. And besides, Lea has it too."

"You do?" asked Palma.

"Yes, and it's driving me crazy!" Lea clawed at herself.

"Let's see," said Palma. She undid the buttons of Lea's dress and searched. "What do you see?" asked Lea.

Palma let out a scream. "Ugh! You've got body lice."

"Body lice?" exclaimed Lea.

The three girls shrieked.

"What do we do?" asked Lea, jumping about as she ripped off her clothes. "It's so repulsive!"

Lea heard Maman's feet hurrying up the stairs to where the girls danced about in a frenzy.

"What's wrong?" she asked, her eyes wide.

"They have body lice!" said Palma. "It must have been those soldiers."

"Body lice? But didn't you wash the sheets after they left?"

Lea and Mathilde shared a guilty look. "No," they both said at once.

"Then no wonder you have lice." Maman shook her head and tsked. "Those poor men. The conditions they have to live under."

"What'll we do?" asked Lea. "I can't stand this a moment longer."

"It's easy," said Maman. "We'll have to remove all the bedding and find the clothes you've worn since they stayed. Then we have to wash them all with boiling water, and iron them."

"But that's so much work," protested Mathilde.

"Well, you *do* want to be rid of them, don't you?"

The girls nodded.

"Then get started right away."

They worked all day, washing the sheets, blankets, and all their garments by hand, then hanging them outside. It was near nightfall when they deemed the laundry dry enough to take in. They heated the iron on the wood stove and passed it over the clothes and sheets, small pops and crackles sounding as any surviving louse died an unmerciful death. By midnight they were done.

Lea and Mathilde flopped into their bed, exhausted. Mathilde's breathing became regular as she fell asleep, but Lea remained awake, her mind drifting back to the small soldier with the kind brown eyes. She smiled. He'd had such a gentleness about him, a charming sense of humour; yet such pride. She hoped she'd see him again.

A few days later, they heard a timid knock.

It was Palma who answered, swinging the door open with an imperious swoop.

The two soldiers wore sheepish grins as though they'd been caught doing something wrong.

"So, you're back," Palma said, a decisive tone in her voice.

The soldiers shared an uncertain look.

Napoleon stepped forward. "We wanted to come and thank you for your hospitality last week. It was very appreciated."

"Appreciated! Well, we didn't appreciate—"

"Palma, where are your manners?" She yanked her sister's arm. "Let these men in. They're probably dying of thirst."

"Yes, but—"

"No buts. We must do all we can."

As the men entered, Lea's heart flip-flopped. Napoleon was more handsome than she remembered. "May I prepare you a cup of tea and some pastries?"

Napoleon's face shone with gratitude. "Yes, that would be nice." His eyes roved up and down her form, seemingly pleased with what he saw.

Lea hurried to the kitchen and put the kettle on. It seemed to take forever for the water to boil. When she came back with the tea and *galettes,* Maman stood in the center of the room, her arms crossed, a frown on her face, obviously in the middle of a serious conversation.

"How dreadful! To have to live with lice like that," she said.

"Yes, well what else can we do?" asked Jacques. "They're everywhere."

"Let us help you. If you can strip down, we can at least iron your uniforms to kill what's there."

Napoleon reddened.

"Here." Palma reached into the closet and pulled out two thick blankets. "You can put these on while we kill the little monsters."

The two men were ushered into the back room. When they came out a few minutes later, they were wrapped in the covers, their uniforms

24

in their hands. Lea and Palma took each piece of clothing and thoroughly ironed it, the lice sizzling as they worked.

When the men were once again dressed and fed, Napoleon eyed Lea, then addressed Papa. "Sir, if I could have a word with you."

Papa broke into a small, knowing smile and followed him to the door.

Lea and Mathilde listened as closely as they could, catching a word here and there.

"…your daughter…calling…"

"I think he's asking for permission to court you," said Mathilde, her voice a high whisper.

"I hope so." Lea, moved closer to hear more. When she saw Papa reach out a hand and pat Napoleon on the shoulder, she knew they had reached an agreement.

Papa returned wearing a wide grin. "Seems you've picked yourself up a beau, Lea."

Lea's heart leapt. All the itching and scratching had been well worth it.

Chapter Three
The Ferry

After Lea swallowed the last sip of her soup, she settled herself on the main deck, finding a seat as near to the window as possible. Tucking her suitcase under her legs, she glanced about to see how crowded the ferry was. If there weren't too many people, she might have the entire row of seats to herself, a safeguard from lonely men looking for company. She relaxed when an old woman made herself comfortable beside her.

As they sailed away, the land behind them diminished, the greens fading to misty pale blues that disappeared into the haze. She watched the faint line grow thinner until water surrounded the vessel, lapping against the hull, only gray sky visible beyond. Lea's pulse quickened as she remembered her mother's worries. *Could there still be U-boats left that haven't heard the Armistice has been signed? No! Nap said it's official—the war's over, and if he says so, then I believe him.* To convince herself of his words, she pulled out the stack of letters from her bag that he'd sent over the past year and filed through them until she found the one she was looking for.

My dearest Lea,

I'm sorry I haven't been by to see you for some time. You see, I wasn't given leave, though we've been stationed close to Chatlineau a few times. We've been transporting POWs back to Germany from France and Belgium now that the armistice has been signed. You'd think it'd be easy work, but it's not. It's quite sad, really. These men are so thin and broken, and I worry, even though they're the enemy, that they may not survive. My comrades say I shouldn't concern myself after all the atrocities the Germans have committed, but aren't all men equal? Weren't they serving their country the same as we were? Don't they have mothers and fathers who love them too?

Yesterday, I spoke to a German who told me, in broken French, that he had a wife and a four-year-old daughter waiting for him back home. I wonder if they'll find him changed, the way his hands tremble and the way he starts at the slightest sound. He's a haunted man. We weren't the only ones hurt. It's a terrible thing war, where decent men are forced to kill each other because of decisions made by political leaders.

One of our boys told me a touching story the other day. He said that one Christmas, the Allies near Vimy Ridge heard the Germans singing 'Silent Night'. They were so moved, they joined in. Can you imagine? Germans and Allies singing together, each in their own language? Then a magical thing happened. Slowly, they all came out of the trenches, shook hands, showed pictures of their girls. Some even cried together. Others shared what small portions of food they'd received from back home. Then someone pulled out a ball, and they began playing soccer. Can you imagine? Soccer! But it all ended when they heard gunshot in the distance. Their brief Christmas was over. It was business as usual. They shook hands and then lowered themselves back down into the muck of the trenches and resumed shooting. My eyes fill with tears at the thought. What a terrible thing to befriend and kill your enemy on the same day.

But there is one good thing that has come from this war, my beautiful Lea, and that's you. As I sat in the mud-filled, rat-infested trenches before the armistice, it was you who kept me going. I could survive the cold and damp, the trench foot, and the lack of

food just by filling my mind with thoughts of you, your beautiful blue eyes, your dark hair, your charming accent. It gave me something to hope for—a future.
As always, I love you,
Nap

Lea let out a sigh. Her little Napoleon! She never grew tired of reading his letters! At first his correspondence had related the latest news, but as they got to know one another—be it live or through mail—he began leaving small hints, choice words that indicated they might have a life together! The day came when Lea received a short note saying he'd drop by that night, that he had something important on his mind to discuss with her.

"I think this is it," Lea had said to Mathilde in an excited whisper.

"What?" asked Mathilde, folding dried bed sheets, still checking for the telltale signs of lice—a slight blood stain—though many months had passed since the soldiers had spent the night.

"Napoleon is coming—tonight!"

"Tonight?"

"Yes, and I think he may ask me to marry him!"

Her sister's mouth dropped. "Marry him! You can't be serious. You barely know him! He's only been here a few times to see you."

"Yes, but we've been writing back and forth. I know him well enough. He's the kindest man I've ever met. He's funny, he's sweet, and besides, I would like to see these golden fields and blue skies he talks about."

"But you don't know what'll happen between now and then. You could be a widow with a baby."

Lea mulled her words over. It was true. She'd known three of the town's girls who'd been furlough brides only to lose their husbands a few months later on the front.

"You can't rush into these things," said Mathilde. "And what if you marry him and then don't fit into his world. Remember, you're Belgian. And he's asking you to move to Canada, an untamed country."

Lea weighed the consequences of her decision, then replied. "Yes, but I love him."

"But Lea…" Mathilde dug her hands into her hips and gave her a condescending look.

A timid knock at the front door brought an abrupt end to the conversation.

"It can't be him already!" whispered Lea. She pinched her cheeks and bit her lips.

Her sister did a quick fold of the sheets and shoved them into the cupboard while Lea smoothed out her dress. Papa opened the door.

Napoleon stood on the steps in full uniform, his chest pushed out. He reached up, took off his hat and smiled. "Good day, *Monsieur Decorte*."

Papa turned and shot Lea an amused hint of smile. "Lea. Are you in the mood for Mr. de

Montigny's company? Or are you too tired today?" Without waiting for an answer, he said, "I think she's too tired." He made as if to close the door.

Lea rushed forward before her beau had time to flee from Papa's wry sense of humour. "Of course I have time for Napoleon. Come in, come in." She grabbed his arm and dragged him to the sofa where they sat side by side holding hands.

Napoleon looked uncertain.

No wonder! After what Papa just put him through.

They made small talk until dinner was served. When they sat down to eat, he barely touched the fish and potatoes Maman had prepared, wiping his forehead over and over again with his napkin and taking sips of water as though his mouth were dry.

When the dishes were washed and placed in the cupboard, Lea led him to the sofa again while everyone conveniently disappeared except Papa who made an occasional entrance to cast a wary eye on the couple.

"So the war is over now and as soon as we're done transporting the POWs, I'll likely be discharged," Napoleon said after the older man left the room for the second time.

"Oh?" said Lea.

Nap cleared his throat. "Yes, and then I'll be going home to Canada. I'll join my father and brothers in Saskatchewan."

Lea moved closer, hoping for an arm to encircle her. "I'll miss you."

"As I will you." He slid his hand over her shoulder only to remove it again when Maman wandered in and began polishing the silverware.

Lea flashed her an impatient glare, but Maman ignored it and continued rubbing the cutlery until every individual piece shone before leaving.

"Tell me more about Saskatchewan. Have you applied to the government for your *homestead* yet?" She loved pronouncing the English word. It seemed so worldly.

"No, not yet. I'll do that when I get home." Napoleon's face paled. "But I...I...I was wondering if..."

"Yes?"

Papa sauntered in and began sweeping the floor.

Napoleon let out a frustrated sigh and then changed the subject. "We've been lucky with the weather, haven't we?"

"Yes, indeed," replied Lea, throwing an angry look at her father.

Papa pushed crumbs into the dustpan and poured it into the trashcan, oblivious.

"It'd be nice to go for a picnic," suggested Lea.

"Ah, yes, it would. We could pick up a baguette from the boulangerie, then take it to the park."

"That would be lovely."

The grandfather clock that stood in the corner of the room chimed. *Ten o'clock.*

"And we could get some *fromage bleu* too," she added. It was getting late. If Maman and Papa didn't leave them alone, Nap would never propose.

Papa cleared his throat and eyed Lea.

Lea hurled him a desperate glare, the effect obviously not working because he dragged a chair to the grandfather clock and began winding it.

On seeing his actions, Napoleon took in a sharp breath and stood up. "I'm sorry. I didn't realize it was so late. I should be going."

Lea's heart fell. Her lips pressed together in a tight line as she walked Napoleon to the door.

He squeezed her shoulders, and cast a glance toward Papa, before saying, "I'll be back as soon as I can. Maybe in a couple of weeks." He kissed her cheek, then retreated into the night.

Chapter Four
England

Lea spied the pale escarpment in the distance and nearly bolted from her seat. *The Cliffs of Dover!* It was true. They really were white, just as Napoleon had described! She grabbed her suitcase and hurried to the deck. A strong wind tossed her hair about and whipped her clothing. The smell of the sea filled her nostrils. If only she had a camera so she could take photos to send home.

The precipice loomed high above the horizon as they approached. Lea watched in awe, rehearsing the English words she'd practiced for when they landed. She was actually in Dover. Dover! No one in her family had ever been here.

As the ferry docked, the sailors lowered the gangplank while a crowd of people waited to disembark. When the walkway landed on the wharf, Lea took a deep breath and followed them on the wobbly footbridge until she reached solid ground. With excitement in her step, she looked for the signs that led to immigration.

"Passport, please?" said a man in uniform, his hand outstretched when she arrived.

Lea noted the similarity between the French and English words and handed him the document Napoleon had sent her.

"Leopoldine Sylvie Decorte?"

She nodded.

"How long are you planning on staying in England?" he asked, scrutinizing her face and comparing it to the photo in the document.

"I go to Liverpool and then to Halifax. I marry Joseph Napoleon de Montigny."

The man closed the passport, the corners of his mouth drawn up in amusement. "My own sister did the same—married a soldier she met during the war."

His words rushed past her, foreign gibberish. Lea opened her mouth to say, "I'm sorry. No speak English," but before she had the chance, he tipped his head toward the gate and allowed her through.

Leaving the terminal, she took tentative steps forward, and then paused. *Where do I catch the train?* She glanced about, searching for someone to help her who wasn't male.

A woman walked past her, gripping a child's hand.

"*Excusez-moi, Madame.* The train to Liverpool, please."

The woman's eyes were kind. "Yes, it's over there," she said, pointing. "Come, I'll show you."

Lea picked up her bag and followed her to another building.

"This is it." The woman pulled the door open. "See that sign that says Liverpool? Line up there."

"Thank you," said Lea.

It was a slow queue. Her stomach rumbling, Lea checked her watch. When was the last time she had eaten? If only she had the lunch Maman had packed for her, she might nibble on it. The line seemed barely to crawl. Her stomach growled continuously. After twenty minutes, she reached the ticket agent. Taking out her money, she handed it to the man.

"No, I'm sorry," he said, pushing it away. "We don't take Belgian francs here. You need pounds."

Lea's mouth dropped. Her eyes scanned the room for a place to exchange money. Seeing none, panic rose within her. Could her trip be over already?

"But I…need go Liverpool." Her voice quivered.

"I'm sorry ma'am. You need to get some money changed. This is England."

"But…"

"Is there a problem here?" asked a loud, boisterous voice.

It was the woman with the child.

"She's trying to pay with Belgian francs and we don't take 'em," said the man.

"Well, how much is the ticket?" The woman asked, indignation creasing her forehead.

He named his price.

"Then I'll pay for her. Here." She shoved the English pounds forward. "Imagine that, giving immigrants such a difficult time. Have you no heart?"

The man mumbled something incoherent, then produced the necessary ticket.

"I pay you back," Lea said, her voice filled with gratitude.

"Not a problem," said the woman. "Are you hungry?"

Lea gave her a blank stare.

"Hungry." The woman raised her hand to her mouth, pretending to eat.

Lea nodded.

"Well then, let's have lunch, and then I can take you to the bank."

Finding a bench, the woman settled her child first, then sat down. "Here," she said, pulling small pasties from a paper bag and breaking one of them in half. "You can share this with me."

Lea sunk her teeth into the tender crust of the beef pie, desperate to fill her empty stomach.

"My name is Elizabeth," said the woman, pointing to herself. "And this is my son, Henry."

"I am Leopoldine."

"Leopoldine. That's a very Belgian name. It's the feminine of Leopold, right?"

Lea stared at the woman, her lips slightly apart, confused.

"Leopoldine—for woman." Her hands traced a female form in the air. "Leopold—for man?"

Lea gave an enthusiastic nod.

They ate their fare, using gestures to communicate, giggling at mistakes, and mutually admiring the boy. After they finished lunch, the woman led Lea to a bank where they exchanged a portion of her francs to pounds.

"Here you go," said Elizabeth. "That should get you to Canada."

"Thank you," said Lea. "You good person."

"Oh, I'm not much different than anyone else, really. War just brings out the kindness in folk. We have to help each other out." She paused, her eyes meeting Lea's. "So where are you going after Liverpool?"

Lea nodded at the familiar word *where*. "Canada. My fiancé…soldier. We live on homestead."

"A homestead?" said Elizabeth. "You're so lucky." Her eyes grew wistful. "My husband died in the war." Her finger pointed at her chest to indicate a soldier being shot.

"I am sorry," Lea replied.

"It's okay. I still have my Henry." She drew the child close and rested a gentle arm around his shoulder. "At least I have something to show for it. Now," Elizabeth said, gathering up her things and motioning Lea to follow. "Let me walk you to the train."

Lea was glad to have female company. Elizabeth reminded her of Palma, the same self-assured personality. When they arrived at the appropriate platform, the woman waved good-bye. For a moment, Lea felt a twinge of fear at being alone again, but hardened her resolve. After all, in ten days, she'd be with her beloved once again.

Her thoughts drifted to the day when he made an unexpected appearance at the door, his chin thrust forward with determination.

When Papa had answered the door, there was fire in Napoleon's eyes. "Monsieur Decorte," he announced, "I wish to take your daughter for a walk." Before Papa could give his usual smirk and teasing comment, Napoleon added, "To the boulangerie…ah…to buy a cake."

"A cake?" Making a slow turn, he nodded to his daughter. "Napoleon wants to buy a cake. Do you like cake?"

Lea's heart pounded. Could this be it? Time was running out. Napoleon would be headed home soon.

"Oui!" Lea responded, her voice eager.

She pulled her coat off the hook, slipped on her shoes, and stepped outside, taking Napoleon's arm. "What's the occasion?" she asked as they hurried along the brick road toward the bakery.

"Er, I thought we'd have that picnic we'd talked about."

"But a cake—that's expensive, isn't it? And it's not anyone's birthday."

"Ah…"

Their footsteps echoed off the narrow façades of Chatlineau's tidy brick houses as they sauntered past.

"I…ah…"

"You what?" asked Lea, her voice encouraging.

"I…ah…" He twisted his body to face her, his eyes filled with passion. Then he caught his foot on a paving stone and hurtled backward, landing on his behind.

"Napoleon!" she cried, stifling a laugh. "Are you okay?"

His face clouded with frustration and burned a deep red. "No!" he snapped. "I'm not okay." He pushed himself up to kneeling position. "And I won't be until you agree to be my wife!"

"Your wife?" Lea pretended to be surprised.

"Yes. I want us to be married before I leave. We could see the priest—tonight!"

Lea reeled. "Married tonight? Are you sure?"

Napoleon rose to his feet, rubbed the dust off his hands, and then took her into his arms. "I couldn't be more sure of anything in my life."

"But tonight?" She led him to a bench and they sat down.

"Yes. I leave in a week's time. It's the only chance we'll get."

Lea gazed at her suitor, remembering Mathilde's words. "Napoleon, I love you with all my heart. But I don't want to be a furlough bride."

The fire in his eyes gave way to desperation. "But...the homestead...we could be..."

Lea took his hand in hers. "My dear Napoleon, I *will* marry you, but not tonight. Go home to Canada and think on it. You may feel very differently in your own country. You may even forget me."

He gave his head a fervent shake. "I could never forget you," he said, his eyes pleading.

"But you don't know. Go home, and if you still love me after six months, send for me...and then I'll come."

The wind taken out of his sails, Napoleon lowered his head for a moment. Then his eyes met hers, his determination renewed. "So then, can we consider ourselves engaged?"

A small squeak escaped Lea's lips as she threw herself into his arms. "Yes, oh yes!"

Napoleon held her close and kissed her. The kiss was long and passionate and Lea wished they could spend the afternoon in each other's arms—but not until they were properly wed.

"Shall we go back home and tell everyone the news?" asked Napoleon when the kiss had ended.

"Yes, but what about the cake?"

"What cake?"

They shared a laugh.

"Oh, that cake," said Napoleon.

They rose from the bench and walked the final block to the boulangerie. As they entered,

Napoleon seemed to grow a few inches taller, a proud man to contend with. "We'd like your fanciest cake, please, to celebrate...our engagement!"

The boulanger's face lit up. "Engagement! Congratulations! When's the big day?"

"Not for a time," replied Lea. "He's going to return to Canada first to make preparations."

"That's wonderful news," said the boulanger, sauntering over to a line of *patisseries*. "Now, let's see, our fanciest cake. Aha! This one is fit for such an occasion." He pulled it from the shelf and laid it on the counter before them.

Lea eyed the cake. It was two layers thick decorated with white frosting and pink marzipan roses.

"It has strawberry jam in the middle," said the boulanger.

"What do you think?" Napoleon asked Lea.

"It's perfect! How much?"

When the boulanger named his price, Napoleon nearly choked.

"But for our Lea and her husband to be, it's half-price. After all, it *is* near the end of the day."

Napoleon gave a relieved smile and reached into his pocket for the coins.

When they arrived at the house carrying the fancy box, they were met with expectant stares.

"What's the cake for?" asked Papa, a brow raised.

"We're engaged!" Lea announced, clapping her hands together.

"Engaged?" Maman rushed forward and hugged the couple while Papa shook Napoleon's hand and the others offered their congratulations.

"When is the big day?" asked Papa.

Lea explained the plan. When she was done, both parents nodded in agreement.

"You're very wise," Papa said to Napoleon. "And I thank you for taking my daughter's needs into consideration. We're pleased to welcome you into the family."

Supper that night was a thick soup followed by the most delicious cake Lea had ever tasted.

Chapter Five
Liverpool

The train to Liverpool was crowded and damp. The stench of wet clothing and mold hung in the air. Lea looked around until she found the one available seat in the midst of a large family. It was between two children whose noses ran and whose coughs rumbled deep in their chests. She hesitated before sitting down, making one last sweep with her eyes in case someone had given up their spot, but no one had.

The train chugged from town to town, past small villages whose chimneys pumped out black smoke while people huddled inside battling the cold February air. Trees stood bare, their branches stretching into the bleak, grey sky awaiting the warmth of spring.

It wasn't long before the train slowed and snaked its way through London.

London! Again, Lea wished she had a camera so she could send photographs home to her family. Instead, she'd have to compromise by mailing postcards.

The resplendent city she'd always dreamed of was anything but beautiful. Sure, the parliament buildings were majestic, as was the large cathedral that stood close by, its tall clock tower hammering out the time. But the narrow streets were lined with small houses and thin, haggard children bundled up to play in the streets. How difficult it must have been to feed one's family here during the war. Lea shook her head in sympathy, glad of her decision to leave Europe for the pristine but wild Canada.

She reached into her suitcase and pulled out the stack of letters Napoleon had sent. Finding the one she'd marked with a heart, she unfolded it, and began to read.

My dearest Lea,

It's been several months now since I returned to Canada, and it turns out you were right. I did meet another girl. She's not as pretty as you, though, weighing in at a few hundred pounds, and her hair is reddish-brown, but she adores me and follows me everywhere. Unfortunately, she doesn't speak French or English which makes it hard to talk. All she knows is one word—moo! She moos when she wants to be milked and moos when she wants to go out to pasture. And her milk makes the best cheese I've ever tasted. But alas, she doesn't hold a flame to you, Lea.

As you requested, I've taken the time to think things over and have come to the conclusion there is no other woman for me. I still want you for my wife. And the good news is, I've been working on a ranch for several months as a cowboy and have now

saved enough money for your safe passage
to our country. If you still want to come,
then please write to me and I'll fill out the
immigration forms to get your passport.
Papa and Maman are very excited to meet
you. I eagerly await your response.
   Love,
   Nap

Lea recalled how she'd wiped the sweat from her brow when she'd reached the bottom of the letter, totally taken in by his joke. When she read it to the family, they'd all laughed too.

Later, Lea had found Maman hiding behind the kitchen door, wiping her eyes and blowing her nose into her handkerchief.

"What's wrong?"

Her mother took a deep breath and replied, "I'm losing a daughter to the war."

"What do you mean?" Lea asked, laying her arm over her mother's shoulder. How odd their roles had reversed—Lea now mother, Maman now child.

"I was blessed not to have lost a son in battle, nor to the Spanish Influenza, but now I'm losing you to a soldier."

Lea's eyes filled with tears. She blinked them away as best she could. "But Maman, I'll write often. And maybe someday you can come to Canada."

"You know we can't afford that," Maman whimpered through a sob. "Not on a miner's salary."

"But perhaps we'll pay your way. We have a bright future in the new country. We might even get rich."

Her words seemed to soothe her mother who wiped her eyes and offered a brave smile. "That would be very exciting."

Lea gave Maman a warm hug. "Now, let's get these dishes done, all right?"

Her mother nodded and together they washed away the remains of the supper, making small talk as they worked.

A week later, Maman led Lea to her room and shut the door. "I have something for you," she said, handing her daughter a pink box. "Since you won't have a real wedding gown."

Lea thought of the dress she'd chosen to wear the day she would be joined in matrimony with Napoleon. It was her best one—navy blue with small, embroidered flowers.

"What is it?" She sat down and lifted the cover. Lea let out a small gasp. "It's beautiful!" Pulling out a cream-coloured nightgown, she fingered the intricate Belgian lace around the collar.

"It's for your wedding night," Maman said. "I made it for you. Wear your old nighties on the boat and train, but save this one. Then when you get to Regina, wear it. You only have one wedding night, and I want it to be special for you and Napoleon."

"I will," Lea said, throwing her arms around her mother.

The train's rumbling drew Lea from her reverie. She took the letter, and lovingly folded it, placing it back into its envelope, its surface smooth on her fingers. Funny how even just an object Nap had touched could fill her with such a depth of feelings. She reached down and carefully returned it to its place in the stack.

Peering out the window, she watched the landscape glide by—lazy brown hills untouched by war, patches of half-melted snow, forests that reminded her of things to come. How scenic the English countryside was, though winter held fast. She imagined the green foliage and flowers that spring would bring. Too bad she wouldn't be there to see it.

"Would you be likin' a sandwich?" The woman who sat opposite her asked.

Lea observed the meagre offering in the lady's hand, two pieces of bread torn from its loaf, and a rough-cut piece of cheese between. She noted each of the children nibbled on their own sandwich, contented, though one boy coughed through a full mouth, portions of his food spattering on the floor. Her hunger overcoming her fear of consuming a possibly infected lunch, she gave a polite nod. "Yes, thank you." After all, she'd been breathing the same air as the children. What difference would it make? Taking a bite, she was surprised at how delicious it was.

"Where you be from?" asked the woman.

Lea paused as she struggled to understand the English words tinged with an Irish accent.

"Chatlineau," she answered. "I go to Canada…get married."

"Ah, to a soldier, no doubt."

Recognizing the word *soldier,* Lea nodded. "Yes. We get homestead."

"Ah, a homestead, you say. Me husband has gone and moved us all up to Liverpool since our own land in Ireland wasn't providin' the crops we need, us havin' so many children and all."

Lea shrugged and shook her head. The woman had spoken too fast.

She repeated her words, slower this time, accompanying them with hand gestures until Lea caught a word or two, filling in the blanks. Lea gave an exaggerated nod to show she'd understood.

"You know, you should be tryin' to learn as much English as possible," the woman said, leaning over to wipe a dirty nose. "You could learn by readin' the paper. Here." With the same hand she'd use to wipe the child's nose, she dug into her bag and pulled out a wrinkled newspaper, tracing sentences with her finger. "Read a bit every day." She pulled out a dictionary. "And look up the words you don't know."

Lea reluctantly took the newspaper and unfolded it, careful to position her fingers in places the woman hadn't left germs. "Thank you." Her eyes traveled over the page, completely stumped. *How foreign! How overwhelming*. But as her eyes scanned the newspaper, words jumped out at her—similar to French.   *Community…police…government.* Lea's mind raced at the possibilities. Perhaps if she applied herself, she could have a small mastery of the language before she arrived in Regina. Wouldn't Nap be impressed?

When the train stopped in Liverpool, Lea disembarked, thanking the lady who led her large brood to the arms of her waiting husband, relieved to leave behind all the coughing and sneezing. Sauntering away, she searched a nearby street until she found a small book shop and entered, the bell on the door tinkling as she stepped over the threshold.

The shopkeeper gave a welcoming smile. "Good afternoon. Anythin' I can help you with?"

Lea thought out her words carefully. "I want to buy *dictionnaire.*"

The man's forehead wrinkled. "A what?"

"A *dictionnaire,*" she repeated, her face warming at her ineptitude.

"Ah! You mean a dictionary?"

Lea gave a frustrated nod. "Yes. *Français et Anglais.*"

"Ah, a French/English dictionary. Right this way." He led her to a row of books and pulled out the biggest one on the shelf.

Lea smiled despite the hopeless feeling that threatened to devour her. She shook her head, then pointed to her suitcase. "Big voyage."

The man's brow furrowed again. Then his face lit up. "Ah, you need somethin' smaller."

He rummaged on the shelf until he found a hand-held dictionary. "Here ya go."

"Thank you," Lea said, turning the book over to read the price. Her eyes rounded when she saw how expensive such a small item could be, but she decided it would be one of the best investments she'd ever make.

Her mind made up, she strolled to the counter where she picked a few postcards to add to her purchase. She pulled out her coins, examining each one to be sure she gave him the right amount. After she'd paid, she asked, "Which way to the *port*?"

"Where ya going?"

"Canada."

"That's a long way away." He reached down and pulled out a sheet of paper and drew a map, scribbling down names of streets. "Go to dock seventeen. You'll get the best rate there." When he'd finished explaining the route and drawn arrows that traced it, his eyes grew solemn. "And be careful. A nice-looking girl like you could get herself in a lot of trouble."

Lea nodded, pretending to understand, then wandered out into the cold, biting wind, following the crude map until she found the right wharf. Showing the official her papers, she purchased her ticket and boarded the ship.

The vessel smelled of coal and oil, and the seats were worn from the transportation of thousands of soldiers.

"Hey, pretty lady!" a dockhand called out, initiating a volley of hoots from his peers.

Feigning innocence, Lea stared straight ahead as though she hadn't heard. When she found the correct hallway, she opened the door of her room to find two narrow bunk beds and a sink. The stench of bleach assaulted her nose. She wondered who she'd be sharing the room with. Laying claim to the bottom bunk, she squeezed the suitcase under the bed and wandered over to the small sink where she scrubbed her hands of the filth of Liverpool. She sat down on the bed and pulled out the newspaper and dictionary, scribbling definitions of words she found. After she'd written twenty-five, she began memorizing them until the door of her room swung open. Lea looked up to find a pretty, young woman with blond hair, carrying a battered suitcase.

"*Allô.*" She smiled. "I am Marie-Ève."

Lea caught the inflections of her speech, her heart quickening. She answered in French. "*Bonjour!* You're from France?"

"Oui," said the young woman. "And you? From Belgium?"

"Oui!"

"Oh, I'm so glad," said Marie-Ève, placing her hand on her heart. "I was so worried I'd be roomed with a cranky, old lady who only spoke English!"

"And who gave constant lectures about how lazy the youth of today are?" added Lea.

Marie-Ève let out a boisterous laugh. "Oui, exactly."

Lea joined her, their girlish voices pitched high. When the laughter faded, she asked. "So where are you traveling to?"

"Quebec City…to get married!" replied Marie-Ève as she dragged her suitcase in and shut the door.

"You too? I'm going to the new province—Saskatchewan—to get married too."

"Oh, my goodness. To a soldier?"

"Yes!"

"Me too!"

They burst into laughter again.

"Then I guess it's providence that we were roomed together," said Lea. "Here, let me help you unpack. When you're done, you can squeeze your suitcase here beside mine under the bed."

"All right," said Marie-Ève.

Lea took her bag out too. Together, they hung their clothes off the various hooks around the room, sharing funny stories as they worked. By the time they were finished, they were solid friends.

Chapter Six
Voyage at Sea

With Marie-Ève in tow, Lea's life had gained a certain degree of comfort. At least with two girls, they'd be safer from the unwanted attention of men. After locking their door behind them, they walked to the deck to watch the ship's departure from Liverpool. Crowds of people stood below, waving to relatives, hankies fluttering in the air.

"I wish my family were here so they could see me off," said Lea.

"Me too," said Marie-Ève, a faraway look in her eyes, "…all of them."

Lea gave her friend a sidelong glance in time to see Marie-Ève brush a tear away, then break into a brave smile.

"I know, why don't we pretend we know some of these people," said Marie-Ève. "Like that man over there with the brown hat. He looks like my Uncle Charles. And that lady over there in the flowered dress, she's fat like my Aunt Adriane." She began waving frantically. "*Au revoir, Tante Adriane. Au revoir, Oncle Charles.*"

Lea let out a mischievous giggle. Seeing someone who resembled the town gossip, she called out, "*Au revoir, Madame Gagnon.* And a good riddance to you!"

They stood back from the railing and laughed for a full minute.

A few moments later, the boat slid away from the dock.

"We're off to the new world," said Lea.

"I know!" said Marie-Ève, pumping a hand in the air.

They watched row houses and brick industrial buildings drift past. The clip-clopping of horses and wagons intermixed with the rumble of smoky automobiles.

Lea stared with interest at the horseless carriages. "I wonder if we'll be able to afford one of those in the new world."

"Anything's possible in Canada," said Marie-Ève.

The image of her and Nap driving in such a vehicle filled her with hope.

As the boat moved away, Lea scanned the port taking in as much as she could. She vowed to sit down and write postcards to her family later on. Then she'd mail them from Halifax. How excited they'd be to see photos of all the places she'd been.

The city grew smaller and smaller until it faded to a pale grey line on the horizon. As they journeyed farther away, the wind picked up, blowing Lea's hair about. She shivered. "It's getting cold. Let's go inside."

When they arrived at their shared room, Lea pulled out the dictionary she'd bought from the bookstore in Liverpool to use as a temporary desk and began writing home. Her words slanted across the card.

> *Dear Maman, Papa, brothers, and sisters,*
> *I have just boarded the ship to Halifax. So far, everything has gone well. There are many people who are very willing to help out a Belgian girl who has no English, especially single men hoping to get a kiss. I've been fortunate to avoid most of them and have made friends along the way. I am sharing a room with a French girl my age named Marie-Ève. If we stick together we should be okay.*

Lea turned the card to write in the margins.

> *I miss you all and will tell you more as I near Halifax. Please send your letters to Napoleon's address in Wide View so they can be forwarded to me.*

She signed her name in the corner of the postcard, then slipped it inside her bag to mail later.

***

Supper that night was a bowl of thin clam chowder coupled with a stale piece of bread.

Marie-Ève wrinkled her nose when it arrived. "It smells like an old pair of shoes."

Lea dipped her spoon in and tasted it. She grimaced. "It *tastes* like an old pair of shoes."

They giggled.

"But we paid for it, so we have to eat it," said Marie-Ève. "It's not like money grows on trees."

"You're right." Lea looked into her bowl and frowned. "But what's that slimy thing?"

Marie-Ève peered into Lea's soup. "I think it's a clam."

"It looks like a slug."

They broke into another fit of giggling.

"It can't be much worse than eating escargots," said Marie-Ève.

"True. But it makes me feel like I'm eating wartime food again," said Lea. "What did *you* have to eat during the war?"

"All kinds of disgusting things."

"Like what?" asked Lea.

"Pigeons."

"Well..." Lea waved her hand from side to side. "It's sort of like chicken, I suppose. What else?"

"Grass."

"Grass?" Lea gave her an incredulous look.

Marie-Ève nodded. "It's pretty good if you prepare it properly. A little like a salad. But it was the bread I missed the most. It was next to impossible to get a baguette."

"We had bread, but more than anything else, we ate potatoes, potatoes, and more potatoes. I got so tired of potatoes."

Marie-Ève laughed.

"But how *was* the war for you?" asked Lea.

Marie-Ève stopped eating, then clasped her hands together, her elbows resting on the table. "As difficult as it was for anyone, I suppose. We were always hungry. And to make matters worse, my brother André was killed at Vimy Ridge."

"Your brother?" Lea's eyes moistened, glad she still had *hers*.

Marie-Ève nodded. "My mother cried for weeks."

"I'm so sorry."

"Then," said Marie-Ève, "the Spanish Influenza came. Several of the townsfolk died, including my father and another one of my brothers." She sighed. "There were so many people who died that they weren't able to give them a proper burial."

"So what did they do?"

"They threw them into pits like common paupers and covered them with dirt."

"That's dreadful." Lea paused before taking another spoonful of the bland chowder.

"And then there was my best friend, Solange," continued Marie-Ève.

"What happened to her?" Lea felt her jaw tighten, fearing what was coming.

Marie-Ève's voice lowered to a whisper. "She was raped by a German soldier."

Lea's hand flew to her mouth.

"She tried so hard to hide, but still he found her and then…"

Lea closed her eyes, unsure she wanted to know the rest.

Marie-Ève was merciful and left out the details. "She's never stopped being frightened since then. She won't even walk to the boulangerie to pick up the bread in the morning."

"Even now that the war is over?"

Marie-Ève's eyes met Lea's, further words frozen in her watery tears.

Lea was glad the Germans had never invaded Chatlineau, though they were close in neighbouring Charleroi. How terrifying to have a strange man force himself on you.

"And how was the war for *you*?" asked Marie-Ève.

Lea let out a sigh. "Many men were executed for standing up against the Germans when they first began marching across our country, creating havoc even though we declared ourselves neutral. One of my brothers wounded his hand in the battle. And we don't know if he'll ever be able to find a job now."

"Oh, no."

"And our next door neighbour lost all three sons."

Marie-Ève shook her head.

"But I suppose some good came out of it. After all, if it wasn't for the war, we would have never met our husbands, and we wouldn't be going to Canada, right?" said Lea.

"That's true," Marie-Ève replied. "And for that I'm grateful."

"So am I." Lea smiled. Staring down at her spoon, she picked up her napkin and wiped her mouth, then dropped it into the bowl. "I can't eat another bite of this. Shall we go back to our room?"

Marie-Ève shoved her bowl aside. "Yes. Enough of this bucket water."

They let out a last high-pitched giggle as they rose and left the cafeteria.

***

During the night, Lea awoke to the smattering of rain against the porthole of their room. The wind howled, and the ship tossed as it rose and fell against giant waves.

Her stomach heaved. Tasting bile, she jumped up and emptied its contents into the small sink in the room. She fell back onto her hard mattress only to hurry a few minutes later to vomit again.

Within minutes, Marie-Ève joined her, running water down the drain as her tasteless dinner expelled itself as well. "I don't know if it's the chowder or the waves that are making me sick."

"Yuck! Please don't remind me of our supper," Lea said.

"I definitely won't ever order that again." Marie-Ève placed her hands over her stomach.

"I sure hope the rest of the food isn't that bad," said Lea.

Miserable, the two girls spent the next hour lying on their beds moaning.

By three AM, Lea's stomach had settled, and she fell into a fitful sleep, beginning an all too familiar dream.

The sound of shells thundered in the distance, the normally green fields mired with trenches hastily built within. The smell of gunpowder fouled the air.

"We have to find Napoleon!" Lea cried to Palma. "I know he's been hit."

"You don't know that," Palma shouted back over the roar of the gunfire.

"Yes, I have to find him."

The two girls stumbled through the battlefield where injured men lay dying. Mud spattered their clothes. "Be careful," said Palma. "There may be unexploded bombs. Watch where you step."

Lea had heard of the undetonated missiles and how one wrong move could end her life. Looking ahead, she picked her route, following the arches of the craters.

Someone groaned.

Lea headed toward the sound, her boots sucked up by the mire. "There's someone over here," she called back to Palma. Finding the man, she handed him an opened bottle of water.

He pushed it away, then rolled his head to one side.

Lea gasped. Part of his skull had been blown away. But how could he still be alive?

"Help me," he cried, breaking into sobs. "I have a girl. She's waiting for me back home. I can't die."

"The medics are coming." She glanced over her shoulder to be sure it was true. "Just wait, and they'll find you." She made as if to move away.

He reached out with his one good arm and grabbed her. "No, please don't leave me here."

"But I have to go. I need to find someone."

"No, please!" His sobs grew louder.

"But my Napoleon. He may have been wounded."

"No!"

"Let go of me!" she shrieked.

"Lea! Wake up! You're dreaming!"

Lea opened her eyes. She glanced about, confused until she realized she was safe within her berth aboard the ship. Pushing herself up to sitting position, she pulled her sticky nighty from her chest and wiped the sweat off her brow. "I had the worst dream."

"I know. That's why I woke you up." Marie-Ève climbed down the ladder and made herself comfortable on the bed beside her friend. "Tell me about it."

Lea wiped her forehead once more. "It's based on something that really happened. It was before the armistice. I hadn't heard from Napoleon for a long time, and I was worried he'd been wounded. So Palma and I decided to go to the battlefield to find him. We went as volunteers. The smell was atrocious." She covered her nose with her nighty as though the stench were real. "Ever smell a stomach that's been sliced open?"

Marie-Ève shook her head.

"It's hideous. We went from soldier to soldier to see who we could help. And that's when I found a young man who was still alive, even though part of his head had been blown away. I offered him water, but he pushed my hand away, then died. I've never been able to get him out of my mind. I keep dreaming about him."

"But did you find Napoleon that day?"

Lea smiled. "Yes, or rather, he found me."

"Well, then, you must have been happy to see him."

Lea let out a sound somewhere between a sob and a chuckle. "Yes and no. He was furious. He scolded me like a naughty child for stepping out onto a battlefield. I was ready to lash out at him because I'd been so frightened, but then he pulled me close and made me promise I'd never do anything so foolish again."

"And did you?"

"No. It was too dangerous with so many Germans everywhere."

"You're lucky to have such a man," said Marie-Ève.

"Yes, I am." She reached over to the light and switched it on. "Would you like to see his photo?"

"Sure."

Lea pulled out the worn picture she had of Napoleon in uniform.

Marie-Ève gazed at the image, raising her brows. "He looks like a very good person. And nice-looking too."

"Thank you." She kissed the image of her betrothed. "That's why I love him. What about you? What does your fiancé look like?"

Marie-Ève rummaged about in her bag and pulled out a small sepia-coloured photo. Friendly brown eyes stared out at them. "His name is Guy."

Lea viewed the photograph, giving an appreciative nod. "He's *very* handsome."

"I think so too." Marie-Ève squeezed her shoulders and giggled. Then she grew thoughtful. "You know, Lea, we have to move forward, you and I."

"What do you mean?"

"We have to forget the war ever happened. I'm through with crying and you should be too. Let's make a pact tonight that from now on, we begin our new lives."

Lea regarded her friend, mulling over her request, then replied, "All right, let's."

"We'll make a toast, then," said Marie-Ève, raising an imaginary wine glass.

Lea raised hers too.

"To Lea and Marie-Ève and their new lives!"

They clinked the invisible glasses. Then Marie-Ève climbed back up to her bunk, and Lea lay down, pulling the covers over herself. The ship had stopped pitching, and she fell into a deep, peaceful sleep.

Chapter Seven
Halifax

Lea awoke to a sore throat and a fever. Her muscles ached, and she felt nauseated. She tried to sit up, but dropped back down on the narrow bed.

"Marie-Ève," she croaked.

Her friend's face appeared at the edge of the top bunk. "What's wrong?"

"I think I have the Spanish flu!"

Marie-Ève gasped. "What? Why?"

"Because my muscles are throbbing, and my throat hurts. Ohhhhh," she moaned.

Marie-Ève leapt down from the top bunk to feel Lea's forehead. "Oh, dear! You're burning up!"

"I know! What if I never see Napoleon again? After all I've been through with this stupid war and this sea sickness, and now we might never be reunited." She broke into heartfelt sobbing.

"Nonsense!" insisted Marie-Ève. "You've probably just caught a cold."

"No, it can't possibly be a cold because it hurts everywhere. I'm sure it's the Spanish flu." Lea wailed.

Marie-Ève looked frozen with fear. Then she sprang into action. "I'm going to get the doctor."

"Yes, please hurry!"

The young woman threw her clothes on and left. Fifteen minutes later, she returned, an older gentleman in tow.

The old man's white, bushy eyebrows rose and fell as he spoke. "What seems to be the problem here?" he asked, his French coloured with a thick, German accent.

Lea flinched at his inflections but decided she couldn't be picky. She was dying, after all. "Everything hurts, and my throat is sore."

"And she's been vomiting too," said Marie-Ève.

"Sit up and let's have a listen." The doctor made himself comfortable on the edge of the bed.

Lea slumped forward.

He pushed the ends of the stethoscope into his ears and laid the diaphragm on her back, tapping and listening. Then he placed it carefully on her chest. His forehead creased as he listened. "And you say you've been vomiting?" he asked.

Lea nodded. "Ever since we left Liverpool."

"Ever since you left Liverpool, you say?" He whistled on the letter 's'.

"Yes." She whimpered.

He tilted his head in amusement. "There's hardly a passenger on this ship who hasn't gotten seasick. The waters *have* been very rough. It's what happens when you travel across the Atlantic in the winter. As a matter of fact, I've been mighty busy treating patients for nausea since we left port."

"But what if it's the Spanish flu? I'll die and—"

"Oh, I doubt it is." He took the stethoscope from around his neck and pushed it back into his bag. "Have you been near anyone with a cold lately?"

Lea's crying stopped as though a great revelation had come to her. "The family on the train! They were all coughing and sneezing…and I ate one of their sandwiches."

"Ah," said the doctor, holding up a decisive finger. "That was probably it. You weren't careful enough. You must wash your hands all the time. Especially since the Spanish flu hasn't been eradicated yet and won't be for some time. Now you get some rest and I'll come back later to check on you, all right?"

"Thank you," said Lea. "But what do I do about the fever and the aches?"

The doctor sighed. "Unfortunately, I can't do much since there is no pharmacy on the ship. Otherwise, I could give you the new miracle drug called aspirin that can cure the worst of fevers. I'm so sorry."

"It's okay." Lea lay back down.

Turning to Marie-Ève, he said, "Keep her forehead cool. Lots of cold compresses. The water from your sink will be nice and chilly."

Marie-Ève nodded.

By the next day, Lea's fever *had* decreased and the aches in her muscles had all but disappeared, but she was left with a hacking cough and a runny nose to go with the nausea from the constant rolling of the ship. She remained huddled in the cabin for most of the trip while Marie-Ève sat on the main deck, making periodic returns to see how her friend was faring.

After an exhausting week, Lea awoke in the night to stillness. The pounding of the rain had ceased as had the relentless tossing and pitching of the vessel. All was quiet. She lay in the dark, listening, wondering, until curiosity called her. Rising from her bed, she slipped her coat on over her nighty, careful not to wake Marie-Ève.

Feeling around in the dark for the handle, she pulled the door open ever so slowly. It groaned in protest.

"Where are you going?" asked Marie-Ève, her voice thick with drowsiness.

"I think we've stopped moving," Lea whispered. "I'm going up to have a look."

"But you can't go alone. It could be dangerous."

Lea paused. "I forgot about that."

"Wait for me. I'll come with you."

Lea stood by the door until Marie-Ève dressed. They slipped into the dim-lit hallways, avoiding anyone who might still be awake.

The corridors of the ship were hushed, an occasional snore disturbing the quiet as the girls crept up the stairs and onto the main deck.

Lea opened the door that led outside, catching her breath at the beauty. Tiny pinpricks of stars like needlepoint and a full rising moon lit up the sky. The waters, like glass, reflected their splendour. A soft breeze caressed her face, a welcome respite from the near gale that thrashed her hair and clothes about. But it was what she saw above her in the distance that filled her with awe.

"The Aurora Borealis!" she exclaimed.

The girls watched as glowing pillars of green and blue lights danced in the sky, rising and falling like giant angels.

"I've always heard of them, but I've never seen them," said Marie-Ève.

"I've seen them once before—on a night like this about a year ago. The guns had been blasting in the distance all day until they finally quit for the night. And that's when they appeared…like some kind of promise that beauty still existed in the world despite the war, and that one day, the earth would heal itself again."

They stared in silence, mesmerized by the play of lights above them.

"Perhaps it's a sign of what awaits us in Canada," Lea said.

"It'd be nice, wouldn't it?"

"Yes."

Her eyes traveling further, Lea spied a ghostly image in the distance. She squinted to see what it was. A shiver ran down her spine. "An iceberg!"

Marie-Ève gasped. "Like the one that sank the Titanic!"

Lea hugged herself. She'd read the stories in the paper about the great ship that had struck an iceberg only seven years earlier and how the disaster took countless lives. Wasn't it on such a night as this—calm and serene? "Perhaps that's why they've got the engines so low," she said. "To navigate through them."

"Maybe."

They watched, entranced, as the ship crawled through the motionless waters, tracing wide arcs around the menacing phantom figures until dawn crept in, a thin line of light hovering over the opposite horizon.

"It's nearly daylight," said Lea. "We'd better get back before the crew rises.

"All right," agreed Marie-Ève.

They made their way down the stairs on quiet feet. When they got to their room, they crawled into their now-cold beds and slept the rest of the night. Lea smiled as she drifted off. Soon they'd be in Halifax and on the final leg of their journey, another step closer to her Napoleon and far from the ruthless ocean that made her life a misery.

***

A few days later, Lea and Marie-Ève stood on the deck with their luggage, watching as the port of Halifax grew larger and larger.

"Something's not right." Marie-Ève frowned.

"What do you mean?" asked Lea.

"It looks like it was bombed, but how can that be when the war was fought in Europe?"

"Didn't you hear what happened here a year-and-a-half ago?" asked Lea.

"No, what?"

"Two ships collided in the harbour. One of them was loaded with ammunition."

Marie-Eve's eyes widened. "Oh, no!"

"It was a terrible thing. First the explosion, and then the tidal wave. Entire buildings were destroyed. More than two thousand people were killed. Some of them were young children on their way to school. Others were blinded by bits of glass when the windows shattered inside their homes."

"Oh, how ghastly!" whispered Marie-Ève.

As the ship drew nearer, Lea scanned the town. City blocks had been wiped clean of any houses, while others were only ghosts of their former selves.

But despite the desolate scene that lay before them, Lea's stomach fluttered as the ship approached. She was glad to be leaving the shifting decks of the vessel for stable ground because it meant she would soon be in Napoleon's arms.

It seemed to take the sailors forever to lower the gangplank and to remove the chain that separated them from the new world. When they finally did, Lea and Marie-Ève hurried down.

After they'd cleared immigration and left the building, Lea knelt and dug her fingers through the snow until she felt the earth.

"First Belgium, then Dover, then Liverpool, and now Halifax," she murmured to herself.

Marie-Ève gave her an inquisitive look.

"Those are all the cities I've passed through on this voyage."

Her friend's face lit up with comprehension. "Okay! For me it's from St-Malo, to Dover, to Liverpool, and to Halifax."

Lea pumped mittened fists in the air. "Do you know what this means?" Without waiting for an answer, she said, "We're almost home!"

"I know. I can't wait to see my Guy! Let's buy our train tickets and then explore the town, okay?"

Lea hesitated. "I don't know," she said, eyeing the wreckage with trepidation. "This reminds me too much of Europe. I mean, isn't this what we're trying to get away from?"

"But we may never return. Let's go see what we can so we can tell our grandchildren someday."

"All right, then," said Lea.

The girls made their way to the temporary structure that had replaced the battered railway station and bought their tickets. Finding a small diner close by, they ate fish and chips. Then they wandered through the streets past lots, empty except for piles of stones that once marked their foundations.

"Look over there at that domed building." Lea pointed.

"It's like a skeleton," said Marie-Ève.

Lea hugged herself. "It must have really been quite a blast."

"I can't imagine how they survived over the past two years."

"Nor I," said Lea.

They continued to walk through streets where mounds of rotting lumber that once housed families balanced precariously, ready to topple, and where dead grass poked through snow. It eventually led them to the graveyard.

"Do you want to go in and have a look?" asked Marie-Ève.

Lea's forehead wrinkled. "But why?"

"I don't know. I like graveyards. Each tombstone tells a story. Like this one, for example." She pulled Lea inside the gates. "This lady died when the Titanic sank, and look, she's buried with her child. Can you imagine the anguish her husband must have suffered?"

Lea shook her head. "It must have been horrible."

"And here's an entire family that died from the blast—an *entire* family!" said Marie-Ève

Lea read the epitaph.

"And look at this really old one," Marie-Ève continued, "a child who died of smallpox."

"Poor thing." Lea's teeth chattered. "Let's get out of here before we freeze to death and join them. I'm so cold."

"Me too."

They trudged back to the station, their breath steaming in the frigid air. When they walked through the door, they clapped their hands to warm them up, then waited for the train that would take them away from the scene of tragedy and death to their new lives far away from any reminders of the war.

Chapter Eight
To Regina

A few days later, the train approached Quebec City from the opposite bank of the St. Lawrence River, leaving the destitute city of Halifax far behind. Lea watched as the town transformed from a thin grey line to an impressive European skyline.

Her friend's eyes were wide with wonder. "This is so much like my *Bretagne!*" she exclaimed, her voice teeming with excitement. "The buildings are almost the same. What a pretty place. And look—there's Château Frontenac!"

"Château Frontenac?"

"Yes, it's a hotel the railroad built!"

"A hotel? Really? Wow! It looks like a castle. Perhaps Guy will take you there for your honeymoon."

"You never know." Marie-Ève wiggled her eyebrows up and down.

Lea watched as they approached the magnificent structure. Every nerve in Marie-Ève's body seemed to have come to life as the train pulled into the station, sputtering out a final puff of steam as it drew to a halt.

Marie-Ève leapt from her seat. "I see him! I see my Guy!" She waved frantically.

Without even so much as a good-bye, Marie-Ève grabbed her suitcase, and nearly bowled Lea over as she slipped past and raced down the stairs into the handsome man's arms. Lea's shoulders drooped as the distance between them grew. She let out a despondent sigh, then reached down for a newspaper to keep her busy for the next little while. But before she had a chance to open it, Marie-Ève reappeared beside her.

"Come meet my Guy!"

Swallowing her disappointment, Lea raced after her into the chill air.

"This is Lea," Marie-Ève said when she found her fiancé again. "We shared a room together on the boat. We're the best of friends, and she's going to Regina to get married."

Guy bowed deeply and kissed her hand. "*Enchanté, mademoiselle.* Perhaps some day you can visit us with your husband."

"I'd love that." Lea smiled.

"Yes, we must exchange addresses," said Marie-Ève, opening her bag to find a pencil and a scrap of paper.

The train whistle blew.

Lea gasped. "Oh, no! It's leaving."

"Wait. Don't go yet." Marie-Ève rustled inside her bag. "I didn't get your address. We have to keep in touch."

Lea shot a frantic look over her shoulder. Steam puffed from the train's smoke stack. "But I've got to go!"

"Quick, Guy. Do you have something to write with?"

Guy dug in his pockets, desperately searching.

The side rods of the train began to move.

"It's leaving!"

"But Lea…" Marie-Ève called, her hand in mid-air.

"Good-bye!" Scrambling up the stairs, Lea hurried back to her seat and waved to the distraught couple until she couldn't see them anymore.

Wiping a tear, she bit her lip. What would she do now that Marie-Ève was gone? She had four days to go until she arrived in Regina.

I might as well make good use of my time.

Taking the dictionary out of her bag, she began circling words in the newspaper, looking them up, and memorizing them.

"I am Lea," she practiced. "Robert Borden is the prime minister of Canada. Last week, the police arrested a criminal. Buy a Ford Model T for only $2,168. A made-to-measure dress from Eaton's department store."

After she'd concocted a few phrases, she took out a piece of paper and attempted to write a practice letter in English.

Dear Prime Minister Borden,

I am a Leopoldine from Belgium. I am coming to Canada because your government is good and because your policemen catch many criminals. Also, I

want to buy a Model T Ford for only $2,168
and order dresses from Eaton's.
Leopoldine Decorte

She chuckled to herself as she reread the letter. How odd the prime minister would find her if he were to receive such a correspondence. Reading through it one more time, she erased the last name and changed it to de Montigny. Satisfied, she folded the paper and put it away.

The carriage she traveled in had numerous empty seats. Lea had placed her bag in the space Marie-Ève had left beside her in her usual attempt to prevent unwelcome male company. Her strategy proved useful, enabling her to sleep lying down that night, bundled up in her coat, hat, and gloves to combat the freezing air of the train. She stirred several times in the night, drawing her limbs closer to conserve heat. When she awoke the next morning and stared out the window, her eyes widened. Vast expanses of forest stretched before her, frozen streams and lakes, and skies a bluish hue caused by tiny snowflakes that fell softly to the earth. Occasionally, she spotted peculiar animals with large, brownish humps and wide antlers who scraped hooves through the snow, searching for bits of grass to chew on.

"Excuse me." She turned to the woman who sat in the seat behind her. "What was that animal?"

The woman smiled. "It's a moose."

"Thank you," said Lea. "A moose," she repeated, writing it down in her notes.

From time to time, the train rolled into a forlorn station surrounded by a smattering of shacks and a water tower. Lea felt a rush of fear. Was this what life had in store for her? But it got worse. As they arrived in Manitoba, miles and miles of flat land spread before her, no vegetation in sight, just white emptiness.

What have I gotten myself into? Do I even know this man? Perhaps Mathilde was right.

The familiar longing for Maman rose inside her, along with a stinging in her eyes. How she would give anything to hear her voice again. She fought a hardness in her throat and wiped her eyes from time to time. Then she remembered Palma's words—*Be strong. I'd come too if I could. I so envy you.* Drawing strength from her sister, she sat up and pushed her shoulders back. She'd made a choice, and she had to go through with it.

A couple of days later, the train pulled into Regina. Lea heaved a sigh of relief when she saw the brick and mortar buildings that lined the streets and the tall church steeples that rose above the town. A domed edifice crowned the city, and telephone poles lined the streets, an assurance of electric lights.

Her body tingled with excitement and trepidation. It had been so long since she'd last seen Napoleon. What if she discovered she didn't care for him anymore? Or worse yet, that he didn't care for her? Taking a deep breath, she grabbed her suitcase and stepped off the train. When she walked into the monumental station, she gazed in awe at the splendour of the marble floors and the dome overhead. Several people milled about, from simple farmers to men in suits and stylish women wearing the latest fashion trend. She scanned the crowd, searching for her Napoleon. Then she saw him…and reeled. This wasn't how she remembered him! Had she been so blinded by love that she didn't realize how bowed his legs were? Had the war marred her vision? He didn't seem near as handsome as he had back home. Her heart pounded. She took slow, uncertain steps toward the man. He flashed her a crooked, leering smile.

Someone called from behind. "Lea!"

She wheeled about, wondering who on earth would know her in Regina besides her betrothed.

It was Napoleon! Her chest rose as she heaved a sigh of relief. She had been mistaken. The other man hadn't been him at all.

Lea ran into his arms and they held each other tight until he took her chin in his hands and kissed her deeply.

"My Lea," he said, over and over. "I've been counting the days, and you're finally here."

"Oh, Napoleon," she cried. "It was so difficult on the ship. I thought I'd caught the Spanish flu and that I'd never see you again.

And I was so seasick the whole way, and…" Tears spilled over her cheeks.

Napoleon wiped her eyes with his clean, white handkerchief, then placed his nose and forehead against hers. "Shhhh. You're here now, and I'm going to take care of you." Releasing her, he took her hand, then hoisted up her suitcase.

"Where are we going?"

"To a friend's house. Then at six o'clock tonight, we're going to be married at the church."

"Tonight?" Lea raised her brows in astonishment.

"Yes. And then afterward, we're going for supper and to see a show."

"Supper and a show?" Lea smiled, thankful that at last she was back in civilization.

***

The marriage ceremony Napoleon had planned was to be simple, the bishop with two priests as witnesses. Lea took out the navy blue dress with the embroidered flowers she'd packed so carefully for the big day and smoothed out the wrinkles the best she could.

When she came down the stairs, Napoleon's face lit up with admiration. "You're so beautiful!"

Lea felt her face warm. "Thank you."

After helping her with her coat, he took her arm and led her to the carriage that waited outside and gave her a hand up. He turned to his friend and thanked him for his hospitality. The man nodded, standing on the sidewalk as they drove away.

When the couple arrived at the cathedral, Lea broke into a grateful smile. What a beautiful church Nap had chosen—St. Mary's—constructed of yellow stone, its one steeple rising above the rooftops.

Nap helped her down from the carriage and led her inside. Lea marveled at the church's grey, marble floors and Gothic arches and at the rosetta window that lit up the altar. A carved crucifix hung beneath it.

They walked up the aisle to where the bishop awaited, flanked by the two priests.

His smile was kind. "You've traveled a long way, Leopoldine."

"Yes." She gave a shy nod.

"And you're sure you want to marry Monsieur Joseph Napoleon de Montigny?"

Again she nodded, remembering how relieved she'd been the man in the station hadn't been him.

"And you?" The bishop turned to Napoleon. "You've come of your own free will?"

Napoleon gave a vigorous nod. "More than my own free will."

"Then let us proceed."

The bishop recited the sacred words of the ceremony, the words that joined Lea for life with the soldier she'd fallen in love with and had waited what seemed an eternity to marry. Lea's heart was filled with elation. How long she had dreamed of this, and now they would be as one. When the bishop finished the final prayers and they signed the documents necessary, he congratulated them.

Lea and Napoleon left the church hand in hand to the carriage that awaited them, their smiles ecstatic. When they arrived at a quaint hotel close by, Napoleon led her inside.

"This is where we're staying and where we'll have supper."

Lea watched as he checked in at the front desk and handed their luggage to the footman.

Dinner was exquisite. She marveled at the high ceilings in the dining room and at the beautiful stained glass windows. Napoleon ordered stew while Lea chose the chicken. She was awed at the ornamental paper ruffle attached to the drumstick. But what surprised her most was that her new husband ordered two glasses of red wine and dessert!

After dinner, they attended the Regina Theatre where they watched *A Dog's Life* with Charlie Chaplin and laughed themselves silly. When it was over, they returned to their hotel.

"You can take a bath if you'd like." Napoleon set down her suitcase by the tub with a soft thud. "I'll prepare myself for bed out here."

"Thank you," she replied, her voice timid.

Lea's heart quickened. She was a married woman now and she had to be perfect for her husband.

Removing her dress, she hung it on the door, and then ran water into the claw-footed bathtub, careful to pour the special bath powder supplied by the hotel. Then, opening her suitcase, she pulled out the small package at the bottom where the pretty nightgown her mother had given her lay.

"Thank you, Maman."

She stayed in the tub for a long time, enjoying the luxury and the foam until the water cooled. Then she got out and dried herself, slipping into the nightie she'd saved for this special day. She brushed her hair using long strokes, tried several hairdos, deciding in the end to let her hair down. Admiring herself in the mirror, she whispered, "Not bad for a girl who's just gotten off the train."

But when she finally left the bathroom and made her entrance into the bedroom, Napoleon was fast asleep on the bed.

Lea's face twisted into a scowl. *On our wedding night!*

Giving a small huff, she turned out the electric lamp and lay down beside him, nestling close to him under the blankets. It'd have to wait until tomorrow.

Napoleon suddenly jumped up. "You thought I was asleep, didn't you?" He let out a laugh.

Lea squealed, then threw herself into his arms.

Chapter Nine
New Life in the Prairies

Two days later, Lea and Nap boarded the train west, waving good-bye to Nap's friend who'd shown them the sites around Regina. Lea had been impressed by the rotunda in the legislative buildings that had recently been built and was mesmerized by the grand hotel, Chateau Qu'Appelle, still under construction. But after a brief time in the modern city, she was ready to begin her new life in the prairies.

The train stopped at various villages until they arrived in a town called Ponteix.

Napoleon stood up and grabbed their bags from the rack. "This is it," he said, wearing a wide grin. "There is where we'll live."

Lea looked with dismay at the dilapidated buildings with peeling paint near the station. Small children with smudged faces peered through frosted windows. "Which house?" she asked, her tone guarded lest she hurt her new husband's feelings.

Napoleon flashed an impish smile. "Not here, silly! We'll be staying on the Gilberts' farm, but you'll like Ponteix. Look, over there through the branches. See that church?"

"Yes," said Lea, admiring the brown brick building.

"It's called Notre Dame d'Auvergne. It's fairly new. Most of this town is. As a matter of fact, Ponteix is only eight years old."

"Eight years old?"

"Yes. It was begun by Père Royer, the parish priest. You see, Saskatchewan's such a new province that the government is busy opening up land and incorporating new towns for homesteaders. There's even a hospital and a convent here."

A relieved sigh escaped Lea despite her desire to hide her misgivings. "But what language do they speak?"

"French, of course."

Thank goodness.

He took her hand and led her down the stairs of the train, lifting her off the final step to where an older couple waited. Lea hugged herself and trembled. She'd never felt this cold before.

"Mr. Gilbert," said Napoleon, speaking in his native French, his arm resting on his bride's shoulders, "This is Leopoldine, my wife." He looked as though he'd burst with pride.

Mr. Gilbert tipped his hat, then squeezed Lea's hand. "My goodness, what a beautiful woman you've married."

"Thank you."

Mr. Gilbert turned to the woman standing behind him. She was tall and robust, her hair pulled back in a tight bun, and her forehead grooved with consternation. "Oh, and this is

Madame Gilbert," he said as though it were an afterthought.

"*Enchanté.*" Lea bent forward to exchange kisses as was the tradition in Belgium, but the woman stood as cold and stiff as a statue, tolerating the peck on each cheek.

"I'm pleased to make your acquaintance," she replied, her voice icy as she glowered at her husband.

Mr. Gilbert squirmed under her stare and grabbed the suitcases, clearing his throat. They walked hastily to where a sleigh and two horses waited. Lea admired the black geldings attached to the harness. But as they drew near, Mr. Gilbert surprised her by hurrying past them to a vehicle.

"You have an automobile?" asked Lea, thrilled at the wealth mere farmers could attain in the new country. Certainly, she and Napoleon would have one too before long.

"Yes, but it's difficult to drive in the winter," said Mr. Gilbert still angling his head away from his wife's murderous glances. "We nearly had to take the cutter."

"The cutter?" Lea entwined her gloved fingers with Nap's.

"It's a sleigh," Napoleon explained.

"Why is that?" Lea asked Mr. Gilbert.

"Because it's quite an ordeal to get the car to run in winter."

"How so?" asked Lea.

"Well, first we have to boil water to put in the radiator, and then we have to throw a blanket over the hood and run the car until it warms up. Otherwise it'll keep on stalling. Not to mention that if the snow is too deep, we'll get stuck, our tires spinning and spinning. More often than not, the only way to travel in winter is by cutter. But I thought since we're having a cold snap and you're a Belgian bride that you'd be more comfortable in the automobile."

"Thank you. I appreciate it," she said.

They passed through Ponteix where tidy businesses lined the streets and a single gas station stood on a corner, a promise of prosperity to come. Row upon row of houses gave the place a homey atmosphere. Lea eyed the general store, imagining the things she'd one day buy, but when they passed the cemetery, a feeling of foreboding overtook her. Would they one day be buried there?

After leaving the town, they forged through miles of snowy roads, surrounded by flat, white fields that stretched to the horizon. The occasional farmhouse caught her eye—a soddy, surrounded by a few extra sheds and a barn. She'd heard of these dwellings where people on the prairie oftentimes lived until a real house could be built, how they piled up layer after layer of sod broken from the earth to form walls, making holes wide and long enough to fit the precious glass windows and doors they'd brought from Regina. Lea shuddered at the thought of her children walking on a cold, dirt floor in the winter.

Her eyes followed the fences that lined the crude road. "Are these fences surrounding the homesteads?"

"No," said Nap. "They build them to stop the snow from drifting and to mark where the road is."

"It snows that much here?" she asked.

"Yes, it does."

Lea envisioned being trapped in an automobile during a blizzard. How could one get help? She'd heard that sometimes you couldn't see more than two feet ahead.

The vehicle continued to crawl on the crude tracks. Lea spied a home in the distance that blended in with the ghostly landscape. It was dug right into the slope of the hill. Yet a merry spiral of smoke plumed from its chimney.

When they finally rolled onto the Gilbert homestead, Lea clutched Napoleon's arm so hard her nails dug in wondering what awaited them. But as they approached the structures, she loosened her grip. A large farmhouse graced the land, flanked by a red barn and a small clutch of cabins nearby. Navigating through the various bumps of the road, they pulled up alongside of the main house.

Mr. Gilbert stopped the car and opened the trunk, pulling out the suitcases while Madame Gilbert stomped off in the other direction, her arms folded. Ignoring his wife, he tipped his chin toward the largest of the cabins, his breath steaming. "This will be where you'll stay as long as you work for us."

Lea gazed at the small house with the protruding stovepipe. *From Belgium, to Dover, to Liverpool, to Halifax, to Regina, and now to our first home here in Ponteix,* she thought as she followed Mr. Gilbert to the entrance, resisting the temptation to dance.

Mr. Gilbert opened the door. The snapping and popping of burning wood greeted them. She searched the room for the fireplace, but instead a black, cast iron stove graced the room. Lea smiled at the sight, glad she wouldn't be cooking over an open hearth. Her eyes roved about. Pots and pans and a kettle sat neatly on a shelf. The largest of the pots had been placed on the stove, filled with thawing snow. *Drinking water?* A little farther away stood a table large enough to fit six people. In the middle of the room, an oval rag rug covered much of the wooden floor. Against the opposite wall, a green velvet camelback couch and a matching chair filled the space.

"I love it!" she exclaimed.

"I thought you would. But you haven't seen the bedrooms yet. There are three of them!"

"Three? That's as big as our house in Chatlineau!"

"Yes. One for the girls, one for the boys, and the best one for us."

Lea giggled, then melted into his arms. He held her close, his cheek nestled against her forehead.

When he released his hold, he said, "Now, how about if you unpack. Our bedroom is through that door. I'll go help Mr. Gilbert empty the radiator of the car so it won't freeze."

They exchanged another kiss, and Napoleon followed Mr. Gilbert, closing the door behind him.

Lea's heart filled with joy as she wandered into the bedroom. A double bed was pushed up against a wall covered in a pretty quilt decorated with tulips. A low ceiling sloped up from the bed, an obvious addition after the original cabin had been built.

A lean-to.

Against the wall stood a dresser large enough to fit all their clothes. On either side of the bed were two matching night tables. A porcelain chamber pot with small rose patterns poked out from under the bed.

She took their suitcases to the bedroom and hoisted them onto the mattress, then opened the drawers of the dresser. Napoleon's clothing already filled three of them. She took out his shirts and folded them before replacing them. Then she laid all of her things in the remaining drawers.

It had grown darker, so she fumbled about near the stove until she found matchbook. Lifting the glass chimney of the coal oil lamp, she struck a match and lit the burner. A soft radiance filled the room.

With the new light, Lea was able to explore the cabin more thoroughly. A broom and dustpan rested in one corner.

"This room could use a good sweep," she muttered to herself as she grabbed the broom and began cleaning the floor. She worked her way from one end of the cabin to the next. When she reached the oval rag rug, she lifted it and discovered a trapdoor.

"Wonder what this is." Bending down, she pulled the ring up to reveal hidden stairs.

Curious, Lea took the lamp from its hook and descended to the basement. When she reached the bottom, she held up the light and explored her surroundings. Against one wall rested a perfectly stacked line of firewood. On the opposite side, she found potatoes, carrots, beets, and onions. A bushel of apples stood close by. Dried corn hung in clumps from the ceiling as did herbs. She took the time to smell each cluster, identifying them as best she could. A large pail of lard stood on the floor with blocks of butter piled on it. She loaded various items in her skirt—an onion, a few potatoes, a couple of carrots—and carried them back up the stairs, careful not to lose her footing. When she got to the top, Napoleon was at the door, smiling.

"I brought supper," he said, handing her a headless chicken, feathers and all.

Lea eyed the carcass. She'd never plucked a chicken before, nor had she ever been handed one complete with claws and neck. But this was the new life she'd chosen, so she reached over and accepted it, offering a tentative smile. She tugged at the feathers as best she could, but when she pulled a large one from the wing, the chicken flew over her head and smacked against the wall.

Napoleon burst into laughter.

"What's so funny?" Lea cried, seizing the chicken from the floor.

"That's not how you do it."

"Well, I don't know!" She slammed the carcass on the table. "In Belgium they come from the boucherie already cleaned and plucked.

Nap bit his lip, the occasional pfft slipping out. "Here, let me show you."

Lea thrust the bird at him and crossed her arms, waiting for her husband to reveal a special tool that would render the job simple, but instead he added more wood to the stove. When it grew so hot that the snow in the pot had melted and begun to steam, he added more snow. When that had melted, he added more again and waited. He repeated the procedure until the pot was two thirds full of hot water. Then he turned and smiled. "Now watch." He took the chicken from her and, grasping it by the feet, immersed it in the water.

Lea stared in fascination.

"The first thing you need to do is loosen the feathers." He dipped the chicken in several times and swished it around. "Once you've done that, they'll come out easily." He peeled back the down with his fingertips, then yanked out the larger feathers. Taking the butcher knife, he removed the feet and neck. Setting them aside, he reached inside and removed the organs.

"But what do we do with the feet and the innards?"

"The pigs will enjoy them," replied Nap. "They eat anything."

Lea took what remained of the chicken and prepared it as Maman had taught her. She salted and peppered the meat and placed it inside the newly washed pot, creating a temporary oven. She added the onions, potatoes, and carrots. Making another trip to the cellar, she came back with lard and herbs. Within the hour, the aroma of roast chicken filled the cabin. When Nap returned later on, they ate their first homemade meal together by coal oil lamplight, while gazing into each other's eyes. Once the dishes were cleaned, they retired for the night, neither of them feeling the slightest bit sleepy.

***

A few weeks later, Lea didn't feel well. Napoleon had woken early as usual to build the fire in the stove that would heat their small home, but when she rose, instead of greeting him with his morning kiss, she ran for the door, and threw up in the melting snow.

"Are you okay?" asked Napoleon, holding a frying pan filled with bacon in mid-air. "Breakfast is nearly ready."

"No thanks. I'm going back to bed."

She returned to their room and slept away the morning, but by lunchtime she felt much better. Slipping down to the cellar, she retrieved the hearty soup she'd prepared the day before, and heated it on the stove. She devoured three bowlfuls. She'd missed the bread-making, but didn't mind the day old bread one tiny bit. They shared their lunch, pleased the nausea had spent itself so quickly and that a doctor hadn't been needed.

The next day, the whole thing began again, and the day after that. Lea broke into a soft smile when she understood what was happening.

She waited until Nap left for the day, then baked a special chocolate cake, icing it with whipped cream. Taking candles, she counted the number of months she had left before the baby would arrive and placed the appropriate number on top.

When Nap arrived, he eyed the cake. "What's this? Is it someone's birthday?"

"It will be," she replied, "in about seven months."

Nap's eyes shot open and his mouth hung. "Really?"

"Mm-hm."

"We're going to have a baby?"

"Yes." Lea laughed.

Nap picked her up and twirled her around. "I can't wait to tell the family in Wide View. They'll be so thrilled. Let's see, I'll build a crib, and a high chair, and a little dresser."

The news traveled fast. One morning as Lea stared out the window at the grey patches of snow that still lingered over the muddy ground, she saw Madame Gilbert making her way to their cabin. It was spring and it'd only be a few weeks before Nap and Mr. Gilbert would begin plowing and seeding the fields. Lea's muscles tensed as she wondered what the woman wanted. Their relationship had always been cold since Mr. Gilbert had made the mistake of telling Nap he'd married a beautiful woman.

Lea cautiously opened the door. "Good morning."

"And a good morning to you," Madame Gilbert replied, a warm smile replacing her previous coldness.

Lea was taken aback at the sudden change in the older woman's attitude. "So what can I do for you?"

"I heard you were with child," she said, her opened lips revealing less-than-straight teeth.

"Why, yes, I am."

"Then we must prepare. Why don't you come to the house? I have some old clothes left over from when our children were small. Perhaps you can use some of it."

"That would be lovely," said Lea, relieved the ice between them seemed to have melted, at least for the time being.

"Besides, I need help churning the butter. My shoulder's bothering me today."

"I'd be glad to help," said Lea, having no idea how butter was made since it was always brought to the house in Chatlineau by the deliveryman, but this was a chance to learn a new skill and befriend the employer's wife.

When they entered the main house, Lea was awed. The kitchen was large with a full stove, complete with oven. A water pump emptied into a sink that could be stopped to wash dishes. Next to the kitchen, a room full of fashionable furniture surrounded a stone fireplace; a piano was tucked in the corner. Lea could see doors that led into at least four bedrooms, but was careful not to stare for too long in case Madame Gilbert found her nosy.

"Here's the container we've been collecting the cream in," the older woman said, unscrewing the cover.

Lea's nose wrinkled at the smell. She had seen Nap lowering the canister of milk into the well every day to separate the milk from the cream, raising it up and taking it to the main house. Oftentimes, they were given cream for their tea too.

"I think it's gone bad," she said, bile threatening to rise in her throat. She pinched her nose and breathed through her mouth.

Madame Gilbert smiled, revealing her anything-but-straight teeth again. "It's *supposed* to go bad. That's what the churning's all about." She ladled the sour cream into the wooden cask, tightened the lid, and began turning the handle with both hands until she was grimacing with pain.

"Here, let me do it for you." Lea took the wooden dowel from her, still breathing through her mouth. She wound it round and round. After a time, she began to sweat, but dared not complain lest Madame Gilbert find her spoiled and resume her cold attitude toward her.

A half hour later, when Lea felt she could handle it no more, Madame Gilbert signaled her to stop and undid the cover.

Lea looked inside to find a large glob of yellow butter surrounded by a cloudy liquid.

"It's ready now," said Madame Gilbert.

"But what do we do with the watery stuff?"

"The buttermilk? We'll give it to the pigs. They'll eat anything."

Lea laughed, pleased she'd finished the laborious job and that now she could resume breathing through her nose once the pigs had been fed. She waited for Madame Gilbert to lead her to one of the bedrooms to show her the baby clothes, but instead, the older woman poured another batch of sour cream into the churn. Lea gave an inward groan.

Three hours later, the job was done and Lea could once again breathe normally.

Madame Gilbert boiled hot water to make tea and cut a generous portion of cake for Lea. She wolfed it down.

Afterward, she took Lea to what had once been a girl's room and opened the wardrobe. Two old boxes covered in dust rested inside. Madame Gilbert hauled them out, pulling out tiny nighties of varying sizes.

"They're lovely!" Lea made a mental note to sort them out later.

"They belonged to my three children—Thomas, Eric, and Cécile," she said, her gaze traveling far away. "And I have more for when your little one gets bigger."

Lea admired the clothing as they sorted through the next box. "So where are your children now?"

Madame Gilbert didn't answer for a time, then said. "Thomas and Eric have gone to Heaven."

Lea's chin dropped. "What happened?"

Madame Gilbert let out a brave sigh. When she answered, the timbre of her voice had changed. "The war. Vimy Ridge. They were in the same platoon. They joined against my wishes."

"I'm sorry," said Lea. "It must be so hard for you."

"It was for a while, and it didn't help that my Cécile rarely comes home, but now you're here, and you have a young one on the way. Life moves forward, *non?"*

Lea regarded the old woman through misty eyes. No wonder Madame Gilbert had been cold to her. She must have been suffering terrible heartache. Lea's arms encircled her.

Madame Gilbert returned the hug and whispered, "I'm sorry I was rude to you at first. It's been so hard living alone here on the prairie, especially in the winter. And I'm not young and pretty like you, but I *am* glad you're here."

"I'm glad too," said Lea.

Chapter Ten
The Mysterious Guest

The snow had all but melted by the time Easter arrived. Chicks pecked about in the yard, and piglets trotted after their sow, hoping for a meal.

Lea and Napoleon had been invited to the Gilberts' after church for the leg of ham that had been saved over the winter for the occasion. Lea looked forward to it, particularly since she and Madame Gilbert had become such good friends, enjoying each other's company daily. Of course, Monsieur Gilbert never made the mistake of commenting on Lea's beauty ever again.

"I'm going to milk the cows before church," Napoleon said, throwing his arms around Lea's shoulder and nuzzling her neck. "What are you going to do?"

"I'm making bread for tonight. A very special loaf like at the boulangerie in Chatlineau—the really expensive type."

"Oh? What kind of bread will it be?"

A smile touched her lips as she imagined the work of art she'd create. "It's going to be braided."

Nap nodded in approval. "I'm sure it'll be beautiful." He drew her close and kissed her on the lips before slipping on his coat and boots and heading to the barn.

Lea watched him through the window as she did every morning and then set about her task. She measured out the flour and sifted it into the large bowl she used for baking. Glancing back, she checked the consistency of the yeast she'd prepared earlier that morning.

"Hmm," she said. "Maybe I could make a sweet glaze to go on top." She shook her head since Madame Gilbert had already claimed the privilege of making dessert and she didn't want to ruffle any feathers. "I know. I'll add some sugar so that it'll taste a bit like a *beigne.* That'll be really Belgian."

She picked up her measuring cup and stirred the sugar into the flour. Then she mixed in the yeast and kneaded it into a ball. Covering the bowl with a damp cloth, she set it aside.

Wandering into the bedroom, she pulled out the same navy blue dress with embroidered flowers she'd worn for her wedding. Since it was the first time they'd be attending church in Ponteix, she wanted to look her best to meet the townsfolk. She placed her hand on her stomach and felt the bulge as the little life within her grew, glad she wasn't showing too much yet.

When the automobile was ready, they drove the few miles to town. Lea marveled at the broad sky that touched the horizon far away. Only on the prairies, where the land was flat, could such a thing of beauty exist. *A myriad of castles where angels dwell.*

She gazed farther to the town where the green grain elevator rose in the distance. Bells rang from the church's steeple announcing Easter mass. Buggies and horses surrounded the church, ladies and girls descending wearing white hats and dresses while men and boys followed in their best trousers and shirts.

When mass began, Père Royer welcomed Lea personally, as well as other war brides, and commented on what a long winter it had been and how grand it was that so many people could make the Easter Sunday mass. He also bowed his head in memory of sons who had been lost.

Lea enjoyed the sermon, grateful it was in French. It made her feel as though she were back in Belgium.

After mass, the congregation moved to the hall where ladies brought out cookies and cakes of every type. Children ran about sampling the fares before leaping away in games of tag while grownups sipped tea. After spending time with such a pleasant crowd, Lea was reluctant to go back home where solitude would once again greet her.

When they arrived at the farm, she opened the door to their cabin and went straight to the bowl to check her dough, but the bread had hardly risen.

"What on earth!" She kneaded it again just in case she hadn't mixed the yeast in properly, then set it aside. A half-hour later, a hard lump of dough still sat on the bottom of the bowl.

She shook her head. "Maybe I didn't put in *enough* yeast." Preparing more rising agent, she added it to the existing dough along with more flour. But the result was much the same—flat bread.

"Ugh, what a flop! This isn't good for anything." Taking the entire mess outside, she threw the clump of wet dough on the ground, then slammed the door.

With a sigh, she took the hot water from the back of the stove and made herself a cup of tea. "When things aren't going well, it's time for a break," she muttered to herself. She sat for a time sipping the hot drink. On her second cup, the solution came to her.

"It's the sugar!" she exclaimed. "I've never put in that much before!"

Her morale renewed, she tied her apron on again and remixed the flour and yeast. An hour later, it had risen into the puffy dough expected. She grinned with satisfaction, then broke off small clumps that she rolled into strands and braided, laying them in pretty patterns on top of the loaf. Then she added wood to the fire until she deemed the temperature hot enough. Placing her creation inside a cast iron pot, she clapped the lid on and let it cook. When she lifted the cover later on, a perfect, round, golden loaf met her gaze.

She wiped her brow with relief. "Just in time for dinner."

As she turned the pot over to release the bread, a burst of laughter from outside startled her. She dashed to the window where she saw Napoleon and Mr. Gilbert slapping their knees and guffawing. Lea swung the door open to see what was so funny. Several small chicks flapped about, their feet stuck in her discarded bread dough.

"Were you trying to catch a chick or two for the supper tonight?" asked Napoleon. "Madame Gilbert is cooking a ham, you know."

"No…I…the dough…it wouldn't rise. I had to throw it out..."

Her face burning, she grabbed a rag, then scrubbed all the chicks' claws with slush while Nap and Mr. Gilbert shoveled up the remaining dough, tears still streaming from their eyes.

"Next time," said Mr. Gilbert, "feed it to the pigs."

"I know," said Lea. "They'll eat anything, right?"

At dinner time, Lea brought the second loaf and handed it over to Madame Gilbert with pride, though the odd snicker still escaped the men.

Madame Gilbert accepted the gift with a gracious bow as she welcomed them into the big house and led them to the kitchen. Lea grabbed an apron off the hook and tied it around her waist. When she turned, she noticed an extra guest—a young woman in her mid-twenties. She was an attractive girl with chestnut brown hair tied back in a ponytail, but her eyes were sad. Lea glanced at Madame Gilbert, questioning.

"Napoleon and Lea, I'd like to introduce you to my daughter, Cécile."

Lea stepped forward, a welcoming smile on her lips. "I'm so pleased to meet you."

The young woman eyed Lea resentfully for a moment before extending a reluctant hand. "Likewise."

They exchanged polite pecks on each cheek before Cécile shook Nap's hand.

"She came all the way from Regina to be with us today," said Madame Gilbert, donning a fake smile.

"Yes, it was a wonderful surprise," Mr. Gilbert said, his voice a little too exuberant like he was trying to be nice.

Cécile huffed without meeting their gaze and began setting the table as though they hadn't spoken while the others exchanged uncomfortable glances.

Lea helped Madame Gilbert with the finishing touches of the dinner, cutting the braided bread into thick slices and placing them into a neat row in the basket while Mr. Gilbert carved the ham.

When all was ready, they sat down at the grand table as Lea and Madame Gilbert laid dish after dish before them.

"How ever did you make such a tender bread?" asked Madame Gilbert.

Napoleon turned his head, disguising a snicker as a cough.

"The secret is in the amount of sugar," said Lea, throwing her husband a warning glance.

"This ham is delicious too. What do you think, Cécile?"

"I haven't had such excellent ham in a long time," the young woman replied, taking her napkin and dabbing her mouth. Without warning, she burst into tears.

The room fell silent except for the sounds of her sobs.

"I'm sorry," said Cécile. "I really miss them…It's just not the same."

Madame Gilbert was the first to speak. "I know. We all miss your brothers." She picked up her napkin from her lap and wiped her eyes.

"And I hate the big city. There are too many people," Cécile continued, her voice bitter.

"Then why don't you come home?" Mr. Gilbert asked. "Planting season will start soon and we could use as much help as possible. We could pay you the same as we do the others."

"I don't know." Cécile wiped her nose. "You see, there's a man."

"Oh?" Madame Gilbert's eyebrows arched.

"It's nothing, Maman. It's been over for quite some time, but I..." She erupted into sobs again.

"You hope he'll come back to you?" asked Lea.

Cécile nodded.

Lea regarded the young woman with tenderness. "You know, Cécile, I miss my family…and my country too, but the whole world has changed, and we have to change along with it. I met a girl on the ship coming over. She lost most of her family and saw things too horrible to describe, but even so, she and I made a pact that we'd move forward. There's simply no other place to go. You could join our pact."

Cécile's eyes met Lea's. "Well, maybe."

"Not maybe," Lea said. "Say yes."

"Well, all right, then. Yes!"

"Then you'll stay until at least after the harvest?" asked Mr. Gilbert.

Madame Gilbert shot Cécile a hopeful look.

"Okay. I could use a break from the city." Cécile nodded.

"Then that calls for a celebration!" Madame Gilbert rose and retrieved an angel food cake iced with whipped cream she'd kept hidden in the cellar.

"Oh, you shouldn't have," said Lea.

"But it's Easter. Why not?" Madame Gilbert smiled as she dished out generous portions.

Lea couldn't get enough of the cake, devouring two pieces.

After the dishes were cleared and washed, Cécile made her way to the piano and tested it out with two fingers. "Needs to be tuned after such a cold winter."

"I agree. We'll send for the piano technician next month when he comes through Ponteix," said Madame Gilbert.

Cécile sat down and began her own rendition of *"Plaisir d'Amour."*

"That's my favourite song!" said Lea, dropping her dishcloth and racing to Cécile's side. Her heart was filled with loneliness for her family as she sang the words. She thought of her parents, Camille, François, Mathilde, and Palma and wondered what they were doing that very moment. The others joined in too, singing with passion.

When the song ended, Lea glanced at Cécile. It appeared the evening had tremendously lifted the young woman's spirits.

***

At the end of April, the earth had warmed up enough that Napoleon and Mr. Gilbert hitched up the team of horses and attached the plow, spending days digging up the fields, then disking and harrowing them until only rich, brown soil showed itself in perfect rows. Then the seeding began.

The summer weighed on Lea in her expectant state, the heat smothering her. But far worse were the millions of tiny mosquitoes that filled the air in the evening.

"Look," she said to Napoleon as she stared up in the sky. "They're everywhere!"

"I know," said Nap, scratching the welts on his legs. "All we can do is be careful not to let them in the house."

But try as they might, they heard the high-pitched whine of the bloodsuckers hovering over their heads each night.

Lea couldn't wait until the yellow wheat shot up, finally able to witness the golden fields Napoleon had described to her. But more than anything else, she couldn't wait until their child was born. It kicked continuously, often waking her. She'd already arranged the baby clothes Madame Gilbert had given her into the top drawer of the dresser and awaited Nap's promised crib.

"You seem mighty big for a woman who's only been with child for five months," commented Madame Gilbert, her lips turned up into a smile of amusement.

"It's all the good food. We lived with so little for so long. But it's not just my stomach that's grown. If I didn't know any better, I'd say I've gotten taller too."

"I noticed that," said Madame Gilbert.

Cécile's forehead creased as she regarded her. "But that's impossible. You're nearly twenty. I stopped growing at fourteen."

"That's what I thought too until I noticed that Napoleon and I are closer to the same height. I used to be so much shorter than him. I'm wondering if maybe the lack of food during the war stunted my growth."

Madame Gilbert's eyebrows rose. "I've never heard of such a thing, but it could be."

When the shafts of wheat were ripe and ready for harvest, Mr. Gilbert came back from town with a carload of young men whose raucous voices filled the yard. He unlocked the doors of the other cabins, assigning six men to a room. Lea was surprised to see that the other dwellings only contained a woodstove and bunks in sharp contrast to the love nest she and Napoleon had made for themselves.

With the men's arrival came long days of cooking and cleaning as it was the women's job to feed the hungry workers. Beginning with baking bread at sunrise, then making breakfast—frying three dozen eggs and three pounds of bacon—they then made a couple dozen sandwiches. After that, they prepared supper, making pies, cooking a large roast, and boiling fifteen potatoes each night. Of course, that didn't include all the dishwashing. By the end of the day, Lea was completely spent.

It was on one such night, as she lay exhausted in bed, she heard Cécile giggling outside their cabin. A man's voice mumbled. Lea sat up, unsure if what she was hearing was real. Sneaking to the window, she peeked out. The full moon lit up the night, casting long shadows from the nearby fruit trees. Lea strained her eyes in the direction of the voices. She spotted Cécile's pink dress near one of the trees. Who was she with? A red ember glowed from a cigarette next to her. Lea just barely made out the outline of a man. He leaned in and kissed Cécile. Lea gasped and tiptoed back to her bed. Waking Napoleon, she whispered, "Cécile has a beau!"

"You mean you didn't know?" A smile tinged his voice despite being heavy with sleep.

"No. She never said anything. Who is he?"

Napoleon rolled over. "His name's Claude. He's been talking about her for weeks."

"Claude?" She curled her lip. Lea knew exactly who Nap was talking about. He was the most dashing of all the workers with a sweep of jet black hair, a crooked smile, and a brash sense of humour, but Lea had been shocked at his coarseness. She'd once overheard him using profanities while talking with the men, but at least he'd had the decency to clean up his language immediately when he'd noticed her presence.

"What's he been saying about her?"

Nap paused before answering. "It's just guy talk. You don't want to know."

Lea's lips tightened. "What's he like?"

"Well, he's not the most upstanding guy, but he's thinking of getting a homestead."

"I suppose that's a good sign," Lea said despite her misgivings. She felt uneasy. Perhaps he wasn't the sort of man she'd want, but who was she to judge? Maybe he was just what Cécile needed.

Indeed, Cécile's mood had changed considerably. She seemed more animated, laughing easily at jokes, not minding the hard work, and making an extra effort to cook up special things she imagined the men would enjoy.

When September arrived, the men turned their attention to harvesting the apples and pears. The women were kept busy peeling, canning, and storing until jars of fruit lined the shelves of the basement. Then the workers began digging up potatoes, carrots, and beets, leaving bushels near the cellar door to be carried in. Lea had grown so large, she could no longer bend over to lift the baskets so that Madame Gilbert and Cécile had to take over.

The night before the men were scheduled to leave, Cécile accompanied Claude to town for dinner. When they returned, several hours later, they woke everyone up with boisterous shouts. Lea and Napoleon dressed and hurried to the house.

As Lea suspected, Cécile stretched out her hand, showing off a ring. "We're married!" she squealed.

"Married?" Mr. Gilbert's expression was the epitome of astonishment.

"Yes!" said Cécile. "We wanted to surprise everyone. We figured the less fuss, the better."

Madame Gilbert stared at her blankly, then quickly added, "Well, congratulations!"

"Where will you live?" asked Mr. Gilbert. "Are you going back to Regina?"

"We were hoping we could stay on here in one of the cabins," said Cécile.

"Oh, forget the cabins," said Madame Gilbert. "You can stay in the main house. Claude can move in tomorrow."

They broke open a bottle of wine to celebrate. Lea refused a glass, her pregnancy making the taste repulsive. Claude gladly took her share.

Later, as she lay in Napoleon's arm, she asked, "Do you think they'll be okay?"

Napoleon hesitated before answering. "I sure hope so.

Chapter Eleven
The Butchering

Lea's heart skipped the day Nap came from Ponteix with a letter in his hand.

"It's been forwarded from Wide View. It's from your sister, Palma."

"Palma?" With a bounce in her step, Lea took the letter from his hand and tore it open. She began reading.

Dear Lea,

I am so happy to hear you are expecting your first child. Do you hope for a boy or a girl?

Things have changed a great deal here in Chatlineau since the armistice. I've gotten a job at the boulangerie making bread. It's difficult since I'm required to be there at four in the morning to start the dough. But I suppose it's better than staying at home listening to Papa rant and rave.

He's in such terrible humour these days. Maman says it's because his back aches from working in the mine. He has insisted that Camille take over his job until he is well enough again. Camille has obliged, but spends far too much time in the tavern after work. In the meantime, Papa has gone back to repairing shoes, and he's training François as well since a shoe is small enough for François to hold with his damaged hand while he sews with the other.

Lea, I'm terrified! Papa has threatened to arrange marriages for both Mathilde and me. He says we cost too much to keep and that he has no intention of supporting two old maids. He told me he has found an Italian man quite suitable for me, but I've seen him, and he's old. Papa says I can't be too choosy since the war has taken away so many of our sons. Oh, Lea, you must help me! I'm beside myself. I'm thinking of running away to Canada, but I haven't saved up enough money with my new job yet. Would you and Napoleon have dollars to spare that you could send me? I'm desperate. I can't bear to be married to such an old man.
Palma

Lea folded the letter.

"I can't believe it," she said to Napoleon. "Papa wants to arrange marriages for Palma and Mathilde."

Napoleon's eyes bulged at the news. "Arrange marriages?"

"Yes. Palma says he's found an older man for her. Apparently, there aren't many young men left since the war."

116

"Well, we have plenty here. Perhaps she could immigrate to Canada."

"But how? She says she has a job, but she can't possibly raise that kind of money in that amount of time. Couldn't we help her?"

Nap sighed. "But we have to save all we can for the homestead, and with the baby coming…and besides, there's the paperwork."

"Oh, poor Palma." Lea wrung her hands. "How could Papa do this to her?"

"We wouldn't have enough room for her anyway with that big tummy of yours always in the way." His eyes twinkled. "She wouldn't be able to get past you to go to her room."

Lea laughed. It was true. Her stomach had grown the size of a pumpkin, just in time for Halloween and that new tradition in town where children disguised themselves in costumes, knocking on doors and demanding candy.

"Perhaps I should draw a jack-o-lantern face on my tummy. That would certainly make tongues wag."

Nap let out a chuckle. "Yes, it would. By the way, Mr. Gilbert says we're doing the butchering of the pig tomorrow."

"Oh, no," said Lea, feeling every aching bone in her pregnant body. She'd been dreading the day, but knew it was coming since the cellars were full, and the men had all left for the winter, save Claude. And that meant the harvest was over and it was time.

"Madame Gilbert wants your help making *boudin*."

For a moment, Lea forgot her fatigue and licked her lips in anticipation. It had been a while since she'd tasted blood pudding.

"She says she'll teach you how to make it."

"Well, all right then. It'll be fun to spend the day with Madame Gilbert and Cécile puttering about in the kitchen."

When Lea arrived at the main house, the next morning, she was put to work chopping onions and bits of apple while Cécile mixed cloves, nutmeg, cinnamon, and salt in a large pot.

"So how's our bride doing today?" asked Lea.

"Oh, fine." Cécile sighed.

"I heard Claude come in late last night."

"Yes, he does that sometime."

"He was drunk." Madame Gilbert flashed a sour look as she separated the cream from the milk.

"He wasn't drunk, Maman. He was just a little tipsy. You have to give him a chance. After all, he's been single all this time. He has to get used to being married."

"Whatever you say." Madame Gilbert shook her head. "How are those onions and apples coming along, Lea?"

"They're ready."

"And are you finished with the spices?" she asked Cécile.

"Yes."

"Good, then. Let's throw them all together."

The three women poured their mixtures into a large pot and carried it out to the barn.

When they arrived, Mr. Gilbert tossed grain into the pig trough while Claude and Nap watched. "Come on, Charlie. This is your last supper."

The pig grunted, his cloven hooves scuffling as he made his way to the food and poked his greedy nose in.

"I can't stand to watch this." Cécile covered her eyes with her hands. "It's so cruel."

Lea instinctively turned away.

A shot rang through the air, and Lea heard the pig drop.

"Quickly, now," said Madame Gilbert.

When Lea looked down, she saw Mr. Gilbert make a gash in the pig's throat. Madame Gilbert shoved the pot under the boar's head where the blood flowed, stirring it in with the mixture of spices, salt, onions, apples, and cream.

"You have to keep it moving so it won't coagulate. Here, you take a turn now."

Lea grasped the wooden spoon and stirred until the pig's blood had run dry. When Madame Gilbert deemed it to be the right consistency, they took the concoction back to the house and into the kitchen.

"And now, we put it into the casings," said Madame Gilbert.

Lea eyed the long cow intestines that lay on the table, wondering how on earth they'd get the mixture inside them.

She soon found out when Madame Gilbert swished around the intestines in a vat of water until they were clean and turned them inside out. Then she twisted one end while attaching the other to the meat grinder, pushing it up as far as it would go. She spooned a portion of the mixture into the machine and turned the handle. The casing slowly filled.

Lea watched with fascination as the sausage took shape. When it was nearly full, Madame Gilbert detached it from the grinder, twisted the top, and coiled the sausage into a spiral.

"Voilà! Now you try, Lea."

Lea attached the casing to the machine, took a spoonful of the boudin, and stuffed it in the main body, but when she rotated the handle, the pudding seeped out the other end of the intestine and onto the table.

Cécile broke into a fit of giggling. "You forgot to seal it."

Lea reddened. "I'm sorry."

"Here, start again." Madame Gilbert squeezed out the pudding and rewashed the casing.

This time, it turned out near perfect. Lea admired her work, pleased she'd learned a new skill.

When all the sausages were ready, they cooked them slowly until they oozed juices when pricked. Lea marveled at the delicate flavor.

Stifling a yawn, she was about to excuse herself to take a nap when the door flew open and Mr. Gilbert trundled in, carrying a crock full of cut meat and another filled with lard. "Here you go. All ready for preserving."

Lea took a giant breath, then pushed down her fatigue yet again.

"All right, now," said Madame Gilbert. "You and Cécile are going to fry the meat while I melt the lard."

Madame Gilbert placed the fat in a large pot and added more wood to the stove.

Lea watched as it melted, taking some of the lard and forking in as many chops as her pan could fit. The sizzle threw up flecks of fat as the aroma of pork chops filled the room making her stomach growl. When the meat was well-done, she turned to Madame Gilbert.

"Now watch what we do," said Cécile. "This is the important part." Ladling some of the melted lard into a crock, she waited until it hardened, then filled the space with chops. Adding another layer of lard, again she waited until it turned white, then placed more meat on top.

Lea and Cécile took turns cooking and preserving. A few hours later, they were done.

"That should last us through the winter," said Madame Gilbert, brushing off her hands with satisfaction.

"But what about the rest of it?" Lea felt as though she couldn't last another minute. "Where are the legs?"

"The men are smoking them in the barn," said Cécile. "And they're storing the rest of the pig in brine until we need it. Later, we can make headcheese and *creton* with the edible parts of the head and the feet."

Lea wanted to ask how they prepared headcheese and creton, but was too tired to hear anymore. Excusing herself, she waddled back to the cabin where she slept until well after the sun had risen the next day.

***

Lea tossed and turned as images of injured soldiers ran through her head. Where was Napoleon? She called his name. Only a dying soldier's moans answered her. A sharp pain stabbed her abdomen. She doubled over in agony, falling to her knees in the deep mud. Had she been shot? She pushed herself back up. It didn't matter. She had to find her beau.

"Napoleon!" she screamed.

A German soldier loomed over her. "He's dead!"

"No!" shrieked Lea. "You're lying."

"It was me who shot him…right through the eyes!"

"Noooo!"

She awoke with a start. Something wet trickled between her legs. An agonizing cramp gripped her stomach. Lea sat up.

"Napoleon," she whispered. "The baby's coming!"

Her husband groaned in his sleep.

"Napoleon!"

122

He rolled over and moaned.

"Quickly, get the doctor."

As though her words suddenly registered, Nap leapt up. He threw on his clothes, lit the lantern, and left the house. A half hour later, he returned, followed by a young doctor.

"Lea, this is Dr. Lupien."

"Pleased to meet you." Lea eyed the man with curiosity. A handsome gentleman, he had the fine features of a nobleman. His brown hair was combed back, his eyes a pale blue. She'd heard stories about how he was the first doctor in these parts, summoned by Père Royer himself. He'd looked after the people of the town when the Spanish flu had stricken, going so far as to build them fires and cook their food. The nuns in the convent declared his heart was made of gold.

"How are you doing?" he asked her.

A spasm gripped her belly. "Not very well at the moment."

"How far apart are the contractions?"

"I don't know." She let out a wail.

He turned to Nap. "Boil some water. And we'll need clean rags—plenty of them."

Napoleon left the house to fill the water pot. When he came back, he built the fire in the wood stove. Grabbing the bag full of clean rags Lea had prepared in advance, he handed them to Dr. Lupien before returning to the stove. "Darn, that snow's taking so long to melt," Lea heard him mutter.

As Lea's contractions grew closer, they became more painful. She gritted her teeth.

"Hurry up, water!" she heard Napoleon say.

"Here, let me examine you," said Dr. Lupien.

Lea complied.

After a few minutes, the doctor raised his head. "It shouldn't take long now. You're fully dilated."

"What does that mean?" Lea asked, innocently.

"It means you've opened up enough to give birth. The next time you have a contraction, I want you to push."

Lea waited for the gripping pain, then heaved with all her might. Sweat poured off her forehead, dampening the pillow beneath her. Then respite. A few moments later, it began again. Lea clutched the sides of the bed in agony and pushed for all she was worth.

An hour later, a tiny cry rang out in the room.

"It's a girl!" said Dr. Lupien.

"A girl?" said Lea.

Napoleon rushed to Lea's beside, his face twisting at the sight of all the blood. But his attention was drawn away by the tiny little baby with wet, brown hair.

Lea watched as Napoleon lifted the child in his arms, his eyes glowing. The baby girl returned his gaze.

"She looks like a little Emma," he said. "We could name her after her grandmother."

Lea smiled. "That's a good idea."

"Then Emma it is. And now that's she's been born, we can go to Wide View to meet the family."

"That would be wonderful!" said Lea. Her face contorted as another contraction gripped her.

"Hmmm," said Dr. Lupien. "I believe there's another one on the way."

"Another one?" Napoleon's eyes magnified.

Lea pushed until the second child came into the world.

"Another little girl!" said Dr. Lupien.

"Two girls?" Tears of joy filled Lea's eyes as the doctor cleaned the second baby, wrapping her in a blanket. "Oh, she's beautiful too…and they're identical!"

"What shall we name this one?" asked Nap.

Lea thought a moment, then said, "Let's name her Palma after my sister."

"Then Palma it is," replied Napoleon.

Chapter Twelve
The Dead of Winter

"I don't remember last winter being as cold as this." Lea rubbed her hands over the stove as it heated up. Napoleon, as usual, had risen and built the fire. The wood crackled and emitted its familiar scent. She turned and glanced at the baby girls who still slept in the crib, swaddled tightly, wearing little hats and mittens.

"Well it *is* December," he said. "And you arrived at the beginning of March. It was a little warmer then."

"True."

Lea gazed out the window, noting a bluish hue to the overcast sky. *Clouds of blue send blankets of white.* She turned to Nap. "Could you please bring in lots of snow so I can wash the nappies?"

"Certainly." He dressed himself in layers despite the short trip to fetch snow, lacing up his boots and pulling his toque and gloves on. Bending down, he grabbed the bucket by the door and left.

Lea despised doing the laundry. It seemed to be a never-ending task—hauling snow from outside, melting it until there was enough water, filling the washtub, scrubbing against the washboard for what seemed hours, wringing out the wet clothes, and hanging them to dry on the lines Nap had nailed crosswise into the walls of the cabin. It had been so much easier in Belgium with the faucets and the large sink in the back room. She longed for the spring when they could retrieve water from the well and hang the laundry to dry in the sun, freeing up more space inside.

She heard Nap's feet stomp outside before the door swung open. "Here's the first bucket," he said.

Lea grabbed it, dumping its contents into the large pot on the stove. She handed it back to Nap. A few minutes later, he returned with another. After three trips, she had three pots of snow all melting at once.

But before it could all be heated, Emma awoke, screaming from hunger. Palma soon joined her, her cries outdoing her sister's. Lea shuffled on two feet between the stove and the girls, indecisive. How could she do everything all at once?

"It's okay," said Nap. "I'll make us breakfast while you feed the girls."

Giving him a grateful smile, Lea reached down, taking Emma first in one arm, then Palma in the other. She balanced their tiny heads on her chest as she made her way to the chair in the living room. After they had both latched on, she watched them feed, feeling calmer.

Such beautiful little babies! she thought, her heart swelling with love. *If only we had a camera so I could send pictures home.* But she knew that was out of the question until she and Nap had saved up enough money. She gazed at their perfect heads. She never knew how deeply she could love her children, more than anyone or anything, even her Napoleon.

Though her breakfast was late, she enjoyed the eggs and toasted bread Nap prepared for her. When she had finished eating, she poured hot water into the basin she'd used to bathe the girls, adding enough cold water until the temperature was just right. She undressed Emma, being quick to wash her and wrap her immediately afterward. She did the same for Palma, then placed them both in baskets close to the stove.

"That should keep you warm," she said in a sing-songy voice.

The girls cooed, their bright eyes shining.

Napoleon bent down and gave each baby a kiss before leaving. "I'll be out in the barn tending to the animals. See you at lunch?"

"Oui, mon homme." Lea stretched her face forward to receive his kiss.

She waited until the door had closed, then began the unpleasant task of doing the laundry. First, she added Ivory Flakes to the girls' bath water and stirred it up. Retrieving the basket of dirty clothes from their bedroom, she took out Nap's shirts and threw them in, wrinkling her nose at the sour smell of the armpits. She rubbed the fabric against the washboard. When they were done, she set them aside and picked out another pile.

"I swear these socks could stand up on their own," she said, feeling how stiff they were. "He must have worn them for three days in a row." She scrubbed them, then threw in his undergarments.

After they were all clean, she began on her own clothing and then the nappies. When she opened the bucket that contained the girls' soiled nappies, a foul odour assaulted her nose.

She gagged. "Oh, my! How is it such cute little things like you could create such a smell?" Lugging the nappies to the basin, she scoured each one separately until they were clean.

"Thank God that's done," she said, stepping outside with the washtub after everything had been rinsed. Soft snowflakes had begun drifting down from the skies. Shivering at the cold, she dumped the soiled water out, careful not to toss it all in one place, producing an accidental skating rink. "My, but that's going to smell awful when the spring thaw comes."

She began the arduous task of wringing out the laundry—something that took a great deal of muscle power—then hanging it on the lines around the cabin. By the time she was done, the babies had awoken once more.

Lea let out a sigh. "Again?" She felt their wet nappies and changed them.

Her stomach growled. Nap would soon be home for lunch. Glancing outside to see if he was there, her pulse quickened. The snowflakes had thickened and the wind had picked up. An uneasiness welled up inside her. Wondering what she would prepare for lunch, she descended the stairs into the cellar and cut pieces of ham that she brought back up with a couple of apples. She sliced four pieces of bread off one of her loaves and proceeded to make sandwiches.

Napoleon never made it back for lunch.

Lea watched out the window, biting her bottom lip. "Where are you, mon homme?"

She squinted and peered through the sheet of snow to see if she could pick out his outline, but only blinding white met her gaze. Apprehension filled her. She knew that in a blizzard, a walk from the barn to the house could result in losing one's way and freezing to death.

Panicked, she opened the door. Cold wind blasted her, depositing snow on the floor. She called, but no answer came.

"Napoleon!" she shouted again, but the driving wind drowned out her voice.

Lea shut the door and clapped her hands for warmth. "Oh, please God. Make him come home!"

She listened for what seemed hours for the comforting thump of his boots at the door, but all she heard was the whistling wind over the soft gurgles of the girls and the snapping of the wood in the stove.

By three o'clock, she became frantic, imagining every scenario possible.

"I've got to keep myself busy or I'll go crazy." She hurried down to the cellar to get meat and vegetables to make supper. The chopping of the vegetables calmed her and soon a rich stew simmered on the stove.

By nightfall, he still hadn't returned.

Lea waited on the couch, clutching her babies while wiping her eyes with a sleeve and whispering fervent prayers for his safe return.

After feeding and changing the girls once more, she finally nibbled at her supper, dipping her bread in the gravy. She bundled up the girls for the night and retired to her own bed, her tears wetting the pillow.

***

Emma and Palma's cries woke her in the night. She stretched out her hand to feel the warmth of her husband, but instead, her fingers touched cold sheets. Jolting awake, she lit the lantern, rose, and gathered the babies in her arms, taking them back to the bed where she laid them down beside her, her eyes filling with tears.

Emma and Palma suckled contentedly while she whimpered.

"Please, God, bring my Napoleon back home safe and sound." As the minutes passed, her cries grew more desperate. What would she do if he didn't return? Where would she go? Would she return to Belgium? Did she even have enough money for such a trip?

After a time, she fell asleep. When she awoke, the lingering warmth of the dying embers of the night before had given way to the freezing temperature of morning. Careful not to wake the girls, she crept to the stove and lit the fire. She cut what was left of the bread, smeared jam on it and ate it.

"I have to eat to keep my strength up," she said to herself.

When the girls awoke, she fed them and changed them, using lukewarm water from the stove for their bath. They screamed in protest.

"I know it's cold, but it'll be over before you know it." She kept her promise, swaddling them and replacing them in the basket by the fire. Then she turned her attention to the world outside.

The sun had just begun to rise to a scene of scintillating beauty. Diamonds glittered in columns of light that stretched across the glistening earth below a pale blue sky—a world transformed into a fairyland. But despite its splendour, Lea was filled with trepidation.

"Is it possible that something so beautiful could claim a human life?" She scrutinized the landscape, terrified lest she see a lump the size of Napoleon's body.

She clenched her fists. *I have to be strong. I'm not a child anymore!* She gazed past the snow to the big house. Surely they would help her find Nap now that the storm was over. Making sure the girls were settled, she bundled up and made her way to the Gilberts. It was so cold her steaming breath froze in her hair.

"Monsieur Gilbert!" she called as she trudged through the snow. "Please help! Mr. Gilbert!"

The door of the house flew open revealing the older man. He squinted in the bright sun. "What's wrong?"

"Napoleon didn't come back last night!" Her voice trembled.

"Didn't come back?"

"No!" She sunk down to her knees despite the icy snow.

"Hold on. I'm coming." He threw on his coat, gloves, and toque and carefully picked his way down the slippery stairs while Madame Gilbert and Cécile watched from the window. "Where did he say he was going?"

"To the barn like he does every morning."

"Then that's where we'll look first."

They plodded through the deep snow, their teeth chattering until they came to the barn door. Mr. Gilbert tried to yank it open, but ice blocked its path.

Lea bent down and began clearing it away with her hands. Her fingers stung despite the gloves she wore. Together they dug until they forced the door open, breaking the seal that had further debilitated their efforts.

"Napoleon, are you there?" Lea called, her voice pitched high. She held her breath as she listened.

"Napoleon!" called Mr. Gilbert.

Lea heard a rustle. "Over there."

They hurried to the horse's stalls.

"Napoleon?" called Lea.

The top of the stall door flung open revealing her husband's grinning face. "I'm right here."

Lea flung her arms around his neck, kissing his cold cheeks and nose. "Where have you been? I was so scared!"

"I'm sorry," he said, holding her tight. "I was going to come back, but I couldn't see the cabin from here, and I didn't want to take a chance. I had to spend the night with the mare in her stall. Look." He stepped back and showed her the straw bed he'd made for himself. "I had to use that old horse blanket to keep warm." He pinched his nose. "And boy, does it stink!"

Lea laughed through her tears. "You can change your clothes when you get home. I did all the laundry yesterday."

"Well, thank goodness for that."

"Are you hungry?" she asked, taking his hand.

"I sure am. If I'd been stuck here a day more, I'd have had to think about eating the mare."

Lea laughed again. "Then come on home and I'll make you a really good breakfast."

"Gladly. I can't take another minute of this mare's flatulence." And with that, they walked back to the cabin arm in arm.

***

134

Lea was humming Christmas carols as Napoleon pulled up in front of the door a week later, leading the two bay geldings attached to the sleigh. Her stomach fluttered with excitement. They were finally going to Wide View to meet the relatives.

"Look at the *chevaux*," she said to the girls. "Papa is taking us to meet your uncles and aunts for Christmas."

Palma let out a squeal at the hairy equine faces.

"I've put the heated rocks in the front," said Napoleon. "We can lay the girls there in their baskets and cover them up with blankets."

"Good idea." Lea handed him Emma first, then Palma. She took Nap's hand as he hoisted her up to the seat and covered her with a thick quilt.

"It'll take us about three hours to get there in the cutter," he said as he shook the reins.

"Hopefully we won't be frozen alive," she said, amusement in her voice.

The horses plodded through the snow, the sleigh sliding with ease through ruts already made by other farmers. Lea's ears stung from the cold. She pulled her toque lower. The freezing wind coloured Napoleon's cheeks to a bright red.

"You look like *Bonhomme Noël*," she said.

"Ah, but I am Bonhomme Noël. And have I got a special gift for you." He puckered up his lips and pulled her close.

"Bonhomme, really! I'll tell *Bonne Femme Noël.*"

"If you do, you won't get any presents."

"Oh, well. I guess I'd better be naughty then." She allowed him to kiss her deeply, her arm encircling his waist.

When they arrived in Wide View three hours later, they resembled icicles with their frozen hair. Nap jumped down from the sleigh and tied the horses. Lea handed him one baby at a time. When she lowered herself down beside them, she took one of the girls and together, they strode to the door.

It was a small house, not much larger than their own cabin, but well-built. It was obvious Nap's father was a fine carpenter. The door flew open before they had the chance to knock.

"Napoleon!" cried a bald-headed man with a round belly, holding his pipe in hand. "Finally we get to meet this bride of yours. And your two baby girls!"

"Papa, this is Leopoldine." Nap beamed with pride.

Levi grabbed Lea by the shoulders, planting a kiss on either cheek. "I thought you said she was ugly."

"I never said that!" Napoleon protested.

A figure with short, grey hair wearing a colourful apron came from behind Levi— Napoleon's mother, Emma.

"Bonjour! I'm so pleased to meet you, Leopoldine. Now where's the little girl who was named for me?"

"Right here, Maman." Nap handed her the correct baby.

"Why she's so beautiful!"

"And this is Palma," said Lea.

"Oh, my. They're as identical as can be!" exclaimed Emma.

"I know. I intend to dress them the same when they're older."

"Oh, won't that be fun!" Emma said. "I just love twins."

The sound of a fiddle caught Lea's attention.

"Come in. They're just tuning up the instruments!" Emma took Lea's coat and hung it in the closet.

"Go ahead," said Nap. "I'll put the horses in the barn."

"All right."

When Lea entered the room, excitement exploded from every direction.

"Everyone," declared Emma, "this is Napoleon's beautiful Belgian bride, Leopoldine, and their new baby daughters, Emma and Palma."

Several exuberant hellos shot out.

"And Leopoldine, these are our sons—Levi, Hector, and Euclide, and my daughters Maria, Bibianne, and Lumina."

Lea did her best to memorize their names but had soon forgotten them, particularly after Emma named all their spouses and children.

"It's okay," Emma said. "You'll get to know us quickly enough. I'm certain you'll remember all these names by the time you leave."

When Lea had been given a seat, the aunties passed the new babies around while children bounced about trying to glimpse them.

Uncle Emory picked up his fiddle and began a *quadrille* accompanied by Euclid on banjo. Soon, the other brothers joined in on their fiddles too.

"You never told me you had such a musical family!" Lea told Nap when he came in from the barn.

"I wanted it to be a surprise." He bowed to her. "Would you like to dance, Madame de Montigny?"

Her hands free of the little ones, Lea jumped up. Napoleon's feet skipped from left to right. When Lea got the hang of the steps, he twirled her around so fast, she felt dizzy. She squealed with laughter. Levi tapped Nap's soldier. It was his turn. One by one, each of the brothers asked her to dance. By the time the music had ended, Lea had danced with every man in the room.

When it was nearing midnight, Levi stood up and made an announcement. "It's time to go to church."

With his words, everyone rose and headed to the door where they dressed themselves in their warmest attire. Lea followed suit, bundling up the twins and herself. They rode in cutters to Wide View where the church lay nestled in the snow. Tiny flakes fell from the sky, small feathers dusting their clothing.

They crowded into the nave, taking up three pews in total. Candles lit the apse near the altar, filling the air with the smell of paraffin. An advent wreath stood close to where altar boys knelt in red and white cassocks.

The congregation sang Christmas carols in between the priest's sermon and the saying of the mass. Lea's heart soared when she recognized the traditional Christmas songs they sang back home. Her voice rose above the others. "*Il est né le divin enfant. Jouez hautbois, résonnez musettes.*"

Levi turned and stared at her, astonished. "Why you have an amazing voice!"

Lea felt her face warm. "Really? Why thank you."

"No, I mean it. You must sing for us the next time we play music."

"Do you think so?"

"Yes."

When the service was over, the family climbed back into the cutters and returned to the farm, caroling the whole way.

Levi sat beside Lea in the sleigh. "It must be quite a thing, moving all the way from Belgium to such a lonely place as Saskatchewan."

"It's certainly been an adventure," she said. "But it's not so lonely. The people we live with are more than just employers. They've become friends."

"I'm glad to hear that. Emma's found it trying at times. When you come from a place like Quebec, it can be hard to adjust to the solitude, but it helped once the rest of the family moved out here."

"I'm glad."

"You know we're thinking of giving up the farm and moving to Ponteix."

"Why?" asked Lea, her brows raised.

"Well, you know, I'm not getting any younger. I came out here more for my sons than anything else, to help them get started. It's not every day you can get a big chunk of land for next to nothing from the government. Has Nap applied for his homestead yet?"

"No, not yet."

"Tell him to hurry up. All that work he's doing for the Gilberts could be put toward your own land."

"That's true."

When they got home, the ladies laid out the food on the table for the *reveillon—tortière, creton*, *tarte au sucre*, *paté*, and ham. Lea savoured a slice of tortière that melted in her mouth, then refilled her plate with a piece of sugar pie. Then they opened their gifts.

Her eyes lit up at the pile of presents presented to her and Nap. She took her time opening each one, carefully undoing the ribbons that held them together and folding the paper afterward. Each time she unwrapped a gift, the aunts oohed and ahhed at the twin baby clothes each one contained. Lea smiled. She wouldn't be wanting for anything now.

"We've all been busy knitting sweaters and booties of different sizes for you," said Emma. "And Lumina made you plenty of nighties."

"Thank you, everyone," said Lea, admiring the fine embroidery on one of the sweaters. "It's all so beautiful."

"Wait. There's one more," said Levi. He handed Lea a large package.

Lea undid the wrapping, then opened the box. Her eyes rounded. It contained two of the prettiest baptismal dresses she'd ever seen.

"And there's more," said Emma. "We've arranged for the twins to be baptized tomorrow morning at the church."

"You have?" Lea exclaimed. "Napoleon, did you hear that?"

Her husband grinned from ear to ear. "Surprise again!"

Beds were found for everyone. After reclaiming her babies, Lea laid them to sleep in their basket, then climbed under the covers, cherishing each moment of the evening. For the first time since she arrived in Canada, she hadn't even thought of her family. It seemed she had found a new one in Saskatchewan. She hoped it was true that Levi was planning on moving to Ponteix. How nice it would be to have them so close.

Chapter Thirteen
The Theft

A weak moan roused Lea from a deep sleep several nights later in the Gilbert's cabin, a tiny, helpless sound that tore at her soul. Groping around in the dark, she made her way to the crib, her fingers searching until she found Emma. Shock ran through her at the searing heat that emanated from the tiny baby's body.

"Nap," she cried. "Wake up. I need light. Emma's sick."

Nap fumbled for the matches. "What's happening?"

"She's burning up!"

Nap broke off a match, then struck it, a glow lighting the room.

Lea pulled off the child's mittens and examined her. "Her hands are freezing. Quick, go build the fire. We need to keep it burning all night."

Napoleon rushed to the stove and laid the kindling inside. Soon, heat radiated in the cabin, but the baby still made the soft, pitiful sounds.

"Why don't you try feeding her?" he asked.

Lea lifted her nighty, and positioned the baby, but Emma wouldn't latch on. Instead, she arched her back, let out a feeble cry, and vomited.

"Oh, no!" Napoleon reached for fresh rags to clean her up.

Lea's heart raced. *What's wrong?* She searched her memory. What would Maman have done back home in Belgium? If only she had listened when other women talked about their children's ailments. She paced around the room, jiggling Emma. Then she remembered what the doctor had said on the ship when she'd been sick. "We need cold compresses to keep the fever down."

"I'll get one." Napoleon took another clean rag, dipped it into the half-thawed snow on the stove, and handed it to Lea.

Lea covered the baby's head with the cloth. Emma gave a pathetic cry, then burst into a fit of trembling.

"Keep the rest of her body warm," said Napoleon.

"That's what I'm trying to do."

To add to their troubles, Palma's cry erupted from the crib.

"Here, give me Emma so you can feed Palma," he said, reaching for the sick baby.

Lea handed him the child and took the other twin into her arms, relieved Palma showed no signs of fever. When she'd finished nursing her, she changed both girls. Emma's nappy was dry.

"I'm going for Dr. Lupien!" said Napoleon.

"We should all go together."

"No. It'll take too long to prepare the sleigh. I'll go with the mare."

"Hurry, then!"

Napoleon dressed quickly and left the house. Lea heard his feet crunch through the snow and the barn door slide open. A few minutes later, she listened as the sound of the mare's hooves broke from a trot to a canter. Looking out the window, she saw Napoleon gallop away. He hadn't even saddled his mount.

The wait was torturous as Emma grew weaker and fussier. By the time daylight crept in, Nap and the doctor hadn't arrived yet, nor had Emma's fever diminished. Lea applied more compresses with little effect. She tried to hold the baby closer, but Emma fought back, her angry fists clenched.

"Please, God," Lea prayed, "make them come soon."

As the skies brightened, Lea's desperation grew as she held Emma in her arms while Palma slept in her basket by the stove. The thudding of horse hooves in the snow announced Nap's arrival. Peering outside, she was dismayed to see he was alone. Lea hurried to the door and flung it open. A cold, biting wind assaulted her, tiny pinpricks that stung her face.

"What happened?" she cried. "Where's Dr. Lupien?"

"He's out delivering a baby. Madame Lupien invited me to stay inside until he returned, but when it started to get light out, I told her I had to leave. I figured you'd need me home. She says she'll send him our way as soon as he's done."

144

"Oh, Nap!" Her voice trembled. "Emma's not getting better. I'm afraid she may die." She looked to him for reassurance, but when their eyes met, she saw the same cold, helpless fear reflected back at her.

"You mustn't think that way," he said, turning away.

"But I can't help it."

Napoleon tsked. After an uncomfortable silence, he glanced at the main house. "I'll go and see if the Gilberts can help."

"All right. Hurry!" Lea watched as he disappeared into the barn to put away the mare, then plodded through the snow to the older couple's home.

Madame Gilbert came immediately, carrying her own bottles of remedies. When she laid eyes on Emma, her face fell. "How long has she been throwing up?"

"Since the middle of the night."

Madame Gilbert glanced about, then flew into action. "We have to get some fluids in her." She grabbed a clean rag, soaked it in water, and wrung it out. She coaxed the corner of Emma's mouth with it.

Emma whimpered and turned her head.

"She's been refusing milk too," said Lea.

"Let's try again."

She took the corner of the cloth and gently coaxed another spot on the child's lips, but Emma merely fussed all the more and vomited again.

The women hurried to clean her up while Napoleon stood back, clutching Palma in his protective arms.

It was just after three o'clock when Dr. Lupien arrived, his eyes sunken as though he'd been up all night. Napoleon ran to the door, relieved.

"I came as soon as I could," said Dr. Lupien. "Where's the baby?"

"Over here." Lea handed him the hot little bundle.

Dr. Lupien's face turned to ash when he saw her.

"What is it?" asked Lea.

Sitting down, the doctor carefully removed her little hat. When his eyes met Lea's, his expression was grave.

"What?" asked Lea again.

"Your daughter has meningitis."

"What's that?" asked Napoleon, his voice weak.

"It's inflammation of the brain. See, look. You see the fontanelle?"

"Yes," replied Nap.

"It's bulging. That means, her brain is swelling."

"Well, what can we do for her?" Nap asked. "Give us the medicine we need. We don't care about the cost. She's our baby girl!" His voice cracked on the last two words.

Dr. Lupien turned away, his eyelids blinking rapidly as he bit down on his lip. He took a deep breath as though composing himself, then uttered the diagnosis Lea couldn't bear to hear. "There's nothing we can do. We just have to wait until God takes her."

"No!" cried Lea. "That's impossible!" She bent her head toward Emma, hugging her tightly and sobbing.

"Lea," said Madame Gilbert, laying her arm around her shoulders. "Many of us lose little ones. I know it hurts, but there'll be others."

"But they're not my little Emma. I love her so much." Her sobs were uncontrollable.

"I know. But you still have Palma."

"But I want *both* my girls!" Lea shrieked.

The hours were interminable as they waited for death to claim the baby girl. Her breathing grew more and more ragged. Lea whispered prayers as life slipped away from her child. Shortly before eight, Emma took a final breath and lay still. Napoleon handed Palma to Madame Gilbert and collapsed on the couch beside Lea. Together they shared destitute tears as they held the little lifeless body they'd soon bury in the cold ground.

"I'll send Mr. Gilbert to inform your family in Wide View as soon as we know the date of her burial," said Madame Gilbert.

"Okay," replied Lea, her shoulders heaving. "But I don't know what to do with her now."

"You'll have to keep her in the cellar until the day of the funeral."

"But it's too cold down there," Lea cried.

"You have no choice," said Madame Gilbert.

"But—"

"Let's prepare her first." Napoleon rose, grabbing the tub from where it hung on the wall and filling it with water.

When all was ready, they bathed Emma for the last time and dressed her in her baptismal dress, tying one of the new hats around her head, and placing crocheted mittens on her tiny hands. Lea placed the little girl in her basket, but instead of laying her by the stove as she usually did, she handed the baby back to Napoleon who carried her like his most cherished possession down the cellar stairs.

"Good-bye, my sweet Emma," said Lea, squeezing her tiny hand for the last time. "I'll see you in the next life."

After they had closed the trap door, Nap disappeared into the barn, his face intent with purpose while Lea retired to their bedroom. She opened the drawer of the dresser and looked at all the beautiful baby clothes she'd received only a few days earlier, her eyes clouded with tears. Tracing the smooth satin ribbons in one of the sweaters, she hiccoughed. Then rage filled her. Grabbing the tiny, hand-knit garments, she tossed them about, sobbing bitterly.

"God! You stole my child! You stole my baby girl! How dare you! You're a thief! A common thief!" She threw open the closet that held her wedding dress, resolved to tear it to shreds, then stopped. Fingering the fabric, she examined the tiny flowers embroidered into the navy blue cloth. She knew what had to be done.

Nap returned from the barn late that night and laid the small casket he'd built on the coffee table. Bending down, he reached for the handle of the trap door.

"Wait," Lea said.

She returned to their room and came back with the dress and her sewing kit. She measured the box, then the fabric of the skirt. Within an hour, she'd made the perfect lining and a small pillow for Emma's casket.

When they laid the child inside, Lea said, "There, my sweet little girl. Now you'll sleep more comfortably."

***

The funeral was set for three days later. But on the second day, Palma succumbed to the same ailment. The child was laid in the same casket as her sister, wearing her matching baptismal dress, and the two were buried in the churchyard to sad hymns sung by the very people with whom they'd just celebrated the girls' christening.

***

January cut cold and deep. Lea moved about her daily chores and routines, mindless, kneading dough to a rhythm without melody, cooking food to a poem without words. And when the bread was baked and the meals had been prepared, she sat before the window, staring at the snowflakes whipped by the wind, at the drifts forming, her thoughts empty save for the sadness of her daughters stolen by a merciless god and the absence of her family an entire world away in Belgium.

Napoleon moved the crib and the baskets into the barn and boxed the tiny baby clothes so nothing would remind her of their loss, but still she noticed the empty spaces, and it made the void in her life all the larger. She'd lost her two greatest loves, and the people closest to her weren't even there to console her.

Napoleon tried to cheer her up with warm embraces and thoughtful gestures. Each day she met his actions with silence, as though he were a ghost, a mirage of something that had once been. She caught the occasional worried glance he cast before leaving when morning's light called him to work and heard the soft mutterings of anxious conversations with Mr. Gilbert.

When a month had passed, Napoleon, his face contorted in anguish, confronted her, standing tall and formidable like the soldier he'd once been. "Madame Gilbert wants you to come for tea. She says it's been a while since you've visited her and Cécile."

Lea gave a blank nod.

"Apparently, this is the time of year to be making clothes. She says she's bought new fabric you might be interested in."

Her ears perked up at the mention of the fabric. For a moment, her eyes met his. "What time?"

"After lunch."

"All right, then I'll be there."

"And could you please do some laundry this morning? I'm out of shirts. This one smells so bad I'm sure there's a green cloud following me along."

A stray, lifeless giggle escaped Lea. "Whatever you want."

Napoleon hauled in the snow and melted it for her on the stove.

After he left, she proceeded to do the laundry, mechanically scrubbing it as she usually did, but when she hung it all to dry, the missing nappies filled her with emptiness again.

The women welcomed her graciously, placing warm arms about her when she knocked on the door of the main house that afternoon.

"Wait until you see the fabric I ordered at the general store," said Madame Gilbert, her voice overly-animated as she unrolled a length of floral print. "See how pretty it is?"

"Yes, it is." Lea gave a dull smile.

"I said we should all make matching dresses!" Cécile laughed.

"And show up for Easter mass like triplets," added Madame Gilbert.

A slightly amused curve formed on Lea's lips. "But I left my patterns back in Belgium."

"Well, you won't need them here. We make our own…from scratch."

"Really?" Lea arched an interested brow.

"Yes. You see, the fashion nowadays is straight dresses, as you know. So all we need to do is measure your hips, bust, shoulders, and length, then add a bit to each side to make the seams. Like this."

Lea watched as Cécile took Madame Gilbert's measurements and then transferred the numbers to the fabric, drawing lines with a pencil and ruler. After cutting out the forms, they set about doing the same for Cécile.

"I'm going to add a few more inches to this one." Madame Gilbert patted her daughter's stomach. "Just in case."

"Oh, Maman." Resentment creased Cécile's forehead. "Do you always have to be going on about having grandchildren?"

"Well, you can't hold it against me now, can you? They say being a grandparent is one of life's most precious experiences. If only your husband would stay home from time to time."

Cécile let out an impatient huff. "Maman."

Madame Gilbert ignored her and finished drawing the dress. Then she turned to Lea. "Let's measure *you* now. I'll make yours wide as well, but with a belt. Never know when you might need some extra space too."

A brief flicker of hope filled Lea.

After cutting all the fabric, they stitched until the light grew too dim to work anymore, sipping tea and eating cookies as they sewed. Lea admired Madame Gilbert and Cécile's work and hoped her garments would turn out as well as theirs. That's when it dawned on her that for the first time in a month, she was interested in life again.

When she returned home that evening, she gave Nap the warmest kiss he'd received in a long time.

"Did you have a good day?" he asked.

"Yes, I did. Thank you."

"I'm so glad. By the way, you got news from home." He handed her a letter.

Lea grabbed it and read the return address. "It's from Palma." She ripped it open.

Dear Lea,

I'm so sorry to hear about your dear little girls' passing on. I had so looked forward to meeting my namesake, little Palma. What nicknames we could have invented for her. We all cried when we heard the news, especially Maman. She so misses you. Had I been a bird, I would have flown to your side immediately. But of course, boats can't fly. If only they'd invent planes that could travel over the Atlantic.

But oh, have I got news for you. I'm married! Yes, can you believe it? I'm actually married! As you remember, I was terrified at Papa's suggestion to wed old Mr. Georgini, but when I was taken to his home, it turned out it wasn't him at all, but his son Dino that I was to be engaged to! And let me tell you, he's one handsome fellow. Well, I stopped balking at the match and we were married two weeks later. I'm as happy as a clown in a circus. We've rented an apartment, and I'm enjoying getting to know him. When things are settled, in a year or so, I may suggest to him that we emigrate to Canada.

I pray for you each day.
Palma

Lea burst into laughter.

"What's so funny?" asked Nap, his eyes wide with astonishment at her change in mood.

"Palma's married! Turns out it was the old guy's son. And look." She reached into the envelope. "Here's their picture."

Nap, seized the photo. "And here I was trying to put money aside for her."

"You were?"

"Yes, I was going to surprise you when I had enough. I'm so relieved."

Lea squeezed his arm. "She says she's still thinking of immigrating here. I wonder how you and Dino would get along. Maybe Maman and Papa could come to Canada too."

"That would be great."

For the next few weeks, Lea spent each day at the Gilberts, sewing more and more clothing. It was on one of those days, she noticed a familiar sea sickness as she worked the cloth. Lea raised her head from her work and smiled. Another baby was on the way!

PART II – The Homestead

Chapter Fourteen
New Beginnings

Dear Maman, Papa, and family,

I have wonderful news. After all this time, the government has finally granted us our homestead! It was worth the ten-dollar investment to apply.

Nap took me to see it yesterday in the Maxwell. I'm so glad we decided to buy that automobile. It's the handiest thing we've ever owned even though it takes a lot to operate it in the winter, boiling water for the radiator and all. But it gives us such freedom. Nap decided it was a necessity after Baby Roger died. He says that if we'd gotten to the hospital sooner, Roger might have survived the pneumonia that took his life. It still hurts terribly to have three babies buried in the Ponteix cemetery, but at least now we have Pol and Lilian.

The homestead is beautiful. It's near a brand new town called Masefield. There's no post office yet, but there's a blacksmith shop there, and they're planning to build a school. It would be better if the land was closer to Val Marie since that town's French, but we can always travel the twelve miles there on Sunday for mass.

Nap is looking forward to breaking the sod on the homestead, but he assures me we will not be living in a soddy. He has put aside two hundred and fifty dollars to buy lumber for the house and a hundred dollars to build the barn! Claude will help him. They'll start fencing the land as soon as they're finished harvesting the crop for Mr. Gilbert. I'm so excited. It'll be wonderful to pocket the money from our hard work instead of Nap being paid as a hired hand.

Little Pol is growing like a weed. He's almost four years old. He's a wonderful little boy who's very curious about everything. He has so brightened up our lives. But he was sure confused when Lilian arrived. She came so quickly we didn't even have time to go to the hospital, and by the time Pol woke up, there she was. When we introduced Lilian to him, he stared at her with an odd expression, and then picked up his ball as though a toy were more interesting than his new baby sister.

I'm glad the difficult times we faced five years ago when we lost the girls have passed. I still leave wild flowers on their grave whenever I can. They will always *have a special place in my heart that no one can ever take.*

I've enclosed a photo of Nap, Pol, Lilian and me on the new land. It's so nice to finally have a camera.
Love,
Lea

Lea slipped the photo inside the envelope, licked and stamped it. She sighed. It would be difficult leaving the Gilberts after having lived on their farm so long, but she hoped that Claude and Cécile's application for a homestead would land them close by.

The summer passed quickly with its burning heat and never ending work. When the wheat had been harvested and the fruits picked and canned, Nap and Claude set out to Masefield to prepare the homestead. It seemed to take forever since Nap was oftentimes gone for weeks at a time, but when he returned, Lea and the children always welcomed him warmly. Christmas came and went, this time in Ponteix since Levi had honoured his word and retired. In late spring, Lea received the letter from Nap inviting her to join him.

She lost no time in packing up the children and their belongings and made her way to the station.

"Un train, Maman!" Pol pointed at the iron horse whose steam puffed from its smokestack.

"Oui, mon cheri. Un train qui va nous emmener à Papa."

She lifted the children up the stairs of the car, then went back for the baggage. Settling them in a seat close to the window, she arranged the luggage overhead before sitting down.

The rhythmic chugging of the train began. Slow at first, its speed increased. Soon it snaked its way through the prairie countryside, past vast acreages of freshly harrowed fields and rows of green seedlings. Lea gazed up at the magnificent clouds that rose high above them, hiding the sun for brief moments as it traveled across the sky; *like giant statues, majestic warriors,* she thought.

"C'est vite," said Pol, turning to gaze at his mother with adoring eyes.

"Oui. Très vite."

An hour passed before the train slowed, coming to a stop in the town of Killarney. With the help of the porter, Lea unloaded the baggage, descended the stairs, and walked a block away, her feet echoing on the wooden sidewalk, until she found the post office and stepped inside.

"Hello, I'm looking for the mail truck to take us to Masefield."

The man behind the counter scowled at her. "We're not a bus service, you know."

"Yes, I realize this, but my husband is waiting for us there."

"Who's your husband?" he asked, drumming his fingers.

"Napoleon de Montigny."

The man's eyes lit up. "Ah, Nap! How's he doing anyway? Haven't seen him in years. He and I used to work together. I see he got himself a pretty wife…and a couple of kids."

"Thank you," said Lea.

"Come right this way." Smiling from ear to ear, the man rose, and took her suitcases, leading the way. "It's around the back. It leaves at eleven o'clock."

She followed him into the alley where a wooden bench provided a comfortable place to sit so she could feed the children. She pulled out some bread and cheese. Pol reached for it and stuffed it in his mouth, chewing contentedly while she nursed Lilian.

The ride from Killarney to Val Marie began smoothly, but soon turned bumpy, the roads transforming to wagon trails riddled with potholes. Pol shrieked and laughed with every bump while Lea clutched his arm and held Lilian tight against her body.

"Sorry about that," said the driver. "After a long winter, the roads are pretty damaged."

"It's okay," she said. "Pol thinks it's fun."

Lea's back ached by the time Masefield came into sight. It wasn't much of a town yet with only a few freshly constructed buildings, but it meant they'd soon be home.

She saw Napoleon from a distance leaning against the Maxwell. When the mail truck pulled up, Lea opened the door, and Pol broke away from her and ran into his arms.

"Papa!" he shouted.

Nap swooped him up. "Allô, Pol. Were you a good boy?"

"Oui," the child replied.

"Then I have this for you." Reaching into his pocket, he pulled out a candy stick and handed it to his son.

"Merci, Papa."

Lea gazed about her. How different from that cold, blustery day in March when they'd first arrived in Ponteix and the Gilberts had picked them up, the freezing wind numbing her ears, and miles of blinding snow forcing her eyes into a squint. Now crocuses shot purple petals through the wild, green grass. Plowed fields emitted the scent of fresh earth, and the air was warm.

Nap whistled a happy tune as they drove, occasionally throwing an affectionate glance at his wife and children. Lea knew he was excited to show her all he'd done and that she'd better act pleased no matter what. After all, she could always add her own feminine touch after they moved in.

The wagon trail they traveled on veered to the right and rose up a steep hill. Nap stepped on the gas until they'd reached the top. Two small mounds came into view, connected by a barb-wired fence that opened into a pasture. A Jersey cow gave them an inquisitive stare from inside.

"*Une vache,* Maman," said little Pol.

"Oui," said Lea. "A cow."

Napoleon stopped the Maxwell, jumped out, and opened the gate. Once he'd driven through, he shut it and climbed back in. They coasted the rest of the way to where the house and barn stood, the Jersey following close behind.

When Lea opened the door of the automobile, Pol raced to the cow, reached out his hand, and stroked the animal's lowered head.

"She's more like a pet than livestock," said Lea, catching up to her son.

"This is the little Jersey cow I wrote to you about when I sent for you in Belgium. She loves people," said Nap. "I bought her off a neighbour in Ponteix."

"How cute. What's her name?"

"Why Jersey, of course."

Lea laughed and stretched out her hand. "Jersey! Come here, girl!"

The cow took eager steps toward her, flapping its lips as though expecting grain.

"Sorry, girl. I haven't got any food." She ruffled the cow's forehead instead.

"Now come and see the house. Nap tipped his head in the direction of their new home.

Lea turned to admire the cabin that stood a short distance away. It was a tiny house, smaller than the Gilberts', but prettier and newer. Its walls were built of shiplap. A single stovepipe rose from the cedar-shingled roof that sloped down from one end to the other in anticipation of snow.

"It's beautiful," said Lea

"It's kind of small, but it's only temporary. I'll build a better one as we make money. But in the meantime, I have an even bigger surprise for you."

"What?"

"Close your eyes."

Lea did as she was told. She heard Nap turn the handle and swing the door open. The smell of fresh wood met her nose. He pulled her inside.

"Now open them."

Lea's eyes widened at what she saw. The prettiest oven-stove she'd ever seen stood before her. "A Blue Royal Windsor! Oh, Nap! Just think how easy it will be to make bread or bake a cake. And look at all the room to boil vegetables. And there are two compartments to keep food warm. I just love it!"

"But that's not all." He placed his hands on her shoulders and turned her to the right. "Look at the table I built. It has an extension for when our family grows."

Lea gazed at the dark brown dining set, but her eyes were drawn farther to where a matching cabinet stood, her dishes placed carefully inside. "Wow!"

"And here's the living room." He turned her around again. "For now, we can all sleep here until I build the new house." He showed her the sofa bed and the Maurice chair that opened up for Pol. "And we have a cellar too, and…I made a huge wardrobe." He walked over and opened its doors to show her.

Lea smiled. "It's huge."

"Now come outside."

He took her to the side of the cabin to where a hand-operated washing machine stood.

"Nap! A washing machine?"

"Mm-hm. I figured you were probably tired of scrubbing everything in the tub. Now all you'll have to do is push the handle for twenty minutes and it'll do all the scrubbing for you. It'll save you a lot of time."

"I love it!"

Next, he led her to the barn that stood two hundred feet away near the slough. It too was built of shiplap, but instead of a cedar roof, Nap had laid poles that he'd covered with straw.

He took her by the arm and led her while Pol ran to catch his mother's hand. Napoleon slid open the door. Lea stepped inside, allowing her eyes to grow accustomed. Dark figures rose above stall doors.

"Horses!" she exclaimed. "Six of them!"

"Yes. We'll need them to break all that land. I plan to cultivate more ground every year to increase our crops." He moved to the first stall. "This is Old Dick and his partner Belle, and that's Prince and Star over there, and these ones are still a little wild—King and Queen."

"They're gorgeous."

A familiar grunting caught Lea's attention.

"You got a pig?"

"Yup. Sure did. To butcher in the fall."

Lea reached her hand in. "Hello there, little piggy. So glad to have you on our farm."

It squealed in reply, its nose wiggling in search of any food Lea might be willing to offer.

"Sorry, girl."

"Now come out back," said Napoleon.

Lea followed him to where a small chicken coop made of sod stood in the shade of the barn.

"Good! We'll have our own eggs." She eyed the slough. "But what about the well? Will we be drawing our water from over there?"

"Never, my beautiful. Not *my* wife." They walked a few feet to where a round wall of stone stood, covered by a wooden roof. Cranking the bucket up from below, he submerged the dipper. "Taste it."

Lea took a long drink and nodded in satisfaction. "Not bad." Turning around, her eyes scanned the house and barnyard. "So where's the outhouse?"

Nap cleared his throat. "About that…" He gave a sheepish smile. "We'll just use the barn. After all, if the animals can, why not us?"

Lea giggled. "But what about winter when it's too cold?"

"I thought about that too." He walked back to the barn and retrieved a bucket with a lid. "This will be our house toilet. When we're done, we can put the cover on so it doesn't smell. But right now, your job is to unpack and start preparing the supper while I get you a chicken."

Lea laughed, still remembering the hard-learned lesson from their earlier days when she didn't know how to pluck a bird. How innocent she'd been and how far she'd come in seven years. "I'll boil the water."

**

Lea watched from outside the corral as Nap opened the pasture gate, then walked back to the center post he had erected in the middle of the pen. It was horse-breaking day just as it had been last Sunday and the Sunday before. One by one, the horses entered the corral. Old Dick was the last to meander in.

Nap waited, his body flattened against the pole, his rope in hand, until the youngest of the horses, the bay gelding he called Prince, edged closer. Using slow movements so as not to spook the animal, Nap raised his rope, twirled it, and tossed it. The rope landed neatly around the animal's neck. In one quick swoop, Nap looped the other end of the cord over the post before herding the other horses back into the pasture.

Prince screamed in rage and wedged his heels into the dirt as he tugged the rope. It dug into his neck, threatening to strangle him.

Lea gripped the top rung of the fence.

The horse reared and pawed his hooves in the air, then snaked to the side, throwing out his back hooves. He balked, twisted and turned, pulling the post with all his might. It didn't budge. Strangled whinnies ripped from his throat. He paused to catch a lungful of air, then began all over again, writhing and zigzagging until a small trickle of blood seeped from his neck. Lea's knuckles turned white, certain the animal would die. Then, just as quickly as the struggle began, it let out a huff of air and ceased fighting, its energy spent.

Nap took slow steps toward Prince, speaking in a low, soothing voice.

Prince's crazed eyes stared back. He shuffled to the side.

"You know me, boy. I give you hay each morning. You don't have to be afraid." He inched closer, reaching a slow hand out to reveal the oats within, a halter hidden behind his back.

The horse's lips flapped over Nap's straightened hand, nervous as he devoured the grain.

Nap withdrew the other arm and, using calculated movements, slipped the halter over the horse's head.

Prince threw his mane back and shook it while Nap reached up and quickly secured the strap. He pulled out more oats. The horse accepted them, calmer this time.

Taking the lead rope, Nap led Prince around the corral several times, then tied him to the post.

"Okay, it's your turn now, Old Dick," he said, addressing the dapple grey who stood waiting patiently just outside the corral. Nap led him to the wagon, attached the harness, then waved to Lea.

Lea glanced down at Baby Lilian, assuring herself the little girl slept comfortably in her basket. Looking back at Pol, she was satisfied he'd keep himself busy shoveling dirt into his bucket for a good while. She stepped into the corral, taking her place before Dick to hold him steady while Napoleon worked at placing the collar on the gelding.

Prince was spooked as Nap lifted the collar, taking quick steps back, his hooves gouging the dirt.

Napoleon slowed his movements, speaking softly as he lifted the collar again. Prince allowed him to approach, his ears flicking. He balked. Lea held Old Dick's lead as the young gelding dragged her to the left. Again, Nap spoke soothing words, then slid the collar over the horse's head.

"Good," whispered Lea.

"Now comes the difficult part," said Napoleon. "I'm going to attach him to the wagon. So hold on tight."

Lea braced herself, sliding her hand up the reins beneath Old Dick's chin and tightening her grip.

Napoleon laid the harness over the horse's back. Prince bucked, throwing it onto the ground. Nap began again, this time, managing to secure the harness and fastening it to the wagon.

"Okay," he said in the quietest of voices. "When I say *now,* let go, then open the gate."

He carefully hoisted himself onto the wagon, then shouted, "Now!"

Lea released Old Dick's halter and ran.

Prince leapt and off they went. He twisted this way and that while Old Dick continued to trot at a steady pace, obeying the guide of the reins as Nap drove them.

Lea giggled as she watched.

Forty-five minutes later, they returned, the gelding sufficiently calmed down.

Lea clapped her hands. "Well done, mon homme!"

Jumping down from the wagon, Nap grabbed Dick's reins and handed them to Lea. She held Old Dick steady while he unharnessed both horses. Prince cantered furiously away, kicking dust back at them as though he'd been gravely insulted.

"Now I have enough horses broken to clear more land."

The next day, Nap hooked them up to the wagon while Lea held Old Dick. After Prince had settled down, she followed them out to the field, carrying Lilian in her basket and leading Pol by the hand. When they reached the patch of land they were to clear, she placed the children in the shade of the cart, then set to work with Nap to remove the stones necessary to plow the land.

Lea reached into the wagon and took out one of the picks. Spying a stone, she dug it out. She proceeded to find others the same size, piling them as she worked. When she'd made a sufficiently large stack, she loaded them onto the wagon.

"Lea," Nap called her after an hour had gone by. "Come and help me with this one."

She walked over to where Napoleon struggled with a massive stone.

"I've managed to dig underneath it, but when I try to hoist it up, it collapses back into the hole. I'm going to raise it up again, and when I do, I want you to toss some of the smaller stones underneath so it can't fall back in."

"Okay." Lea sauntered back to the wagon, loaded up some of the smaller rocks, and carried them back in her skirt.

"Okay, on the count of three. One, two, three." He lodged the crowbar underneath and heaved it up.

She dropped the stones down the hole. The rock landed higher than it had before. Going back to her pile, she loaded her skirt again.

"All right. One, two, three."

She threw more stones under the large rock. It stood taller.

"Okay, I think this is it. One more try and I should be able to get it out." Taking the tool, Nap pushed with all his might. The stone rose higher and higher. "Almost there!" Nap gave the crowbar a final shove.

A loud scrape ripped the air.

Lea watched in horror as the crowbar catapulted out of the hole and struck Nap in the forehead. He let out a cry and rolled on the ground, clutching his head in anguish. Blood gushed from the wound.

"Nap!"

Visions of the battlefield assailed her—the young man whose skull had been partially blown away, still alive. Lea's breath came in gasps. Frantically turning about, she scoured the horizon for someone, anyone, to help. No paramedics ran to her aid. Only empty fields stretched out before her.

"What should I do?" she screamed.

"Tear your skirt and make a bandage! Quick!"

Of course. She knew that. How often had she bound wounds on the battlefield? Swallowing her panic, she reached down and made a small rip in her skirt. Yanking it, she pulled back a strip long enough to fit around his head. She knelt beside him, first applying pressure until the bleeding slowed, then wrapping the makeshift bandage around the wound.

Napoleon sat up, catching his breath. He took her hand, then gave her a rueful smile. "I think we're done for the day. What do you think?"

"Agreed. Let's go home. This needs cleaning."

"Okay, but only because you say so."

She shot him a disgruntled frown.

Lea left the tools where they lay, loaded the children and Nap onto the wagon, and drove the team home. She removed the harness when they arrived, releasing the horses into the pasture and hanging the tack in the barn. Prince stared back at her, mischief in his eyes.

"Don't even try anything on me," she said in a low voice as she scowled back at the gelding.

Chapter Fifteen
The Card Game

Lea led the Jersey to the barn, tied her to one of the posts and hobbled her hind legs, making sure the straps were tight. The animal let out a protesting moo. Reaching into the corner, Lea grabbed the bucket and placed it underneath the cow's udder. She felt behind for the handle of the three-legged stool and set it down on the left side of the cow. Making herself comfortable, she began milking. The smell of fresh cream filled the air.

"That's a good girl, Jersey. Feels nice, doesn't it? And we'll enjoy your milk. We'll make cheese with it and all kinds of other delicious things. You're such a good cow." She broke into a melody, humming as she worked, its rhythm in sync with the squirting sounds as the milk splashed into the metal bucket. When the cow's udder was empty, she took the liquid, filled a long canister, and walked to the well where she lowered it down the shaft so it would stay cool despite the sweltering, summer Saskatchewan heat. Then she removed the hobbles from the Jersey's hind legs and released her into the pasture.

As the cow sauntered away, Lea turned her attention to the garden she'd planted. How well it was doing! Carrot tops, like green lace, pushed up from the soil. Wide leaves hid potatoes that grew beneath them. Tall stalks rose from onion bulbs. Green sorrel leaves promised a delicious winter soup. And her tomatoes were so plentiful that she had to can every third day to keep up. She was glad red buffalo berries grew nearby so she could pick them with Pol, thus allowing her more time to make jam. Already there were two dozen jars stacked on the shelves in the basement. She looked forward to the frost that would sweeten the remaining berries on the bush.

It had been an excellent summer, despite the overbearing heat and mosquitoes—even Lilian was covered in welts despite Lea's care to keep her chubby limbs concealed. The crops had yielded forty bushels to the acre, and the cellar would soon be full once she'd harvested all that grew in the garden. But there was still so much to do before the chill of winter set in. They'd have to buy wood to keep the stove burning. And because of the bumper crop, they needed a dry place to store the wheat until it could be sold.

Lea's glance shifted to the side of the house where Nap pounded shiplap on the frame of the new lean-to he'd decided to build to store the grain. Perhaps next year, they'd have so much wheat they'd have to take it to the elevators in town. She loved the way Nap's tongue poked out of the corner of his mouth every time he pounded his hammer. Her heart swelled at his skills both as a farmer and a carpenter. He'd already made the decision to build houses over the winter to tide the family over until the following year. And with the breaking of more land, she was that much closer to her dream of going home to Belgium. How thrilled Maman would be, though surely, she'd notice the rough callouses on Lea's hands from the hard work. And how wonderful to see Palma and her little family and to meet Mathilde's new husband, Amadori, even though her sister didn't seem so enthused about him in the letters she'd written. She was pleased Camille had married and wondered how François fared with his damaged hand.

"Lea!" Napoleon motioned her over. "Come here. I have news for you."

"What?" she asked, walking toward him.

"You know that new guy who's just settled a mile south of us?"

"Bourlon? Yes, what about him?" He had stopped by earlier, leaned up against the Maxwell while chatting with Nap for a brief time before continuing on his way.

"Says he's building himself a blacksmith shop, so we won't have to go to town anymore to shoe the horses. And he said he heard there were more homesteaders coming. Soon we'll have so many neighbours we won't know what to do with them all."

"That's wonderful!" Lea said, hoping they'd be French.

"And speaking of which, there's a card social in Val Marie this Saturday night. They've asked that we perform."

Lea smiled. She quite enjoyed the evenings in town, especially when they requested her to sing. It gave her a chance to feel important, like the old Lea of days gone by, before the children, before the farm.

When Saturday evening arrived, they packed up the family in the Maxwell and headed to Val Marie. Lilian cooed from her basket while Pol sat up, staring out the window. Excitement filled Lea. It would be so good to be around other women after a summer of canning and cooking for the coarse men Nap had hired to help with the harvest. She marveled at the golden fields as they drove past. Acres and acres of amber stalks blew lazily in the breeze between the farm and town. They were just as beautiful as Nap had described to her back in Belgium. She wished she could take a photo to send home, but the black and white prints would never reveal the true colours.

When they rolled up to the church hall, Lea bent down to grab the sandwiches she'd made as her contribution to the evening, and the plate of her well-known *galettes*, small, extra-sweet waffles.

"I'll take those," said Napoleon as he came around the Maxwell.

Lea handed him the sandwiches, balancing the plate of pastries on top.

"No dipping into the galettes," she said, casting him a wary eye.

Napoleon flashed her a mischievous grin, making as though he'd pick one up in his mouth.

A woman gave an exuberant wave at Lea as she lifted Lilian from the dusty automobile.

It was Cécile. Grabbing Pol's hand, she hurried to her friend and threw her arms about her. "Cécile! I'm so glad you finally got your homestead in Val Marie. Now we'll get to see each other every week in church."

"Me too." They exchanged salutational pecks on the cheeks.

"So this is the new baby!" said Cécile.

"Yes."

"Oh, she's so cute."

"Thank you," said Lea. "And she's very good too. She hardly ever cries."

The two women fussed over Lilian who smiled and squealed back at them, putting on her own little show. Lea stretched her neck, scanning. "Where's Claude?"

Cécile's face darkened. "He's over there with some guys he met in town."

Lea's gaze wandered to where a loud group of men smoked and guffawed. *The Proux boys!* Her teeth clenched. They were known for bar brawls and other rude behavior. Rumour had it that one of them had even spent time in prison, plus one of the older girls had born a child out of wedlock.

"They're going to play poker tonight, and they've asked that Claude join them."

"Well, it *is* a card evening, and I'm sure they won't try to gamble in front of Père Fortier."

"No. They'll just disappear and play in someone's basement," said Cécile, a sarcastic tone in her voice. "I just hate it." She shook her head. "I mean, we finally get our homestead, and he has to go and risk gambling all our savings away."

"Oh, Cécile, I'm so sorry."

Her friend let out a sigh. "It's my own fault. I was a bit too quick in marrying him. I should have gotten to know him better."

"Why didn't you?"

Cécile squirmed before answering. "Well, harvest season was over, and he was going to leave. And he said if I didn't marry him that night that there were plenty of other farm girls to choose from."

"That's dreadful!" Lea threw a disgusted look back at Claude.

Cécile pressed her lips together in a tight line. "I can't stand the way he goes to town and comes back drunk. How can we raise a family or even start one?"

"Perhaps I can get Nap to talk to him." Lea laid a reassuring hand on her arm.

"That'd be wonderful if you could, but in the meantime, come and sit with us. Maman and Papa are here helping us set up house."

"They are? Then let's go."

The two ladies linked arms and stepped inside the hall. Pol trailed after them.

Lea spied Napoleon placing the galettes and sandwiches on the long table at the back. Other men surrounded him, exchanging humorous stories, slapping backs, and laughing.

"Mom and Dad are over there." Cécile pointed to the edge of the hall where the Gilberts sat, the seats near them beginning to fill.

When they had made their way to the table, Madame Gilbert stood up. "Lea! So good to see you! My goodness, look how much Pol has grown!"

"I know."

"And this must be Lilian." She bent over to admire the baby.

"Yes, it is."

"What a beautiful little girl."

"Thank you."

"It's too bad Cécile and Claude haven't had any yet." The furrow between her brows deepened. "But what can you expect when he's hardly ever home?"

"Maman," Cécile warned.

"Well, it's true, isn't it? Where is he now? No doubt hanging out with his new cronies." She tipped her chin in the direction of the door where bright light filtered in.

"Never mind. Let's just have a good time tonight, all right?" said Cécile

Madame Gilbert sniffed. "All right, then."

The tables were nearly full when Père Fortier stood up to say the blessing. The people rose too, bowing their heads as he prayed. When his last words trailed away, they formed a long line to the buffet.

Lea scooped out a generous portion of sandwiches along with fresh potato salad and *fèves au lard*—enough to feed herself and Pol. When she reached the galettes, her mouth turned up in a satisfied grin to see the entire plate empty. She made a mental note to bring more the next time.

"I wonder if Claude will bother to come in and eat," said Cécile, craning her neck as she searched the crowd.

Lea's jaw tightened. "I don't know."

Napoleon joined them at the table, his plate overflowing.

"Hey, Nap, make sure you leave some for everyone else, eh," called a man from across the room.

Napoleon opened his mouth to object, but before he could, the man shouted, "Hey, you guys, Nap's here. Quick, get your food before it's all gone."

Laughter burst from the surrounding tables.

"But there's plenty left," Napoleon protested, wearing a stupefied grin.

"Quick, quick! Before he gets more."

"Hey, who ate all the galettes? I didn't get any," complained another man sitting nearby. "Naaaapppp!"

Napoleon shook his head. "Not me. Look. They were all gone when I got there. I took some of Madame Segouin's cookies."

Lea hid a smile, knowing full well Madame Segouin was not well-known for her baking expertise.

"Mmm, Madame Segouin's cookies. Heck, I'll just grab a pile of those," said the man.

Madame Segouin, a bulky woman who clearly enjoyed her own baking, giggled with glee along with anyone within hearing range of the banter.

After they'd all had seconds and leaned back in chairs, hands pressed against full stomachs, Madame Segouin stood up.

"Bonsoir, everyone."

"Bonsoir!" Several voices shouted back.

"Before we begin the card match, Mr. and Madame Gilbert will perform a little skit about the joys of marriage on a Saskatchewan farm."

The audience applauded as the couple marched up to the front of the hall, Madame Gilbert wearing a large apron with a deep pocket, Mr. Gilbert sporting his most worn out overalls.

As they reached the small stage, Mr. Gilbert began staggering. "I'm home, dear," he said, slurring his words and hiccupping.

Madame Gilbert's eyes grew wide and her mouth flew open. "Why, you're drunk! How dare you!" She pulled a rolling pin from her pocket and chased him about the hall while Mr. Gilbert scurried away, covering his head.

Peals of laughter ripped the air.

When they returned to the front, Madame Gilbert turned her back to the audience and bent down, fishing for something else in her pocket.

Mr. Gilbert took hesitant steps toward her and slipped on a night cap. "I guess it's safe now. I'll just climb into bed. She won't remember a thing in the morning." He placed his hands under his right cheek and pretended to drift off. Within seconds, he faked loud snoring.

Madame Gilbert turned around again, wearing a hairnet full of rollers. A cigarette butt hung from her mouth. The audience laughed.

Mr. Gilbert feigned waking up, stretching his arms out as he yawned, and faced her. His eyes popped out, and he shrieked in terror at the ugly woman staring him down before running away, his arms and legs pumping as he fled.

The audience roared for a full minute. When they'd quieted again, the couple continued.

"Mr. Gilbert," she called, still wearing the hairnet.

"Oui." Mr. Gilbert simpered back.

"I need to go to the general store today. Could you give me some money?"

"Okay." He took out his wallet and leafed through several bills. "Let's see, how's this much?" He pulled out a five.

"Perfect." She grabbed his wallet and promptly left, throwing a wicked laugh over her shoulder.

"Hey!" shouted Mr. Gilbert.

The audience laughed hysterically, breaking into applause as the couple returned to their seats.

Madame Segouin rose again. "And now, I'd like to call upon Napoleon and Leopoldine to perform a song for us.

Lea made her way to the front of the hall to thunderous applause, Napoleon following close behind, his fiddle in hand. When they arrived, she gave him a nod.

The audience grew quiet.

Napoleon's bow drew softly at first, chugging on double stops.

Lea joined in, singing the opening words of a traditional Belgian song. Her voice began sweetly as she recounted the joyful meeting of a young girl and her lover. Nap added a soulful melody line at the end of the verse, then resorted back to the rhythmic chugging as she began the second. Her voice rose and fell with emotion as the story unfolded—about their courtship, and how her man had declared his love until the end of time. On the third verse, when the girl's papa refused to acknowledge him, Nap's melody line grew more intense. The passion of Lea's voice deepened as she told of the anguish felt by the girl at her father's rejection, especially since a child grew within her. When she revealed the upcoming baby to her father and her intent to marry her love, he banished her from home. Nap gave a poignant pause and Lea dropped her voice to sing the final words as the girl threw herself off a cliff.

When Lea had finished to loud claps, she glanced over to Cécile and saw her sobbing quietly into her handkerchief. Other ladies dabbed their eyes too, while men looked away, blinking. Lea and Nap bowed and strode back to their seats.

"Well done!" said Madame Gilbert as the couple reclaimed their seats. "That was beautiful."

"Thank you," said Lea, shifting her eyes downward in modesty.

"And now," said Madame Segouin, "let's start the card match. And remember, there will be no gambling."

Couples moved tables as they rearranged themselves while children were excused to play outside.

Lea glanced to her left where she saw Claude enter and pick at what food remained on the table. She elbowed Cécile. "Look. Maybe he won't play poker with the Proux after all."

Cécile gave a wistful gaze in Claude's direction. Their eyes locked for a moment in a tense exchange. Then he left the hall to rejoin his cronies.

Chapter Sixteen
Lost

Lea watched Napoleon's silhouette as he left the farm on his way to break more land. A gopher poked its head out of the ground and scolded him as he passed by. She knew the field he was plowing was particularly long and that she wouldn't see her husband for a whole hour until he returned to carve the next furrow. It was on days like this, she'd meet him on one of his returns to hand him his lunch and cigarettes. But today she had other plans.

It was September, and the leaves were changing to russets and gold. That meant it was time to dig up the potatoes. She eyed Pol. He was old enough now—six years old—that he could meet Papa at midday while Lea took charge of other chores.

She heated water on the stove in preparation for the children's bath. Then she prepared the bread dough, covering it with a red checkered cloth, and placing it on the table to rise. Next, she poured the water into the metal bath and scrubbed the children.

Lilian laughed and slapped the water with her tiny hands, splashing Lea.

"Lilian, don't," Pol chastised. "You're getting Maman all wet."

The little girl giggled.

"It's okay, Pol. She's only three. You did the same when you were her age."

Mischief filled Pol's eyes. "You mean like this?" He took a handful of water and tossed it in Lea's face.

"Pol!" Water dripped down from her dark hair, spotting her glasses.

"Well, that's what you said." He grinned, revealing his two missing front teeth.

Lea gave him a warning look, then finished up washing them, patting them down with a towel, and dressing them.

"I have a job for you today, little *monsieur*," she said when Pol had settled to play on the floor.

Pol looked up with interest. "What?"

"I want you to take Papa his lunch and his cigarettes today."

Pol's eyes brightened. "Me? All by myself?"

"Yes. I have to dig up the potatoes this morning. You can help me too if you want. Then you could meet him at the bottom of the hill at noon."

"Okay!"

"Wonderful." She stroked his head. "You're such a big boy."

After kneading the dough, she took the children outside where the leaves of the potato plants had turned to yellow. "See, Pol, when the plants get droopy like that, that means the potatoes are ready. Watch."

She grabbed a pitchfork and turned up the roots, then sifted through the soil underneath with her fingers pulling up five golden nuggets.

"Wow!" said Pol. "That's a lot. Can I try?"

"Sure. I'll dig."

Pol wandered to where she stood, his boots sinking in the soil. Reaching down, he pulled up a plant, but reeled when a carrot came up instead. He scowled. "Hunh?"

"Not that one." She laughed. "Here. It's these ones."

The boy tugged on the correct plant and felt around the soil with his small hands. "Look at this! It's huge!" he exclaimed, holding up a giant potato with a triumphant grin.

"That *is* a big one. Now put it over here in the bucket."

They continued working, harvesting until the sun reached its highest point. Lea straightened herself and rubbed her back. Taking Lilian's hand, she headed toward the house. Pol followed, his two steps to her one.

When they got to the cabin, Lea reached for Nap's lunch, and placed it in a paper bag. Picking up a pack of cigarettes and matches, she slipped them inside, rolled the top of the bag shut, and handed it to her son. "You're sure you can do this?"

"Yes!" Pol gave a vigorous nod.

Lea watched as her little boy sauntered away up the knoll and out of sight. She smiled and shook her head. He was growing so fast.

She pounded the bread dough for the last time and added wood to the fire. She'd make a special bread tonight for her big boy. Maybe even shape it like an animal.

She peeled a few apples, cut them into pieces, and placed them in a saucepan on the stove. "Fresh apple sauce for my little girl," she said, glancing at Lilian.

"Mmm," Lilian said. "I like apple sauce."

Picking up the child, Lea placed her in the wooden high chair Napoleon had built. "Oh, my! You've almost outgrown this chair."

"That's 'cause I'm a big girl now."

"Yes, you are."

Lea cut pieces of cheese and placed them on Lilian's tabletop with a handful of crackers.

The little girl picked up a piece of cheese with her little hands and took a bite.

When the apple sauce was ready, Lea added sugar and stirred it to cool it down. Turning to Lilian, she hesitated when she saw her staring off in the distance, her face contorted.

"Smoke," said Lilian, pointing to the window.

"What is it?"

"Smoke," Lilian repeated.

Lea swung around in the direction the child pointed. In the distance, a single plume of grey drifted up, then disappeared. She frowned. A minute later, it rose again only this time much thicker and darker.

"Pol!" she whispered.

Dropping the bowl of apple sauce onto the table, Lea ran out the door and up the hill. She heard a shriek. Then she saw Pol…and flames.

"Pol!" She broke into a run. "I need water." Racing back, she lowered the bucket into the well, dragged it up, and untied the knot. Hoisting it, she struggled back up the knoll. When she got to the top, the fire had grown to twice its size.

"Maman!" Pol screamed.

She picked up speed despite the weight of the bucket, then fell. Water spilled out all over the grass. Quickly righting it to save whatever water she could, she pushed herself up again. "Oh, please, God."

"*Maman, sauve-moi!*" Pol shouted as the flame he'd just extinguished leapt back to life and ripped across the field.

"I'm coming!"

And then a miracle happened.

Nap appeared. Sweeping off his hat, he beat the flames, moving swiftly from left to right and back again. Lea pushed herself off the ground and ran to his aid, pouring what little water remained in the bucket onto the fire. When they'd finally extinguished it, they stood panting. Then Lea turned with a vengeance on Pol.

"I told you to give the cigarettes and matches to Papa!" she shouted.

Pol backed away. "But I just wanted to try and make a fire!" he whimpered.

"Well, you could have burned down our entire farm! We could have lost everything, you stupid boy!"

"But I didn't know. I was trying to build it in that circle of rocks. It worked the first time, but the second time, it took off."

"Just wait until you get home," shouted Nap. "You are going to get the biggest lickin' of your life!"

"But…" Pol burst into tears and raced away down the hill.

Lea turned and faced her husband, still breathing heavily. "I'm sorry. I thought he was old enough. I should have known he would be curious."

"It's okay," he said, taking her in his arms. "It's over now."

"I know, but we could have lost the house…the crop…Lilian …" She gasped. "Lilian! I left Lilian in her high chair!"

"Go, quick! I'll get more water and make sure everything's drenched in case there are any sparks left."

Lea hurried back down the trail to the house, fearing the worst. Her heart pounded as she neared the cabin. But when she flung the door open, her precious daughter was asleep in the chair, her tear-stained face resting on the tray. Lea let her arms drop to her sides, marveling at how beautiful—and safe—her little girl was.

But where was Pol?

"Pol," she called, her voice stern. Receiving no answer, she called again. "Pol?" Her voice echoed back at her. Shaking her head, she wandered out to the barn. "Pol!" The grunting of the pig met her ears. *Perhaps he's in the potato patch.* She peered from the door of the barn, but there was no one in the garden. Lea frowned, then threw her hands up. "He'll come home when he's ready."

Returning to the house, she put the bread in the oven, and woke Lilian, giving her the promised bowl of apple sauce. Lilian devoured it, though much of it landed on the tray of her high chair. After she finished, Lea gathered her up and brought her back out to the field where she dug up more potatoes, only revisiting the house to remove the bread from the oven when it steamed golden brown.

When her watch read four o'clock, she washed the potatoes in the slough and spread them out to dry. She'd bring them to the cellar later. She picked fresh vegetables from the garden and carried them into the house. Descending to their cache, she took some pork chops from one of the crocks, and brought them up.

By five, her son hadn't returned. Lea stood at the door and called again. The boy didn't answer. "How far can he have gotten?"

Napoleon arrived just short of six, brushing the dirt off his pants and leaving his muddy boots at the door.

"Have you seen Pol?" she asked.

"No. I thought he was here with you."

She shook her head. "No, he hasn't come back yet," she said, noting the lengthening shadows.

Nap cupped his hands and called.

"What if he's lost on the prairie," said Lea. "Those fields go on forever."

"I think he's just hiding out until it gets dark."

"But the coyotes might get him…or a badger…or even a rattlesnake." She clasped her hands, her eyes wide with fright. "What if he's been bitten and is lying dead in one of the fields?" Hurrying to the door, she shouted again.

They called over and over until Monsieur Bourlon, the blacksmith passed by on his horse from town. "What's wrong?" he asked.

"It's Pol." Lea's voice quivered. "We can't find him. You haven't seen him, have you?"

"No. Did you check the slough?"

Lea's heart quickened at the implication.

She hurried to the water's edge, her heart hammering in her chest. "Pol!"

The chirping of the crickets was growing louder.

She heard Nap and Mr. Bourlon calling his name in the distance.

By ten o'clock, they still hadn't found him.

"What'll we do?" asked Lea.

"Maybe we should start a search party in town to help," said Mr. Bourlon.

"We might have to," said Nap, his expression grave.

An idea struck Lea. "You know, we never checked under the couch. He's hidden there before when he's in trouble." She ran back into the house, bent down, and looked underneath the sofa. A tear-stained face met her gaze.

"He's here!" she cried, her voice filled with relief. "Come out from under the couch! We've been so worried about you."

"No! Papa's going to give me a lickin'."

"No, he won't." Tears of joy ran down her cheeks. "We're just so happy to find you safe and sound."

Pol slid out from his hiding place, but hesitated when Papa entered with Mr. Bourlon.

"It's okay," said Nap. "You're not in trouble. But promise me you'll never play with matches again, okay?"

"I promise."

Nap lifted the boy into his arms and gave him the warmest hug ever.

Chapter Seventeen
The Crash

In January, the cold bit deep. It created perpetually frozen patterns on the edges of the window and chilled the cabin despite the hot fire that burned in the stove. Lea watched Pol and Lilian play quietly with their toys, wearing thick sweaters and slippers, and hoped they were warm enough. Wondering what it was like back home in Belgium, she realized it had been a while since she'd written to her family. Taking out a sheet of paper and a pen, she sat down and composed a letter.

Dear Maman, Papa, and family,

I so miss all of you, especially now that it's winter and we can't go outside except to care for the livestock. It's so cold we dare not even attend mass on Sundays and instead stay home to pray the rosary. How I miss the days when I could just wander over to the Gilbert's house and spend the day puttering about with Madame Gilbert and Cécile. It's not quite like the excitement of summer when we had that bumper crop and Napoleon decided I could finally travel to Belgium. I was so excited back then. Ah, but it'll be so good to see you all when I go.

Nap and I have cleared and broken another seventy acres, and when that crop comes in, that's when I'll board the train to come home.

It's not easy work clearing all the rocks and breaking the sod. There's one really huge stone that's just too big to move. Pol enjoys climbing it, but I worry that one day he'll fall and crack his little head. Then there are the circles of rocks where the Sioux Indians once built their camps. Nap says he doesn't want to touch those, that somehow they're sacred, and I agree. I oftentimes wonder what it must have been like seeing teepees long ago. Memère Emma once told me she remembers natives traveling across the prairie on their travois. Travois are kind of like carts only they have no wheels, just long sticks attached to the horses that they bundle their supplies on. But the Indians don't come around anymore, although there is one Métis family that lives in Val Marie.

Nap has found a job building a school in the next town. We'll use that money to order new clothes from the Eaton's Catalogue. I love Eaton's! It's so easy, just picking and choosing what you'd like to order instead of making it all by hand. And it's like Christmas when it arrives, opening up the boxes to take out the things we've dreamt about for so long. This year, we

194

ordered pants, dresses, jackets, toques, mittens, and plenty of other things for winter. Perhaps when I come to Belgium, I'll stop in Winnipeg and shop in the real Eaton's department store. Can you imagine?

Palma, congratulations on the birth of your little boy, Roberto. I can't wait to meet him. And Mathilde? Courage. I'm sure you'll soon have a child to join our little throng. It'll be so fun when the children all meet each other.
Leopoldine

Lea folded the letter, placed it in the envelope, and sealed it. She'd get Nap to take it to town when he returned from Rosefield on the weekend. She sighed. How lonely it was when he was gone. Thank goodness she had the children to keep her company.

Pol swooped his toy bi-plane down from above, nearly grazing the floor before sweeping it upward again. Lilian rocked her doll in the wooden rocker Nap had built for her.

She marveled at her husband's woodworking skills, how he could dismantle the dirty slats of barrels, soak them, and straighten the wood to make polished toys for the children fine enough to grace the window of any Belgian toy store. Christmas had been wonderful. She was glad she'd insisted on keeping the traditions of the old country this year, celebrating on December sixth, St. Nicholas' Day instead of

December twenty-fifth. The children's excitement was worth it as she wrote their names on slips of paper and laid them on their Christmas plates awaiting Bonhomme Noël's visit. After they had fallen asleep, she'd made fudge and cut it into squares, placing an ample piece next to a Christmas orange and a shiny red apple in each child's place. How their eyes had sparkled when they awoke the next morning to the treats and the wooden toys Bonhomme Noël had brought them.

Lea let out a long, sorrowful breath, her warm feelings evaporating. Writing the letter home had made her feel more alone than ever. She gazed out the window to the darkness that surrounded the cabin, the light of the coal oil lamp a small comfort against the vast expanse of prairie. How she craved conversation with another adult. What she would give to have Madame Bourlon, the blacksmith's wife drop by for a cup of hot tea or even better, Cécile, or Madame Gilbert.

She clenched her teeth at the thought of her friend's dilemma. Though Claude had won the pot that day of the social that summer, he'd squandered it on more poker games. Yet Cécile hung onto his empty promises of a life of luxury like a naïve little girl waiting to see what Bonhomme Noël might bring *her*. But what else could Cécile do? She was so unlucky in love.

But is it really a whole lot different than what I'm experiencing right now? A pang swept over her at the thought of her husband's

196

absence. If only he didn't have to live in the next town during the week, she wouldn't feel so isolated. A stray tear fought its way down her cheek. She attempted to wipe it away lest the children see, but against her wishes, more slid down her face. Before she knew it, she was sobbing.

At hearing her cries, Pol stopped and watched her for a time, his eyes as wide as saucers. Laying the biplane down, he crawled over to her and placed his hands on her knees. Lea reached out and smoothed his hair, then caressed his cheek. Lilian followed, climbing into her lap and throwing her arms around Lea's neck. Soon, all three were crying. Far in the distance, a lone coyote let out a long, sad howl. His companions joined him, and humans and animals lamented together. Lea cried until there were no more tears. Then she laid the children down to sleep and curled up in her own bed, wrapping the blankets around her head to keep warm.

***

When the darkness of winter changed to spring, Napoleon ploughed and seeded the fields for the upcoming season. They waited with anticipation for the much larger crop they'd yield, since Napoleon had broken so much more land. As expected, acres of green sprouts shot out from the earth filling Lea's days with dreams of when she would board the train and make the journey back to Belgium, stopping at Eaton's in Winnipeg, or in Quebec City where she might run into her old friend Marie-Ève and her husband Guy, or passing through Halifax where surely the city had been rebuilt. But more than anything, she dreamed how wonderful it would be to see her family again, to introduce her parents to their two grandchildren.

"Maman and Papa," she'd say, "this is my son, Pol, and my daughter, Lilian."

Maman would sweep her arms open as the children dressed in their newest Eaton's clothes threw themselves into her embrace while Papa stood by, proud of Lea's success.

One of the neighbours passing by would exclaim, "Why, those are the most beautiful children I've ever seen!" So enthralled would that neighbour be that everyone on the street would pay a visit just to glimpse the fine, healthy Canadian children their little Leopoldine had born.

They'd be celebrated each night, invited to a different home where food would be set out on delicate plates.

But in June, the weather turned hot, dashing her dreams. At first, it hadn't concerned her. She knew it changed often, hot one day, a lightning storm the next, but by July the wheat had dried up into limp, brownish threads.

She waited a few days to see what her husband would do, but when no solution seemed in sight, she approached him. "Is there anything I can help with, mon homme?"

Napoleon pressed his lips together. "No. We need irrigation." He glanced at the meandering water of the slough close by. "But that would be a huge project in itself. All we can do now is save the garden." He patted her shoulder. "That'll feed us through the winter, and then I can get more work to support us."

It was difficult hauling water each day from the slough to the garden, carrying bucket after bucket while Nap cleared more land hoping next year might be prosperous. If only the children were old enough to help. But Pol wasn't quite seven yet, and Lilian had only recently turned four.

Still Lea managed to can her fruits and vegetables, make her butter and cheese, and fill the cellar. The only thing that was lacking was the usual store of buffalo berry jam. The dry earth had withheld its usual bounty of the bright red fruit, and Nap had felt it was more important to use what he could to make buffalo berry wine, much to her chagrin.

"We need it for when company comes," he had said.

"But what if the Mounties come instead?"

"Lea, we're French. It's not our fault the Canadian government has decided we can't drink wine. The French have been making it for centuries."

Lea had grudgingly agreed.

In the autumn, he let four of the horses go. "They can look after themselves," he said. "We won't be able to feed them over the winter anyway."

"But won't they go wild?"

"Probably, but it's okay because in the spring, I'll find them and break them again. We can use Dick and Belle to get us to church and to town since it'll be too cold to run the Maxwell."

"Okay," Lea said, pressing his hand in hers.

On October thirtieth, Nap returned from town, his walk brisk, his face twisted with consternation.

"What's wrong?" When he didn't reply immediately, Lea's voice grew frantic. "Nap, answer me!"

His eyes reluctantly met hers. "The stock market crashed."

"The stock market?" She shook her head in puzzlement. "You mean in New York? What does that have to do with us?"

Nap took a huge breath. "You see, in America, people invest in the stock market. The idea is that they put in so much money and their investment grows so they get far more in return."

"Yes, I understand. A lot of people have made their fortune that way. But isn't it like gambling?"

"A little, but the problem is that many people were borrowing money they didn't have from their brokers and letting *them* invest it on their behalf."

"But wouldn't they be able to pay them back once the stocks rose in value?"

Napoleon shook his head gravely. "No, because it turned out that a lot of the investing going on was speculative." When Lea gave a blank stare, he continued. "It means that what they were investing in didn't actually exist yet. And because of that, there were some huge fluctuations in the market. Investors panicked and tried to sell everything all at once…and the market crashed."

Lea frowned. "So how will that affect us?"

"They say the brokers will call in their loans. And if they do that, it'll wipe people out. They'll have to sell their businesses to pay for it. Then there'll be far less jobs." He shook his head in despair. "This is a disaster. It could mean I won't find any work either."

Lea pondered his words before straightening herself. She dug her hands in her hips. "But we're farmers. We grow crops. We make our own food. Our garden survived, plus we have the pig and the Jersey."

"But we had no crop this year."

"There's always next year. The rains will come again. You'll see."

Napoleon cleared his throat. "Except that I won't be able to send you home."

Lea's spirit fell at the truth of his words.

"And I know how much you wanted to see your family." Napoleon draped his arm over her shoulder and pulled her closer. He pressed the tip of his nose against hers and kissed her. "I'm so sorry."

"It's okay. It can wait a year or two," Lea finally said.

Holding each other close, the autumn winds blowing their hair, Lea felt little arms wrap themselves around her legs and waist. She reached down for Lilian while Nap hoisted up Pol. Together, they walked back to the cabin.

Chapter Eighteen
The Drought

It was shortly before planting time the following spring that Lea awoke feeling the familiar sensation of nausea. She bolted from the bed and ran out the door, arriving just in time to empty the contents of her stomach in the pasture. Jersey, close by let out a woeful moo, her hooves thudding the ground as she came up beside Lea and nuzzled her ear. Lea laid her hand on the cow's cheek, then rested her head on its neck as she recovered.

Napoleon stood at the door, a frown creasing his forehead. "Are you okay?"

"Yes," she replied, raising her head and rolling her eyes.

A slow smile formed on Nap's lips. "Another baby?"

She gave a tentative nod. "I think so, but not the best timing."

"It doesn't matter," he said, holding out his arms. "Any child is a gift."

Lea left the cow and reached for the warm hug her husband offered. "Yeah, but it'd be nicer if we'd had a bumper crop."

"We'll get by," said Nap, his arm around her as they walked back inside.

Lea busied herself preparing breakfast, frying the fresh eggs Nap had collected for her and toasting yesterday's bread on the stove.

Still giddy at the discovery of her pregnancy, she savoured the thought of a new baby, one to fill the void of having lost the other three. An unwelcome sadness enveloped her at the thought of the twins and Roger. If only they had more doctors in these parts, they might all still be alive. She clucked her tongue. She wished there were telephones. That way it would be so easy to call a doctor, or the relatives in Ponteix, but it would be a while before the town would even think to install electricity. And with the crash of the stock market, there wasn't a chance they'd get a phone soon even though eight years had passed since Alexander Graham Bell's death. She'd ask Nap to put the question to Bourlon. He'd be the man to push Val Marie into the twentieth century.

As the weather grew warm enough for Napoleon to plant his crops, Lea threw her attention to her garden, teaching the children how to dig small holes in the ground to lay the potato pieces inside.

"It's like magic," she said. "You put in one small piece, and presto, later on, several others appear. And soon, you have a whole bushel of potatoes."

"Can we make *frites* with them?" asked Lilian.

"Yes, we can," said Lea.

Lilian clapped her hands at her mother's words. "Oh, boy, we're going to have frites for supper tonight after the potatoes grow, Pol," she said before burrowing into the soil to place the spud she'd claim as her own.

"It takes a little longer than that," said Lea. "We'll dig them up in September. But in the meantime, I can still make frites tonight with the last year's crop."

"Hurray!" said Lilian.

After the potatoes had been planted, Lea pounded poles into the ground, stringing them together with lines of cord. She dug furrows underneath. "Come and see now, kids."

The children dropped what they were doing and rushed to her side.

"You have to put the seeds for the green beans just under the soil so that when they grow, they'll grab onto these strings just like a little person and keep on climbing right to the top."

"Like Jack and the beanstalk?" asked Pol.

"Yes."

"Jack and the beanstalk!" A look of terror flashed on Lilian's face. She began to cry.

"What's wrong?" asked Lea.

"I'm scared of the giant. What if he comes down and eats us up?" She sat back in the dirt.

"He won't come down and eat us up," said Pol.

"Yes, he will," Lilian sobbed.

"No he won't because Jack and the Beanstalk is just a story."

"No, it's not." Lilian screamed.

"Yes, it is," insisted Pol.

"Pol," warned Lea. "She's just a little girl. Lilian, I promise you there'll be no giants coming down the beanstalk. It's just a fairytale. The beans won't grow that tall."

"Are you sure?"

"Yes."

Grabbing their shovels and seeds, the children planted several rows under Lea's guidance.

For the next two weeks, they watched the garden each day and were rewarded when small shoots poked their heads out of the wet soil and stretched out, growing taller and taller until they curled around the strings.

"Pretty soon they'll be bigger than you," Lea said to Lilian.

But by mid-summer, all the sprouts began to dry up before they had the chance to reach maturity.

Lea panicked when she realized they had fallen right back in the hated drought of last summer. It meant another year without the money to return home to Belgium. And even worse, they might starve…unless she found a way to save the garden. She became possessed, rising early each morning to haul water from the slough, bucket after bucket filled to nourish the struggling plants of her garden, but as the summer wore on, the slough grew shallower.

Finally, on a particularly hot day, she stopped, laid down the bucket, and rubbed her belly, then slumped down.

"This is too much for you, isn't it?" asked Nap, passing by on his way to the fields.

"I'm just so tired," she said, fanning herself.

"Why don't you get Pol to help you?"

"He's too small." Lea's voice trembled as she eyed his thin little arms and legs.

"No, he's not. He's almost eight years old. Besides, it'll build character."

Lea weighed her child's freedom against the fatigue of her pregnancy, guilt playing at her emotions. She heaved a sigh. "Pol, come here."

And so Pol hauled buckets of water, his arms straining under the weight and his breath heaving as he tipped the container, allowing the water to find its course through the little waterways they'd built. Lilian trailed after him, a small, tin can held in her hand, splashing anything that looked dry, including weeds.

By the time August arrived, intolerable heat had settled over the farm. Hot, dry winds blew each day, creating drifts of soil against fences and buildings. Russian thistles claimed the prairie, replacing the usual grass that had been so abundant.

Nap scowled. "I don't know how we'll feed the animals this winter. They need hay."

"I guess we'll just have to let them loose again in the fall like last year. That's all we can do."

"Yes, but if there are only thistles out there for them to eat, how will they survive?"

"I don't know," said Lea. "If only cows and horses were like our pig and would eat anything. It'd be so much easier."

Nap stared at the ground as though deep in thought. "We could sell the Maxwell."

Lea's heart skipped at his words. "Sell the Maxwell? But didn't we agree that had we had an automobile, we might have saved Baby Roger?"

Napoleon let out an anguished sigh and raked his fingers through his hair. "Yes, but what else can we do?"

Lea mulled his words over in her mind before answering. "Then do it. We can always buy another one when the crop comes in."

By September, Lea's garden was ready for harvest. She dug up the potatoes, splaying her legs as she bent to avoid pushing up against her growing belly. More often than not, she'd sink back onto the wooden bench Nap had built her, wiping the sweat from her face or filling her hat with water she'd dump over herself. Pol helped, but Lea knew she'd be working alone before long since school began in a few days. Her son was nearly eight, and he'd never attended school. Most kids began at six. They couldn't put it off any longer.

The day after Labour Day, she prepared Pol's first packed lunch, slicing two thick pieces of bread and filling them with scrambled eggs. She wrapped the sandwich in a cloth and placed it in a five-pound lard can, adding an apple and some cookies. Then she searched through the wardrobe until she found the one Eaton's outfit that still fit him. After dressing him, she brushed his hair and washed his face.

"I don't want to go, Maman," whined Pol. "I want to stay here and play in the garden with Lilian."

"Non, Pol," said Lea, "You must go. You need an education."

"Non!"

The jingling sound of reins interrupted his cries as Napoleon brought the horses alongside the house. Lea gave a resentful glance at the wagon, wishing they still had the Maxwell. How much quicker it would be to get to school.

"Come on, now, Pol." Nap jumped down from the wagon and took him by the hand while Lea picked up Lilian and climbed into place.

"Non, Papa."

Ignoring the boys cries, he hoisted the child up on the seat beside his mother.

Lea grabbed the reins and gave them a good shake. Old Dick and Belle broke into a trot and headed off to Masefield, two-and-a-half miles away.

"I don't want to get an education." Pol's complaints grew louder. "I want to be a farmer like Papa."

"But you have to go," she said. "Besides, there'll be many other children there for you to play with."

"But I can play with Lilian."

"Pol…" Lea tipped her head and gave him a warning glare.

When they arrived in Masefield, she led him to the new building she knew housed grades one to four.

A young woman with dark hair and warm, brown eyes greeted her as she entered. "Hello, I'm Miss Moiny," she said as she laid a piece of paper on each desk. "And who might this young man be?"

Lea searched her memory for the words. If only she'd kept up her self-taught English studies, she wouldn't feel so stupid. "I bring Pol for school," she said, feeling her face grow hot. "He eight years old. No speak English."

Expecting Miss Moiny to roll her eyes at her ignorance, or at least grow impatient, Lea was taken aback when the woman replied, *"Ah, vous êtes de la Belgique!"*

Lea gasped upon hearing her country's name. "Oui!"

"Ma mère aussi!"

The two women broke into excited chatter, their voices animated as they shared stories of their Belgian roots until the children began to trickle into the classroom. Then Lea turned to Pol and said, "I'll come and pick you up at the end of the day."

"Non, Maman," pleaded the boy.

"Oui." She pointed a stern finger at the child.

"Maman," cried Pol, looking after her, his eyes desperate.

Lea grabbed Lilian's hand and walked away with brisk steps, climbed into the wagon

210

and shook the reins. When she was out of view, hot tears rolled down her face.

Chapter Nineteen
Baby Claire

Three days before Christmas, Lea's contractions began. Not wanting to make the long, uncomfortable journey to Ponteix in the snow, she'd insisted in advance that they employ a midwife, a Madame Carlier, a woman from France. She knew a midwife couldn't possibly be as good as a doctor, but Dr. Lupien was too far away, and Madame Carlier was reported to have a great deal of experience. Nap had balked at the idea of a midwife, but she'd retorted that Europe was far more sophisticated in their knowledge of medicine than the simple prairie folk. Nap had acquiesced.

Gripped by a vigorous contraction, she sent a telling look toward her husband. "It's time."

Nap jumped to his feet and grabbed the children's packed bags from the wardrobe while Lea bundled them in their warmest clothing.

"Where are we going, Maman?" asked Lilian.

"You'll be staying with the Bourlons for a few days," she told them as she wrapped scarves around their necks.

"But why?" asked Pol. "It's nearly Christmas. Bonhomme Noël won't find us there. And I've been a good boy. Remember, Miss Moiny put me in grade two already after only a month."

"Don't worry. I promise you your gifts will be waiting for you when you get back. Bonhomme Noël has his ways," Lea said as she ushered them through the door.

They'd only gotten a few steps away when Pol hesitated, then asked. "Maman?"

"Yes."

"Why are you so fat?"

Lea laughed. "It's Bonhomme Noël's fault. He said that if I ate a little extra each day that he'd bring a special surprise for the family."

"Maybe he'll bring me another dolly," said Lilian, her face lighting up.

Lea cast a furtive smile at Nap. "You never know."

Closing the door, Lea watched Old Dick and Belle lead the cutter away. Then she set about preparing for the birth, taking old newspapers Nap had brought from town and spreading them under the sheets of their bed. She took out the bag of clean rags she'd washed ahead of time and placed them next to her pillow. Slipping on her coat and boots, she went outside to gather snow and put it on the stove to melt. She added more wood to the fire and waited.

The contractions came and went, each one more painful than the last. She groaned as they wracked her body. Watching the hands on the clock make their slow journey, she waited, impatient for Nap to return with Madame Carlier. When her water broke, she filled the bucket and cleaned the floor, all the while clutching her stomach.

It was past midnight when Nap finally arrived with the midwife. Lea's contractions had gotten so close she feared the baby would arrive before they did.

"What took you so long?" she asked between gritted teeth.

"Well, you know Madame Carlier lives far away. I had to travel close to thirty miles in total," he said, sounding injured.

"Well, then you should have galloped!" Lea snarled.

"I went as fast as I could."

The midwife's gaze swept around the room. She took charge. "All right, let's move you to the bed."

Lea did as she was told, relieved to have an expert in her home to care for her instead of that clodhopper of a farmer, her husband. She sent another scowl his way. The newspapers rustled beneath her as she lay down.

"I see you've already lined the mattress," said Madame Carlier.

Lea nodded between breaths. "I was trying to pass the time away until my *husband*…." She shot him another angry glare. "Came home."

"All right. Enough of that. Now." Madame Carlier tapped Lea's knees with a well-practiced hand. "Let's see how dilated you are."

Lea gladly obeyed.

The midwife examined her. "Excellent!" she said. "You're fully dilated. You can start pushing."

Pleased at the woman's expertise, Lea strained her stomach muscles, her fingers gripping the railings of the headboard as she did. With each spasm, the baby advanced a little more.

After an hour had passed, Napoleon shouted. "I think I see the head!"

"Yes, you're right. Time to pull out my baseball mitt." Madame Carlier let out an artificial laugh at her obviously much-repeated joke.

Lea let out a strained chuckle and continued to push.

"One more!" the midwife cried.

Lea thrust with all her might.

"Another."

She pushed again.

A feeble cry rang out into the night.

"It's a girl!" said Madame Carlier. "A beautiful little red-headed girl!"

"A red-head?" exclaimed Lea.

"What's wrong with red-heads?" asked Nap, all smiles despite their earlier quarrel. "There are quite a few of them in my family."

The midwife cut the cord, wrapped the baby in a blanket, and handed her to Lea while

Napoleon moved to Lea's side to admire his new daughter.

"Actually, it's more like auburn," he said.

"Try feeding her," suggested the midwife.

Lea lifted her nighty and latched the baby on. The tiny child sucked, her little rosebud lips like small suction cups. "She's hungry!"

"Look at her go!" Napoleon laughed.

"What a feeder!" said the midwife.

Lea's face winced with pain.

"Here comes the afterbirth! Give it a good push," said Madame Carlier, redirecting her eyes to Lea's lower half.

Though she had no strength left, Lea thrust one more time.

"Good!" said Madame Carlier. "I've got it." She frowned, her mouth slightly open. "Wait a minute." She raised her head, her easygoing expression replaced by a look of sheer terror.

"What is it?" asked Nap.

"I don't know. She's bleeding…really hard!" Madame Carlier's voice had lost its confidence and risen to a frantic pitch. She grabbed a rag and pressed it against Lea's bottom.

"Let me see!" said Napoleon.

"No, no! You musn't be in the way!"

Blackness engulfed Lea's vision, and the noises of the room drifted far, far away. She floated in oblivion, lost, as though she'd been there for an eternity, gliding like wood on the waves of the ocean, no land in sight, only water. When she came to, all was quiet except for the sound of creaking wood. Lea opened her eyes. A woman sat before her, facing away, rocking and sewing. Who was she? Lea squinted in the dim candlelight. This surely couldn't be Madame Carlier. Was it Cécile? Or perhaps Madame Bourlon? Where was Nap…and the baby?

"Who are you?" Lea asked.

The woman didn't answer.

"Excuse me." Lea spoke louder. "Who are you and what are you doing here?"

Startled, the woman sat up on the edge of the rocker, listening. She rose, tiptoed to the window, and parted the curtains with gnarled fingers. Certain no one was there, she returned to her chair, shaking her head, and resumed her work.

Frowning, Lea tried again. "Excuse me!" she demanded. "I asked you a question!"

The woman flinched, then made a slow turn, her wide eyes searching in Lea's direction, unseeing.

Lea's hand flew to her mouth. "Maman!"

She reeled as she recognized the house in Chatlineau—the table the family gathered around during mealtimes, the clock Papa wound each night, the couch where she'd sat holding Napoleon's hand, the cabinet where they kept the silverware. She was home in Belgium. But how?

The woman's eyes darted back and forth, searching.

"Maman, c'est moi, Leopoldine!"

The woman gasped. Her hand shot up to her heart.

Lea heard Napoleon's voice shout far in the distance.

"Napoleon?" Her ears pricked. "Where are you?"

He spoke again, closer now. "I thought you said you were an experienced midwife!"

"I am."

His words yanked her back into reality, spiraling downward through an endless tunnel, an intense pain gripping her stomach.

"Mr. de Montigny, I've delivered many babies. This is the first time this has ever happened!"

"Well, she might have died!"

As Lea regained consciousness, she opened her eyes to find her husband at her knees, one hand pushed hard against her abdomen.

"What happened?" she asked, her voice groggy.

"You bled out," said Napoleon. "And it's a good thing I was here or you would have died!"

"It's like I say, I've never seen such a thing." Madame Carlier was near tears.

"Well, now you have. And I hope you've learned from this!"

"But Monsieur."

"Don't you dare monsieur me. Take your things and leave!"

The midwife packed up her belongings and backed out the door, harrumphing as she left.

When she'd gone, Napoleon drew his attention back to Lea.

"What happened?" she asked.

He shook his head, his voice quivering. "You started bleeding really badly, and she went into a panic. She had no idea what to do. So I moved in and saved you."

"How?" asked Lea.

"It's something I learned a long time ago working as a cowboy before you came to Canada. I was helping a vet with a cow that was having a hard time delivering. When he finally pulled the calf out, the mother hemorrhaged. So he stuck his entire fist up the cow's birth canal and pressed down on her belly. It stopped the bleeding. Thank God I was there to see that so I knew what to do." He clenched his teeth. "Stupid midwife. I could have lost both of you!"

"I'm sorry, Nap," said Lea. "I'd heard she was very good."

"Well, not good enough. The next time, we're not taking any chances. I'll bring you to Ponteix a few weeks before you're due so Dr. Lupien can deliver the baby."

"That's a good idea." She paused a moment, then grew serious, her voice cautious. "You know, Nap…I saw Maman."

"Pardon?" His brow furrowed.

"When I passed out, I saw Maman back in Chatlineau. She was sewing."

Napoleon's eyes grew wide at the implication. He listened as she related her experience, then did a quick sign of the cross.

"So it turns out I did go home after all—in a way."

"Yes, well let's make sure you never visit her again…at least not in spirit."

Lea nodded. "Agreed."

***

On the twenty-ninth, Napoleon brought the children back home. "Come and see the surprise Bonhomme Noël left for the whole family," he said.

Lilian and Pol took off their boots and coats and sauntered over to Lea.

"It's your baby sister," Lea said. "Her name's Claire."

"A new baby sister?" Pol's brow twisted with suspicion. He looked down at Lea's stomach, then back at her face as though a great revelation had come to him.

Lilian stood on her toes and kissed Claire's cheek, then proceeded to the table where Bonhomme Noël had left her gifts. "Lookit! Bonhomme Noël brought me a high chair for the baby!" She grabbed a piece of fudge as she spoke.

"I'm afraid this baby will be too big for that chair. You'll have to use it for *your* baby," said Nap, tipping his chin at the well-worn doll who lay in the toy crib.

"Okay. Come here, baby." Lilian picked up the doll with her sticky hands and placed it in her new high chair. "Here, you can have some fudge." She smudged the doll's face with the sweet.

"Wow! Look what Bonhomme Noël brought me," said Pol, holding up a wooden puppet and a flat paddle. He shoved the end of the board under his seat and bounced the figure up and down on top.

"That's not how you do it," said Nap. "Watch." He reached down and pressed the paddle in an even rhythm. The puppet began to tap dance on its own, its feet rattling with the movements of the board.

"Very nice," said Lea.

After their belated Christmas, cold winds whistled through the house, battering the shiplap with driving snow, the temperature so low they were trapped inside. Lea cared for the family each day, cooking, washing, and hanging Claire's nappies to dry. She loved her new baby, but worried she didn't have enough milk for her.

"I don't understand what's wrong," she told Nap, her voice trembling. "I've never had problems feeding a baby before."

"It takes time," said Nap as he laid more firewood in the stove. "It's just been a while. You've forgotten what it's like."

"No, I can feel it. I can see it. There's not enough for her."

"Then why don't we just give her milk from the Jersey? After all, that's why we have her." He finished stoking the fire before replacing the lid.

"I suppose I could, but I should be able to do this myself. Besides, didn't you tell me the Jersey wasn't producing much milk these days?"

Nap sighed. "That's because she doesn't have the right kind of food. I've been trying to get her to eat the Russian thistles, but she doesn't like them."

"What else can we feed her then?"

"I heard in town that a good substitute for hay is a mixture of straw, wheat, and molasses."

"Straw, wheat, and molasses?" asked Lea. "Who ever heard of such a thing?"

"Certainly not me, but what have we got to lose?"

"Well then, let's try it. We have lots of molasses in the cellar. And if the Jersey doesn't like it, the pig will. She'll eat anything."

Napoleon descended into the basement and came up again with a large crock of the sticky, brown liquid. Bundling himself, he carried it out to the barn under one arm, his other hand following the rope he'd tied from the front door, reassuring Lea he wouldn't get lost in a storm.

A half hour later, when he brought the milk canister into the house, Lea ladled the warm milk into Claire's bottle.

The baby fussed at the unfamiliar nipple and spat it out.

"It's okay, Claire," said Lea. "I know you love Maman's milk better, but you'll get a lot more this way."

The tiny girl gagged, arching her back and throwing out her arms.

Lea changed the angle of the bottle. "Here, try one more time."

After a few attempts, Claire got the hang of it, but an hour later, her frantic cries filled the small cabin.

"She looks like she's in such horrible pain," said Lea, her voice trembling.

"Here, let me take her," said Nap. He hugged the baby close to his chest, but Claire still could not be consoled.

The feeding and screaming continued day after day despite the Jersey's milk. Lea spent much of her time trying to calm the tiny girl until one evening, a terrible thought invaded her mind. *Suppose we lose this baby too.* A sob escaped her. She couldn't fathom the loss of another child. Oh, how she longed to talk to one of her women friends, or better yet Dr. Lupien.

"Why don't you let me try, Maman?" Pol asked.

Lea looked up from where she sat on the sofa. How tall her son had grown. Maybe hauling water *had* done him good, but he was still a child. "It's too hard for you, Pol," she said.

"No, let me try," he insisted. "I noticed she cries less if you hold her a certain way."

"Give him a chance," said Napoleon. "Maybe she'll respond to him better. You never know. Besides, you could use a break."

"All right then." Lea surrendered Baby Claire to her son.

Pol took the little girl and laid her tummy against *his* while her head rested against the crook of his elbow, her little arm dangling below. "Now give me the nipple."

Lea unscrewed the top of the bottle and handed it to him.

Claire whimpered at first, let out a few angry cries, then quieted down.

"I think it's because she gets tummy aches," said Pol, walking the baby about the room. "And if you press on her tummy hard enough, it stops hurting. Kind of like a hot water bottle."

Lea watched her son in awe at the magical effect he had on Claire. She exchanged a grateful look with Nap. "He really has a way with babies, doesn't he?"

"Yes, he does."

The blizzard ended a few days later, only to be followed by another and another, the temperatures so low all they could do was huddle by the stove, drinking hot liquids and wearing as much clothing as possible.

"How is Pol going to go to school?" Lea asked, when a couple of weeks had passed. "With all these storms, we can't get him there. He's going to fall behind."

Nap tapped his pipe into the fire and refilled it with tobacco. "Well, I'm not doing anything until spring. I could teach him. His school books are here."

"But your English isn't very good, though." Lea giggled.

"What other choice do we have?"

For the next few weeks, Lea enjoyed listening to Nap teach in his strong Quebecois accent while Pol repeated the words in perfect English. How well they worked together.

When the blizzards came to an end, Nap hitched up Old Dick and Belle to the cutter to take his family to mass.

The air was frosty, the drifts flowing in straight, perfect lines over fences, reaching to rooftops and nearly covering buildings. Lea breathed in the crisp air. Its coldness burned her lungs. She covered her face with her scarf, allowing the heat of her breath to reduce the sting. Her gaze wandered to the horses that pulled the cutter. How emaciated they were, and how weak. Her heart ached for them.

When they arrived at the church, Lea saw a familiar figure from afar entering with Cécile. It was Madame Gilbert!

"They must be visiting," she said, reaching down to help Lilian from under the blanket where the heated bricks kept her warm.

"They probably never left after Christmas because there have been so many blizzards."

Descending with Claire held close to her bosom, Lea hurried over to greet her friends.

"Lea!" Madame Gilbert's arms opened wide. "So this is the new baby." She pushed back Claire's blanket for a peak. Her expression of admiration turned to one of concern. "Her face is so thin. Has she not been putting on weight?"

Lea's heart fell. "I don't know, Madame Gilbert. I've been so worried. I don't seem to have enough milk for her. We switched her to the Jersey's milk and all she ever does is cry. And I'm so exhausted."

"Have you been to see Dr. Lupien?"

Lea shook her head, a helpless gesture. "Not with all these blizzards. It's been impossible. Pol hasn't even been to school."

Madame Gilbert pressed her lips together in thought. "You know, I've heard of a Dr. Bates in Bracken. It's closer than Ponteix. He has a baby clinic, and he's been known to do wonders."

Lea shot a glance at Nap. "Yes, but we don't have the money."

"Never mind the money. We'll lend it to you. You can pay us back as soon as this year's crops pan out."

Lea turned to Nap as though asking his permission.

He nodded. "Would you really do that for us?"

"Of course. Just as I would if it were Cécile's baby."

"Then we'll take her today," he said. "I don't want to bury another child."

After mass, Nap loaded his family onto the cutter and drove the horses into a canter all the way home. Then he packed little Claire under his coat and took her to Bracken.

Chapter Twenty
The Dark Cloud

For the next six weeks, Lea did her best to keep herself busy making her bread, doing laundry, and sewing clothing for the family to keep from worrying about Claire. But she couldn't stop wondering how her little girl was doing in the hospital. Did she miss them? Did she cry herself to sleep every night, calling for Maman? Did Nurse Cameron cuddle her the way Pol did?

But Lea had other pressing issues to contend with, like how to clothe her children on such a tiny income since the crop had failed. She'd given up on the idea of ordering clothes from the Eaton's catalogue with their meagre income, yet she couldn't afford to buy fabric from the general store either.

The answer came to her one morning while filling the flour box when she stopped and eyed the cloth of the sack. How pretty the fabric was—flowers—and made of cotton too. What a lovely dress this would make for one of the girls. And didn't the other sacks have patterns too? Curious, she lifted the latch under the rug and descended to the cellar, a lantern in hand, where she examined the small pile of bags. They too came in every type of pattern imaginable—plaid, bunnies, stripes, cowboys, baby ducks, and even paisley. But how could she make clothing with this fabric when there was a big logo on it? "Sunbonnet Blue Flour," she read. Perhaps she could use only the back part of the bag.

Still intrigued by her discovery, she slipped on her shoes and coat and went to the barn where she knew more discarded piles of empty sacks lay. Again, she admired the various patterns. Picking one up, she found directions on the back.

To Wash Out Ink
Soak overnight in soap suds and water. Then wash thoroughly in warm soap suds until ink has been loosened. Rinse well, and if necessary, boil for 10 minutes to restore the natural whiteness of the cloth.

Lea let out a triumphant laugh. "So that's how you do it. The companies have known all along how tough times are, so they created special fabrics we can make clothes with."

Enlightened, Lea gathered up all the sacks and slung them over her shoulder. When she got back to the house, she pulled out the old tub and scrubbed them one by one until all the logos had disappeared, then hung them to dry.

When Nap came home that night, he found the cabin draped with every kind of cloth imaginable. "What's this?" he asked.

"I found some fabric to make everyone's clothing with," said Lea, pasting on a clever grin.

"But where?"

"It was in the barn and the cellar the whole time."

"The barn and the cellar?" Nap gave her a puzzled look.

"Mm-hm."

"What? How?" He threw up his arms.

Lea explained to him about the sacking, then showed him the directions on how to remove the logo.

Nap eyed the cloth, and then the children. Letting out a quiet chuckle, he placed a hand over her ear and whispered, "No one will know we're poor now."

Lea spent long hours cutting, pinning, and piecing together shirts and dresses for the family. She was surprised when she discovered some bags even came with sewing patterns on the back side! Using the fabric with the horse images, she made a large shirt for Nap and a smaller one for Pol.

"Like father like son," she said to herself, smiling.

She created matching dresses for herself and Lilian—red flowers on a blue background to match the beautiful prairie sky!

"These will be so cute to go to mass."

But when she came to the cloth that had marching baby ducks, she saved it to make larger nappies for Claire since surely she'd come back from the hospital healthy and strong…or at least she hoped so. Her throat caught and tears threatened to form in her eyes. If only they'd receive word from the doctor, but Nap came home every day from the post office empty-handed. Could that mean good news?

***

When things warmed up, Nap set out to recapture the horses they'd set free in the fall. It took him two days to find them, but when he brought them home, a wave of pity swept over Lea. They were so thin, the hair of their manes and tails matted.

"Poor things!" she cried, as she reached a hand to the bay mare.

The horse pranced and snorted as though she'd never known Lea.

"It's okay, Queen. We're old friends."

The horse backed away nonetheless. Lea coaxed the animal with a carrot laid flat in the palm of her hand until the mare allowed her to stroke its cheek.

"So, what are we going to do now?" she asked Napoleon, as the horse munched noisily. "How are we going to feed them?"

Napoleon let out a frustrated sigh. "I guess we'll give them the same mixture as the other horses and the Jersey, at least until the rains begin and the grass grows again." He slipped the halter over the mare's head and tied it, then paused a moment as though remembering something painful. "You know, they're not so bad off compared to some of the livestock I saw."

"How so?"

"There was one horse who was so bone thin, he tried to gnaw the mane of another thinking it was hay."

"How terrible."

"I just hope whoever owns them brings them in soon before they've starved to death."

For a brief time, the grass *did* rise as the snow melted and the earth warmed. The horses *did* grow plumper, their matted hair shedding with the return of the summer.

One day, while watching Nap re-break the horses, the sound of an automobile in the distance caught Lea's attention.

"Who on earth?" she asked, craning her neck to see.

Seeming tiny at first, the black vehicle inched its way up the road until it stopped near the house. When the doors opened, a man stepped out, followed by a woman carrying a child in her arms.

"It's Dr. Bates and Nurse Cameron!" exclaimed Nap.

"And he's got Claire with him!" shouted Pol, breaking into a run.

"Claire!" called Lilian.

The whole family crowded around the automobile to see the little girl.

"She's gotten so fat," said Pol.

"How on earth?" Lea reached out for her red-headed baby.

"It's because she was having trouble digesting the milk from your cow," said Dr. Bates. "It's too rich for her."

"But everyone knows that Jersey milk is…the richest of all." Lea's voice trailed off on the last few words. "Then what should we feed her?"

"Well," said the doctor, "if you get regular Holstein milk, she should be just fine."

"That's easy enough," said Nap. "We'll trade milk with one of the neighbours."

"Oh, and by the way," said Nurse Cameron, coming alongside them, "Claire's become a little Shirley Temple."

"What do you mean?" asked Lea, searching for similarities between her daughter and the child movie star.

"She won second place in the Bracken Baby Clinic Competition!"

"The Bracken Baby Clinic Competition?" Lea's eyebrows furrowed with curiosity.

"It's a contest we have every year," explained Dr. Bates. "After we cure whatever ails the babies, we have a little competition to determine who's the cutest and healthiest of them all. And Claire came in second. Here's a photo."

Lea took the picture from the nurse and let out a laugh. "That's adorable!"

"What?" asked Lilian. "Let me see."

"Me too," said Pol.

She passed the photograph around to the others. "She's wearing a little bathing suit. Look at her chubby legs.

"Aw, so cute!" said Lilian.

"She *is* a little like Shirley Temple," said Pol.

"How can we ever thank you?" asked Lea. "We were so scared we'd lose her and you've plumped her up like a Thanksgiving turkey."

"It's what we do. But just remember—Holstein milk."

"I promise."

After Nap signed the release papers, Dr. Bates and his nurse climbed back into the car and drove away. Lea watched as they disappeared over the horizon, then carried Claire back to the house, content to have her little girl home.

From then on, Nap milked the Jersey each morning, then sent Pol on horseback to the Devlins, the next homestead over, to exchange a bucketful. Claire continued to flourish, her weak, despondent cries now replaced by smiles and giggles.

When the weather warmed enough, Nap planted his crop, anticipating its success, but was devastated when again the rains halted and the soil began to drift, piling ever so high against buildings and fences. But worse still, something more ominous threatened the farm this year—the water in the slough dried up to the point where it was no longer possible to dip a bucket in.

"What are we going to do?" asked Lea. "I won't be able to save the garden this year if we have no water."

Nap pressed his lips together and shook his head as he mulled over the direness of the situation. "I'll go see if I can get some from the Devlins. I noticed their slough is much fuller than ours. I'm sure they'll be glad to spare some."

"But that's so much work."

Napoleon shrugged. "What choice do we have? I'm not giving up. I promised you golden fields, and that's what I'm going to give you. I'll go every day and bring water back, enough for your garden and enough to keep one field of wheat healthy. That way we'll at least have a small crop."

"Then I'll help you," said Lea, her voice marked with determination.

After receiving permission from the Devlins, Lea took on the daily job of loading the vessels onto the wagon—two barrels, an empty topless beer keg, and a thirty-gallon steel container while Nap hitched up Old Dick and Belle. When she'd placed them all on the wagon, she laid pieces of wood in each one to stop the water from splashing once it had been collected. There was no sense in watering the wagon trail.

When Nap returned an hour later, Lea helped him unload the containers, her muscles straining as together they lowered the water to the ground. "Come on, Pol," ordered Lea. "If you want to eat this winter, you'd better help."

"Why doesn't Lilian have to help?" asked Pol, his face sullen. "It's not fair."

"Because she's looking after Claire."

Pol obeyed, his face in a scowl as he dipped a smaller container into the larger vessel, walked to the garden, and dumped it at the base of the plants.

When they'd finished, Nap placed his arm about his son's shoulder. "Pol, you're getting to be quite the young man, and I'm really proud of you. And because of that, I'm giving you another job in addition to exchanging the milk for Claire."

Pol's shoulders dropped and he let out a huff.

"I want you to water the livestock each morning and night at the Devlin's coulee."

Pol raised his head, looking relieved. "Is that all?"

"That's all."

"Phew. I thought you were going to get me to plow the fields for you."

"I'll help too," said Lilian. "And we can bring Claire with us."

Napoleon sent his daughter a look of approval. "Good girl. The more the merrier."

And so the month of June continued, each family member contributing to the survival of the farm. The small field of wheat held its own as did the garden. Then one day, near the beginning of June, Lea spied a dark cloud on the horizon while watering the potatoes. "What's that?" she asked. "I've never seen a brown cloud before."

Nap stared in the distance, climbed one of the hills beside the pasture, and stretched his head forward while shading his eyes. "I don't know, but I sure don't like the look of that. We'd better finish up."

"Quickly, children!" Lea called. "We have to work twice as fast."

They ran in every direction, drawing water and dumping it on the soil.

The wind picked up speed, the cloud swallowing up the sky as it crept closer and closer. Their hair and clothes were tossed about as the wind grew stronger.

Pol let out a cry. "Ow! Something's in my eye. It hurts!"

"What is it?" asked Lea, but before Pol could answer, thousands of little pins seemed to pierce her skin. She covered her face. "What's going on?"

"I think it's a dust storm!" shouted Nap. "Quick, get inside!" He ran to the pasture where the restless livestock pranced and trotted about nervously and shooed them into the barn. Lea snatched Claire in her arms. After a dash for the door, she waited until the other kids caught up, opened it, ushering them inside with a quick hand before entering and slamming the door. Then she waited for Nap, opening it for only an instant so he could slip in.

236

Within minutes, the entire house was surrounded by howling winds. Brown dust lashed the windows, scraping the glass.

"What do we do now?" asked Pol, staring out the window.

"We just have to wait it out," said Nap.

"How long?" asked Pol, his brows furrowed.

"Don't know. It could last for days."

"Days?" Lea held Claire close to her bosom.

"It's like a blizzard, only this time it's dust," said Nap.

"Well, at least it's not cold," said Lilian.

They huddled for a time watching the furious winds outside until Lea ran a finger along the table. It left a trail. "It's getting in everywhere."

"I better seal the windows," said Nap. Grabbing the bag of rags from the closet, he shoved some under the doors and along the base of the window, but the relief was only temporary. The dust still found its way in, its long fingers reaching inside the cracks of the frame

Lea prepared the dinner despite the storm, placing lids on the pots to keep the dust out. Every few minutes, she wiped a layer off the stove. When the children began to cough and wheeze, she fashioned a bandana for each child to wear over their nose.

The storm continued to rage the next day, a whirling brown mess. Nothing was visible through the window. It was as though their world had ended at the door, the rest cast into darkness. Lea and the children continued to wipe down the furniture and sweep the floor, but still the dust wriggled its way in.

After supper, Nap pulled out his fiddle.

Lea flashed him a look of incredulity.

"We might as well enjoy ourselves," he shouted above the wind, breaking into a grin.

"Oui, Papa!" Pol shot up and ran to the cabinet where he retrieved the wooden puppet and paddle Bonhomme Noël had brought him.

Lea leapt up from her sewing, took two spoons out of the drawer, and placed them back to back. Napoleon broke into a tune. She tapped the spoons together in rhythm against her lap and her other hand while Pol tap-danced his puppet on the board, bouncing it up and down with his left hand. Lilian and Claire danced to the music, laughing and singing as they held hands, twirling in circles. The music lasted until the younger children's eyes, heavy with sleep, begged to close, and Lea led them to their beds, tucking them in for the night.

"That was certainly a fine way to pass a dreadful evening," she said as she took the quilt off their bed and gave it a good shake.

"Made more sense than to sit around being miserable."

"Do you think the storm will end soon?" Lea spread the cover back on the bed.

"I don't know," replied Nap. "I've never been in one before."

238

"Then we might as well sleep in," she said, climbing in beside her husband.

"Sounds good to me," he said, placing his arm around her.

The wind howled all night long. Lea awoke each time an object struck the house or when a particularly wild gust of wind threatened to overturn it. Rolling onto her back, she listened to the turbulent gale. Suppose a tornado hit. Hadn't there been one in Regina in 1912? Yet despite her fretting, she eventually fell back to sleep.

When she opened her eyes the next morning, the peaceful sound of birds met her ears.

Lea rose from her bed and sauntered over to the window. She rubbed it and looked out, but the glass was so thick with dust, she couldn't see anything. She opened the door a crack only to have a bucket's worth of dirt tumble into the entrance. Momentarily scowling at the mess that lay at her feet, she raised her face to take in the scene before her. Drifts of soil had climbed halfway up the barn and covered the fence so high that any one of the horses could have scrambled over it and wandered away. But worse yet, her garden was completely buried.

"No!" she cried. "We'll starve!" Throwing on her shoes, she ran to where the normally green plants shot up and began digging through the dirt, handful by handful. "Help! Quickly! We need to save the garden. Nap!"

Napoleon and the two older children appeared in their pajamas.

"Hurry, Pol!" she said. "Lilian, you look after Claire."

Together, they raced about, clearing the dirt until one by one, they dug out the plants.

When they'd nearly completed the task, Pol's eyebrow wrinkled. "What's happened to the animals?"

Nap stood up and looked around. "I don't know. I put them in the barn. I hope they're okay. Go look."

The boy disappeared inside. Lea waited, her breath held until he came out leading Old Dick by the halter.

"They're all just fine!" he shouted. "Kind of dirty, but fine."

Lea turned, letting out sigh of relief and wiping away tears on her sleeve.

"But there's a really big a mess in there," said Pol. "It's going to take a long time to sweep it out."

Sweep they did. They worked hard, clearing the dust and resumed watering the garden and field with the now murky waters.

Chapter Twenty-One
The Visitors

Lea heard Pol's voice in the distance as she watered the garden. Glancing back over her shoulder, she spied her son hurrying as he dragged along Lilian. Something wasn't right. Lea stood up, shading her eyes from the bright sun.

"What is it?" she called back, laying down the empty container of water she held.

"Indians!" Pol shouted. "Come quick!"

Lea's pulse quickened. She'd seen natives before and had heard they'd once been a problem for settlers, but that was a long time ago. Were they rising again? She ran to meet the children, her heart thudding, but as she neared them, the looks on their faces read excitement, not fear.

"Hurry! They're on the big rock!" said Pol.

"How many?" Lea asked.

"This many." Lilian held up five fingers.

"It's a mother and four kids," said Pol.

"Well, what are they doing?"

He shrugged his shoulders. "Just sitting around."

"Sitting around?" Lea looked past the children into the fields, searching. "Wait here," she said, then ran back to the house and came back with a tin of homemade cookies. She picked up Claire. "Show me."

The children raced ahead, waiting from time to time for Lea and Claire to catch up. When the great rock came into sight, Lea slowed her pace. An entire family sat atop, eating. Lea admired the buckskin dresses the woman and girls wore, decorated with geometric beadwork.

Lea stepped forward. "Hello," she said, offering a carefully placed smile.

The Indian woman seemed to size her up, her eyes sweeping up and down Lea's figure.

Lea felt a shiver, hoping that the woman too was admiring *her* dress. She held up the tin box. "I have cookies."

The woman eyed the container for a moment, then slid down from the rock.

"They're good." Lea opened the tin, revealing two types. "These ones are molasses, and these ones are sugar cookies. Have one." She held them at arm's length.

Looking back at her own brood, the woman eyed the sweets and took one of the darker ones. After nibbling for a bit, she smiled, then turned to her children, motioning them forward.

They scrambled down from the rock.

Lea allowed them each a cookie, then passed the container back to their mother. "You can keep the box."

The woman nodded, tucking it under her arm. From her own buckskin bag, she handed Lea a piece of dried meat. "Pemmican," she

242

said, holding it to her mouth and pretending to take a bite.

Lea looked down at the offering with uncertainty, then accepted the gift. She tore off a strip, chewed it, then nodded. "Mmm, good." When she'd swallowed it, she worded her next question with caution. "Are...are you just passing through on your way somewhere?"

The woman glanced at her eldest son, a boy of possibly thirteen, who translated. "We're going to a pow wow."

"A pow wow?" asked Lea.

"Yeah."

"What's a pow wow?" Lea felt a little uneasy.

The boy exchanged guarded expressions with his mother, then shook his head. "It's secret. Only the Sioux are allowed to know."

"Okay, then. Where will you be having this pow wow?" Lea asked, keeping her voice as pleasant as possible.

"Over there." The boy pointed to the horizon where the sacred rocks Nap had refused to clear sat.

Lea felt a shiver despite the heat. "When will it happen?"

"Tomorrow."

Nodding, Lea turned her attention back to the boy's mother. "If you'd like some water, we have some at the house." She pantomimed drinking.

Shaking her head, the woman pointed to their skins.

"We already have some," said the boy.

Pol and Lilian climbed the rock and waited for the other children to join them. They slid down the smoothest part of the stone, then hurried back up to try again, taking turns. Lea watched them for a while. *I guess children are children despite the colour of their skin. Look at them play.* Smiling, she turned to speak to the Indian lady again, but was surprised when she saw she'd packed her things. The woman motioned her children to follow, ending the game just as quickly as it had begun.

"Bye," called Pol and Lilian, looking disappointed.

The native children waved.

That night, after dinner had been cleared and the dishes washed, the drumming began.

"What is it all about?" Lea asked Nap as she knit socks for Pol.

"I don't know," he replied. "I've never heard them do this before."

"I mean we're long past the days of attacks, and that sort of thing, right?"

Nap let out a chuckle. "I'm certain we are."

The drumming lasted through the evening and long into the night. When they awoke the next morning, the rhythms still pounded away.

"I wonder how long this will go on," said Lea. "I mean, how long do pow wows last?"

"I've heard they can go on for days."

They ate a slow breakfast, listening to the rhythmic pelting. When they'd finished, Lea poured the tea. "Maybe you should stay home today."

"I can't. I have to dig a new well since the old one's drying up."

"But where?" asked Lea, adding milk to her tea. "There's no water left in the slough."

"Part ways to Devlin's coulee."

Lea frowned. "But that's not our land."

"I already spoke to him. He doesn't mind, considering there's a drought going on. Besides, their house is way on the other end of their homestead. They won't lose water because of us."

"Well, do what you have to then."

By nighttime, the drumming still echoed in the distance, keeping Lea on edge though she was somewhat comforted knowing that nothing bad had happened thus far.

"How is that well coming?" she asked her husband as she loaded up the plates of food when he came in.

"Slowly, but surely. I'll have to dig deep, but I know there's water to be had."

"A well closer by will be a handy thing," she said, laying the dinner on the table.

The next day, the drumming persisted. Lea, as usual, tended to her garden while the children watered the livestock. Near lunchtime, she watched with curiosity as a buggy traveled the road in the distance. How sad to see people's vehicles stripped down to just the body pulled by a horse, the engine and windows having been removed. She followed the vehicle with her eyes for a time, but instead of passing by the homestead, it came up their road and stopped. It was Cécile!

Lea dropped everything and ran to meet her friend. "What happened to your automobile?"

Cécile let out a huff. "It was Claude's doing. We can't afford the gas, and it would take a team of horses to pull the entire contraption, so Claude took out the engine and doors to lighten it. And now we have this funny little buggy. They call it a Bennett Buggy after the prime minister."

"Well, it's better than nothing, right?"

"I guess so. You know, I've heard the government is sending out food and clothing."

"Really?" Lea felt a twinge of hope.

"Yes. Apparently they requested help from all over Canada, and it's on the way. Boxes of coats, canned goods, apples…really, anything will help."

"Yeah, I know what you mean." Lea threw a glance back at the fragile garden. "How's your crop going?"

"Well, about as well as can be expected. We're all in the same boat, but at least Claude is staying home since he has to save the farm. And he hasn't gambled it away…yet."

"I'm so glad to hear that." Lea stopped and listened. "Can you hear the drumming from your place?"

"No, but I heard in town that the Sioux are doing their rain dance, and that the government is turning a blind eye even though it's been against the law for years. I sure hope it works."

Lea gave a skeptical smile. "I wish. But what's a bunch of people dancing going to do? If I thought it would help, I'd dance all day too."

"Well, I'm willing to wait and see. It certainly can't hurt."

"I suppose."

"So is there any news?" Lea winked. "Is there a baby on the way?"

Cécile sighed. "No, not yet."

"Why don't you come in and we can have tea?"

"That would be nice. I think I will."

After a brief visit, exchanging stories of who had left town and what other farmers were doing to save their livestock, Lea walked Cécile back to her buggy. She felt dismayed to see how thin Cécile's horse had become. She hoped it was true the government was shipping out food and clothing because despite her sewing garments from flour bags, they would still need winter clothing.

The drumming lasted all through the night and the next day and ended as abruptly as it had begun. Lea let out a sigh of relief as the air cleared. Gazing up at the sky, her eyes widened at the huge clouds that had formed. Magnificent clouds! Black clouds! *Messengers of hope.* And then it began.

The rain poured down, a deluge, the thirsty ground sucking up the water.

Lea grabbed Claire and ran out into the storm. The other children followed closely behind. She began a frantic dance. "It's raining!" she shouted. "It's really raining!" Tears of joy rolled down her cheeks. From a distance, she saw Nap arrive with the horses. After letting them loose into the pasture, he joined his family. They danced about, singing, laughing, and crying as the wonderful life-giving rain cascaded down their bodies, drenching them to the skin, and filling them with hope for the future.

Chapter Twenty-Two
Old Dick

The thrill of the storm was short-lived as the earth dried up once again, leaving deep cracks in the hardened earth and swallowing up the promise of life. Lea did what she could to save the garden, but the line of canned goods that normally filled her with pride was sparser this year, the potatoes fewer, and the carrots smaller. At least they managed to save a portion of the wheat crop they stored in the barn.

"I'll see if I can find some work in another town," said Nap, upon observing the sorry cache in the basement.

Lea felt her heart drop; it was now or never. "Why don't we go see the Red Cross? Cécile told me they were giving away food and clothing."

"No!" Napoleon's eyes flashed. "We're not that poor. I told you I'd find work elsewhere."

"Yes, but everyone's looking for work! And there's none to be had because there are no crops, and no one can afford to hire anyone!"

Napoleon tsked, eyeing her as though he'd been betrayed. "What? You don't think I can support my family?"

"No, that's not what I'm saying." She raised her voice.

"Then what?" His eyes narrowed.

"I'm saying these are tough times and sometimes you have to accept charity."

"No!" Nap clenched his teeth. "Never!" He turned and left, giving the door a firm slam.

Finding employment proved futile since many hobos rode the rails searching for any job large or small. Lea had seen them in Ponteix, young men, dirty, desperate, huddled around fires, scrounging whatever they could to eat. Nap traveled from town to town, but no one could afford to hire anyone. There was nothing to be had anywhere. The day arrived when he came home with bad news.

Lea watched as he shuffled to the house, his head bent.

She ran to meet him at the door, her heart beating hard in her chest. "What's wrong?"

Napoleon gave a nonchalant smile, but Lea detected the hidden worry in his eyes. "Nothing." He shrugged.

"Napoleon, don't you lie to me. I know when something's bothering you. Now, out with it!"

His smile faded, replaced by an expression of discouragement. "We can't buy the wood we need for winter this year."

Lea's breath caught, his words suspended in mid-air, a life sentence. "Then what will we do? We can't just freeze."

"Well…." He hesitated. "We can do like the Indians—burn cow and horse dung."

"Cow and horse dung?" Lea crossed her arms over her chest. "I will not have dung in my house!"

"You don't have to have it in the house. We'll make a pile along the wall outside. Once it freezes, it'll be odourless."

Lea digested his words. It was true that manure lost its stench if left alone. It was only when one stepped on it that the smell re-emerged, besieging one's nose like a full-on attack of mustard gas, but she understood they had no choice. "All right," she said, the hostility in her voice melting away. "We'll get started today…before the snow arrives."

After feeding the children a humble lunch, she took them into the pasture, balancing a large basket on one hip, Claire on the other. "Okay, kids," she said. "We're going to try something new today."

"What?" asked Pol.

"We're going to pick up manure to burn in the stove."

"But I don't wanna pick up poop," Lilian whined.

"You're not picking up poop. It's manure. It's different."

"But it stinks," said Lilian.

"Only if it's soft," said Lea. "We'll only pick the hard ones and leave the fresh stuff on the ground, okay?"

"No!" Lilian stamped a foot.

"But we need to if you want to stay warm this winter," said Lea, her frustration mounting.

Pol bent over and scooped one up. "It's not so bad. They're nice and hard. Kind of like bricks. Just don't mush them up. See?" He flung the dung toward the basket. It landed neatly inside. "And look, it flies if you throw it just right."

Lilian broke into a smile. "Let me try." She picked up one of the cow pies and threw it straight into the basket.

"It's a goal!" cried Pol.

Lilian laughed and tried again. This time the manure missed its mark, landing on the ground close by. Undiscouraged, she ran to find another.

"Let's see who can get the most points," said Pol, hurrying after her.

They gathered all they could in the pasture, and when that was done, they wandered into the fields and collected more.

It was truly an event that night when they tried out the dung. The children took turns, placing the pies in the fire and watching them burn with fascination.

But Lea had more worries on her mind than the scent of the fuel in the stove. She knew the food from their garden wouldn't last the winter and was losing hope that Nap would find work. Without consulting him, she took the matter into her own hands. Thus, one morning when he had left for the day, his shoulders slumped, his brows knitted with worry, she hitched up the wagon and made a secret journey to Val Marie where the Red Cross was distributing goods.

A lineup of people trailed outside the church basement, tracing the sidewalk for a whole block. Lea scanned the crowd, curious, catching glimpses of familiar faces from Sunday mass and the church socials—many of their farmer friends. How thin they looked. How ragged. Searching farther, she saw strangers with dirty faces and clothes—hobos passing through.

It took an hour before Lea got inside, but when she did, she took two large bags of apples, several jars of canned peaches and pears, as well as pickled beets. She savoured the thought of the Quebecois beets since their own crop had barely produced anything. But when the volunteer handed her salted cod, she hesitated, remembering Nap's words. He'd know for sure she'd been to the Red Cross if she brought this home. She could hide the canned goods in the cellar, but cod? No one ate that kind of fish around here. Stubbornness welling up inside her, she took several packages anyway. They had to eat, didn't they? And besides, he'd probably like a good fish stew for a change.

Lea rummaged through the used clothing, choosing thick coats that would keep Pol and Lilian warm for the winter. Claire would have to wear Lilian's hand-me-downs, and Lea would need to knit all scarves, sweaters, and toques in the evenings from the bits of yarn she had left over.

When she got home, she stored the edible goods in the cellar, then set about preparing the fish stew to surprise Nap. Chopping an onion, she fried up the cod, then added water, carrots, and potatoes.

"Not bad," she said to herself when the aroma wafted to her nostrils as it simmered on the stove, certain Nap would forgive her for accepting charity once he tasted her culinary expertise.

When he came through the door, he wrinkled his nose. "What *is* that?"

Lea thought of concocting a lie, but decided to come clean. She hardened her resolve. "I went to the Red Cross today and got a few things. I figured it couldn't hurt."

"What?" He hurled his coat down on the floor. "I thought I told you not to go there!"

The children stopped playing, their eyes glued to the drama that played out before them.

"Nap, we won't make it through the winter with what we have."

"I told you—I'll find work! We're not hobos!"

"And what if you don't?" She dug her hands into her hips.

"You think I'm no good? Some kind of poor farmer?"

"That's not what I said," she shouted.

"Then what?"

Lea let out a huff of air. "Nap, it's not just us. There were lots of other farmers there too. They're not doing well either."

Nap turned his back to her. "You don't have faith in me."

Lea rushed forward. "Yes, I do." She placed an arm over his shoulder. "But these are hard times. We have to do the best we can. And if that means accepting a small amount of charity, then that's what we'll have to do."

Napoleon's hard stance melted. He turned and faced her, then placed his hands around her waist. "All right, then, but just this once."

"I promise," she said, wrapping her arms around him and placing a kiss on his cheek. "Now, let's try this cod stew I made."

The family seated themselves at the table. Nap lifted Claire into her high chair while Lea dished out the hot food. She watched as her husband blew on a spoonful, then tasted the recipe.

"Mmm, not bad," he said, dipping in for a second taste. Then his eyes popped open and he snatched his glass of water. "Oh, my gosh, this is so salty."

"It is?" asked Lea. She sampled a spoonful and choked. "Ugh! You're right! It's awful!"

"I think it's pretty good," said Pol.

"Yuck!" said Lilian as she spit it into her napkin.

Lea grabbed all the bowls and dumped the stew back in the pot, determined to remedy the problem. After all, they couldn't afford to waste food. "All this needs is a bit of milk to water it down. Nap, can you get me some from the well, please?"

Nap gladly went, returning a few minutes later with the canister.

Lea poured the entire contents of the container into the stew. She waited until the mixture had heated to boiling and added flour to thicken it. "There. It's more like a soup now—a chowder."

She filled the bowls again and set them down on the table. The family ate the dinner very slowly, drinking lots of water between mouthfuls.

"Perhaps what you need," suggested Nap after the table was cleared, "is to soak it first, and then cook it up."

"Humph!" Lea glowered at her husband. Taking the remainder of the stew, she carried it out to the barn where she fed it to the pig.

For the rest of the evening, the family made several trips to the water bucket, taking long drinks from the dipper.

By the next morning, things had simmered down until Pol went to the barn to hitch up Old Dick and Belle before going to school.

Lea heard a scream, then saw her son racing back, his face a mess of tears.

"What's wrong?" she asked, her voice frantic.

"Old Dick's dead!" He blubbered.

"What?"

"He's dead—in his stall!" Pol wailed.

"Oh, don't tell me he ate that stew!" Nap cried.

Lea shot him an angry glare, then hurried out without her coat, Nap close behind. Lilian picked up Claire and raced after them.

When they got to the barn, they found their faithful horse lying on his side in the stall, his body rigid.

"Get up!" ordered Nap, digging his toe into the animal's hide. When the horse didn't rise, he shouted louder. "Get up, Dick! Get up!"

"Papa, he's dead," cried Pol. "He's already stiff."

"Get up!" shouted Napoleon again, this time swinging his leg harder, stopping in mid-air when his son's words registered. Sharing a despondent look with Lea, he crumpled down beside the horse, his eyes blinking rapidly.

"I guess he just couldn't handle the hunger," said Lea. "Oh, poor Old Dick." She stooped down and rubbed her hand against the cold emaciated flesh of the animal.

Lilian and Claire began crying too. Tears rolled down their faces.

"He was the best horse in the world," sobbed Lilian.

"Yes, he was," agreed Nap.

They mourned together, stroking their old friend, saying their goodbyes.

Then Lea rose and clapped her hands. "It's time you went to school, Pol and Lilian. Go get your things. We all loved Old Dick, but life goes on." She strode to the next stall and prepared Belle. "Sorry, girl. Your partner's gone. You'll have to work it alone today."

The mare looked back at Old Dick's body and let out a low rumble, her head hanging.

"What'll we do now? You've already let the horses free," Lea asked Nap after the children had gone inside.

"I guess I'll have to go find one of them, bring it back in to replace Old Dick."

"No one can replace Old Dick." Lea's voice choked.

The ride to school was somber that morning, the sobs of the children accompanying the clip clopping rhythm of Belle's hooves as the mare plodded along in the cold, autumn air led by Lea. When they got to school, Lea went inside and shared whispered words to Miss Moiny to explain Pol and Lilian's morose mood.

Miss Moiny's eyes enlarged. She gave an understanding nod.

Lea spent the rest of the morning helping Nap remove the horse from the barn. When she returned to pick up her children after school, Pol avoided her gaze.

Lea placed her arm around him. "It's okay to be sad, you know."

Her son didn't answer, nor did his eyes meet hers.

Lilian came running from the school, out of breath, exclaiming, "Pol got into a fight!"

"What?"

"It's true. One of the English boys punched him in the eye."

Lea grabbed the boy's chin and turned his face around. A black shiner stared back at her. "What happened?"

"It was one of the older boys. Told me I was a no good French farmer. Says his mother saw you lined up at the church the other day at the Red Cross."

"What?"

"It's okay, Maman. He picks on a lot of the kids. I usually stay out of it, but today, I just couldn't take it, so I threw a punch at him. No one insults my Maman." He clenched his fists. "And no one gets to run me down for being French."

Incensed, Lea contemplated his words. "Perhaps you should tell him you're Belgian."

Pol turned and faced her. "I did, but he said it wasn't any different."

They traveled in silence until Lea couldn't contain herself any longer. "So…how did *he* fare?"

Lilian piped up, her eyebrows raised, her voice sassy. "The other boy had a really bloody nose."

Lea broke into a smile. "Good!" She emphasized the word with a downward thrust of her chin. As they neared home, Lea voiced a thought. "You know, maybe it's time we switched schools. Would you like to go to school in Val Marie instead? It's a little farther, but…."

Pol mulled the thought over before answering. "I don't know."

"You'd get to study French, and all your classmates would probably be French too."

His eyes brightened at the idea. "Maybe."

"We'll discuss it with Papa tonight, okay?"

"Okay."

When Nap came home that night, leading Prince, Lea's heart fell at the gauntness of the gelding. "He's so thin," she said.

"That's because there's nothing to eat out there. You should have seen what it was like," he said, blinking away tears. "So many dead animals—cattle, horses. It's just awful."

"Then maybe we should bring all the horses in for the winter. They'd have a better chance of survival."

"I think I may have to."

Lea encircled her arms around Nap's chest. "You know, this drought *will* end. We just have to keep believing and doing our best."

A few days later, the remaining four horses were housed in the barn. Nap fed them what he could, the Russian thistles, or the straw, wheat, and molasses mixture, but still they grew thinner each day.

At the beginning of the following week, Lea took the children to the school in Val Marie. The principal, Mr. MacMillan welcomed them, asking Pol and Lilian numerous questions. Then he took Lea aside. "Your children are most welcome here, but there's a small problem," he said.

"What's that?"

"We have no desks for them. You'll have to bring your own."

"No desks?" Lea frowned, withholding the information that they couldn't even afford the wood for the stove. "I'll tell my husband," she said, giving a curt nod. Making a quick turn, she motioned for the children to follow.

"Aren't we staying?" asked Lilian.

"Not today," replied Lea. "We have to find desks for you first."

"Desks?" asked Pol.

"Yes. Apparently even the schools can't afford the basics."

The problem of the desks was resolved in an innovative way by Napoleon. Finding an old car door in an alleyway in town, he added legs to it and painted it orange from a variety of leftover paint he had. For Pol's, he constructed a small table out of wooden crates, painting it the same ghastly colour as Lilian's.

The first day they attended school in Val Marie, the makeshift tables stood in the classrooms, bright beacons surrounded by standard desks. Lea cringed at the sight of them, hoping the others might approve of their colour.

When she returned to pick the children up later that day, Pol's head hung. "So how was your first day?" she asked.

Pol squeezed his lips together hard. "Everyone laughed at my desk," he said. "They called it a Halloween desk."

"And everyone laughed at mine too," said Lilian. "They knew it was a car door, and they knew where Papa got it from. They called him the garbage man."

"The garbage man?" Lea repeated.

Lilian gave a miserable nod.

Lea let out a frustrated sigh, then clenched her teeth with determination. "Well, just be glad you have desks at all," she said. "These are hard times and we have to make do."

"I know, Maman," said Pol. "But it's still tough." He thought for a moment. "But at least no one called me a dirty French farmer."

"Well, I'd say that's a step in the right direction."

Chapter Twenty-Three
The Deed and the Jersey

It was nearly spring the day Napoleon burst into the house carrying a large envelope in his hand. Making a quick bend to remove his boots, he untied them and kicked them off, a huge smile stretched across his face. Lea gave him an inquisitive look.

"We got it!" he said, handing her the long, brown envelope.

"What is it?" she asked, reading the return address. "Dominion Lands Office?" She gasped.

"Open it up!" Nap said.

Lea nearly ripped the envelope in two, her fingers trembling. When she read the contents, she lowered the letter and let out a squeal.

"The land is ours!" said Nap, picking her up and twirling her around. "It's ours! We've done it!"

"What's happening?" asked Pol, jumping up from the sofa, followed by Lilian.

"We own the farm!" cried Nap.

"We own the farm?"

"Yes!"

"We own the farm!" shouted Pol at the top of his lungs. "Today is March fourth, nineteen thirty-two, and *WE OWN THE FARM!*" He leapt on the couch and bounced up and down.

"No jumping on the furniture," said Napoleon. "You're too big. You're almost ten years old." He grabbed Pol and flung him around to a soft landing on the floor, then lifted Lilian and Claire in turn, throwing them into the air before catching them. He did a final twirl in the room with Lea, then stopped. "We need to celebrate. What's for supper?"

"Cow pies," said Pol.

Lea giggled. At seeing the dismay on Nap's face, she said, "Don't worry. He's just joking. We're having cod stew, made the right way."

Lea had learned how to soak the fish for several hours, changing the water three times until all the salt had been rinsed out, then cooking the onions and vegetables with lard until soft. Next, she'd boil the potatoes separately, throwing them into the mixture when they were done. Then, and only then, did she add the cod and milk, cooking it for about fifteen minutes until the fish was flaky. Nap had raved about it, particularly after she began adding a small amount of bacon.

"Mmm!" said Napoleon, eyeing the pot on the stove. "Good choice."

When they sat down for the long anticipated dinner, Napoleon ate about half of his serving, then laid down his fork.

"What?" Lea asked, noting the sober expression in his eyes.

"I was thinking we should trade the Jersey for a Holstein. It would save us the trip each day, exchanging milk with the neighbours."

"Not the Jersey!" said Lea, holding her spoon in midair.

"It only makes sense. There's a farmer, a Mr. McGraw that I met in town. He said he'd be glad to make the switch. His wife likes the cream for cooking."

"But we've had her so long. And she's more of a pet than anything else," Lea said. "Besides, she's your old girlfriend."

Nap smiled. "I know, but we'll get used to the new one."

"No," said Lilian, her elbows propped on the table, chin resting on her hands. "Jersey's *our* cow."

"Yeah," said Pol. "How would you like it if we traded you in because you were too short?"

Nap let out a dry laugh. "I understand, kids, but she's barely giving any milk anymore."

"But that's 'cause she's hungry," said Lilian.

"Yeah. I think we should keep her," said Pol.

"I'm afraid not this time. We really need Holstein milk for Claire," said Nap.

A few days later, the family surrounded the cow, petting her muzzle and neck as Nap prepared to lead her away.

"Goodbye, Jersey," said Pol, biting his bottom lip.

"You're the best cow of all," said Lilian, her mouth hanging down in a pout, "and we'll never forget you."

"Ever," said Claire.

They all waved as Napoleon mounted the horse, leading the cow by its rope.

"That's like if we gave away Claire," said Pol.

"I know," said Lilian. "It's not fair."

They watched as Nap took the Jersey away until man and beast had climbed the hill and disappeared from view. Then they retired to the house.

It was a dark day…a Saturday. Grey clouds smothered the prairie. Lea worried that the children seemed a little too quiet, but then why wouldn't they be? They'd just lost their pet.

Nap returned by lunchtime, dragging along a feisty young cow who tugged rebelliously on its rope.

Lea met him in the barn, dangling Claire on her hip, the other two children close behind. "So this is the new cow, then?" she asked. "What's her name?"

"Mathilda," replied Nap, the corners of his mouth twitching.

"Like my sister?"

"Afraid so."

"Well, we'll have to change her name. Let's see now." She put a finger to her lip. "How about Blacky?"

"Blacky," said Pol, sneering. "No way. I know. How about Tar?"

"Tar! But tar's sticky and smells bad," said Lea.

"How about Rose?" suggested Lilian.

266

"Rose? That's a nice name." Lea placed her hand between the slats of the stall to pet the new cow. "Hello, Rose."

It bolted backward in revolt.

"See? She doesn't like that name," said Pol.

"Guess it'll take a while to get used to us, right girl?" Lea said.

And a while it took. Milking that night was quite the challenge. It took the efforts of both Nap and Lea to tether the cow and hobble her hind legs before they were able to calm her enough to extract the milk.

"Whoa, there, girl," said Nap, knotting the animal's rope to a slat of wood in the stall.

The cow tugged at the cord, letting out a fierce moo.

"It's okay," said Lea. "Here, Nap. I'll slip behind her and tie her hoof while you distract her with a carrot." She moved past the cow and slowly lifted its hock into the loop of the hobble, but before she could tighten it, the animal kicked her.

"Ow!" Lea cried, falling back in the straw.

"Here, let me try."

They changed places.

Lea gave the cow a small piece of carrot while Nap grabbed her hind hoof and pushed it into the noose, pulling it taught before she had time to react.

"Ha! Gotcha!"

The young cow mooed in protest while Nap hobbled her other leg.

"She's ready now," he said.

Lea pulled out the stool and pail and began milking the new cow. She managed to fill the canister enough for their dinner that night, but dreaded repeating the routine again in the morning.

She awoke to extreme cold, the next day, her breath steaming from beneath the warm covers. Nudging Napoleon, she whispered, "I think it snowed. I'm freezing."

In response, Nap rose and lit the fire he had prepared the night before, piling dried thistles on paper, followed by cow pies. After he replaced the cast iron lid on the stove, he walked outside to get more manure, a chilly draft blowing through the door as he retrieved it. But instead of closing the door as swiftly as he'd opened it, he stopped, his eyes growing twice their size. "Oh, my gosh!" he said

"What is it?" asked Lea. "Snow?"

Nap gave his head a slow turn, his lips breaking into an astonished smile as their eyes met.

"What?"

Nap clapped his hands. "Kids, get up! Come and see!"

The children scrambled from their warm beds, rubbing their eyes as they ran to the door. Lea picked up Claire and followed.

"What? Did Bonhomme Noël come early?" asked Lilian.

"No. This is better," said Nap.

Lea peered outside and let out a cry.

The Jersey stood by the barn door, patiently waiting to be milked.

"She walked all the way home!" Lea exclaimed.

Grabbing their coats and boots, they ran outside to greet the cow.

"Jersey!" said Lilian as she threw her arms around its neck.

"Told you you should have never traded her," said Pol.

Napoleon shrugged. "But I was only thinking of Claire."

"Yeah, but Jersey loves us. This is her home," said Pol, petting the animal's muzzle.

"What are we going to do?" Lea whispered in Nap's ear as the children showered the cow with attention.

"I guess I'll have to take her back," he answered, his voice equally low, "and explain what happened."

"You're going to make her travel all that distance?" asked Lea. "She was up all night walking. She'll be too tired. She's old, you know."

"I know. Maybe I should go see McGraw on my own."

It turned out to be unnecessary as McGraw himself arrived soon afterward.

Napoleon met him at the door, looking rather sheepish.

"That darned cow broke out yesterday," said McGraw, his face in a scowl. "Can't find her anywhere. Have you seen her?"

Napoleon nodded, tipping his head toward the barn. "She's here. She came home last night."

The farmer shook his head, dumbfounded and followed Nap into the barn. When they came out again, they talked for a while longer, then shook hands, the farmer leaving without the Jersey.

"What happened?" asked Lea.

"He says to keep her, that we can pay him back later on when the crop comes through. He says there's no sense in forcing her to stay on their farm since she'll only break out again."

"So we get to keep Jersey?" asked Lilian.

"Yes," said Nap. "She's our cow for the rest of her life."

"Yay!" Pol cheered.

A few weeks later, Nap's words came to fruition when they found their dear beloved Jersey lying on her side in the pasture. Lea stared at their pet with pity. Could it be the animal had known her time was near and had come home to die?

Chapter Twenty-Four
The Plague

Dear Lea, Napoleon, and children,

How quickly the time passes. Lilian, Roberto, Luigi, and Fernando have grown so much. My Lilian is twelve now and is the star pupil in her class. She's so talented in piano. I wish you could hear her play. Last week, she performed a difficult sonata at the conservatory to loud applause. I was so proud. However, I'm very worried about the boys even though they're only six, eight, and ten.

I daresay you must have heard by now that Adolf Hitler was appointed chancellor in Germany. He says terrible things that make me nervous. He calls for complete obedience of his people saying he'll restore a great nation. And with our country right next door, I pray this doesn't mean war. I couldn't bear to have my own boys called to fight when they're older. What use is it to put children in uniform just to be mown down when the Germans come through on their way to France? This man isn't right in the head. He blames the Jews for all the problems of the country. Is he not aware that the entire world is in a depression? I don't want to be engaged in war again. It's only been fifteen years. I don't think I could ever be ready even if an entire lifetime had passed. You were so right to have moved to Canada, though things are tough there too. I still regret not having followed you.

I'm so happy to hear that you are with child again. Don't worry, the drought will end and soon you'll be living the lives of rich farmers now that you own the land. Perhaps that's when Dino and I might think of emigrating to Canada.

Mathilde is well and sends her love. Her little girl, Charlotte, is doing well. I'm glad you changed your cow's name to Rose, though Mathilde laughed and laughed when she read your letter. Too bad about the Jersey, but think of it this way, you won't have to worry about the 'other woman' anymore.

Camille has recently been diagnosed with cirrhosis of the liver. Too much alcohol. It's not like we didn't try to warn him. His poor wife. Nothing has changed with François. He's still repairing shoes.
Your sister,
Palma

Lea laid down the letter, feeling dread in the pit of her stomach. She turned to Nap. "This new chancellor in Germany has me worried," she said.

Nap lowered his newspaper. "Me too. I suspect he may become a dictator the way he's talking. He's so full of empty promises—and so much anger!"

"I'm scared for my family back home. They could be caught in the middle of a war. Germany could rise again the same way it did in the Great War."

They shared a long, intense look, the silence in the air magnifying their fears.

"We'll just have to pray for their safety," Nap finally said.

When the end of April drew closer, Nap kept his earlier promise of taking Lea to Ponteix for the delivery of their fourth child. Loading up the family, they spent the weekend with the uncles, aunts, and cousins, their usual party of music, good food, and dancing. Lea was again presented with gifts of clothing from the relatives. When Sunday afternoon arrived, she waved goodbye to Nap and the kids.

"I knew Maman was going to have another baby," she heard Pol say as they walked toward the wagon. "Because she's really fat just like before Claire was born."

"Yes." Nap gave his son a pat on the head. "She is. But don't tell her that, okay? You might not survive to live another day."

"She's going to have another girl, right, Papa?" asked Lilian. "And we can name her Gladiola."

"Gladiola!" Pol's nose wrinkled almost up to his brow. "No, Maman has to have a boy to make things even."

"I'm afraid the good Lord will have to decide that," said Nap, as they drove away.

The delivery went well with Dr. Lupien in charge. Lea shook her head in scorn when she thought back to Madame Carlier's ineptitude and wondered if babies had died at her hands.

When Nap returned to Levi and Emma's weeks later with the three children, Lea motioned them over from her bed in the corner of the living room where she lay after her discharge from the small hospital in Ponteix.

"Maman!" cried Lilian. "Did you have a girl?"

Lea smiled, then shook her head. "I'm afraid not. It's a boy."

"A boy? Hurray!" said Pol, throwing his arms into the air. "Now I'll have someone more interesting to play with than just girls."

"What's wrong with being a girl?" asked Lilian, pouting.

"Nothing. It's just that all you do is play with dolls."

"Do not!"

"Yes, you do."

"It doesn't matter." said Lea. "Because I know you're all going to love him. Come and see."

The children crept closer to view the newborn. A tiny, wrinkled head poked out from the blue blanket.

"He looks like an old man," said Pol.

"All newborns do." Lea gave him a patient smile.

"He's got red hair like Claire's," said Lilian.

"Red like mine," repeated Claire.

"What are we gonna name him?" Pol asked. He pressed his lips together in thought. "Hmm. How about—?"

"He's already got a name," said Lea. "It's Denis. I named him after a martyr."

"What's a martyr?" asked Pol.

"It's a saint who was killed because of his faith."

"He got killed because of his faith?" Lilian's eyes widened.

"Yes, but a really long time ago…hundreds and hundreds of years ago."

The children broke into relieved smiles.

After a jovial lunch with the grandparents and several cousins, they prepared for the ride back before long shadows claimed the day, transforming it to night. Napoleon carried Lea's bag to the waiting wagon while Pol took the gifts Denis had received. When they arrived home a short time after dusk, Lea picked up where she left off, reclaiming her role as mother by cooking and washing.

Summer was brutal as it had been for years, the crops drying up, the slough turning to mud, but they continued as they had before, nursing their garden and thus assuring their lifeline of food.

As usual, Nap insisted on making the buffalo berry wine again, filling Lea with apprehension. They argued until she finally gave in with the promise that he would serve it only to guests, never offering it for sale.

Nap took the children to a choice spot by the Frenchman River where the berries were abundant. He instructed Lea and the children to grasp a sheet beneath the bush while he reached up with a hook, struck a branch, the ripe berries tumbling below. They transferred the red fruit to a large ten-gallon boiler. When the container was filled, they returned home where Lea added water and cooked the mixture until the leaves and other twigs floated to the top. Taking half the mixture, she made her usual tasty jam in half-quart jars while Nap bottled his portion into wine bottles he had gotten from the local bar, adding a teaspoon of sugar to each. They hid the illegal wine in the cellar behind a shelf, though the stench dominated the entire room. After a few weeks, popping sounds could be heard from below as the spirits fermented, blowing off corks.

The wine made them a hit with other folk from Val Marie, and they soon began to have a great deal of company during the evening when all the chores had been done.

Lea enjoyed the camaraderie, but worried the RCMP might get word and pay them a visit as they had to others in the town. Fortunately, they never came...or had they simply turned a

276

blind eye because they liked Nap? She didn't know, nor did it appease her anxiety.

To detract attention from the RCMP, Lea became a model citizen, insisting that mass should never be missed. After all, she had to provide a good example to the children.

"Come on, everyone," she ordered one Sunday morning. "We want to get there early so we can get a front seat."

With groans and yawns, the children picked at their breakfast, then dressed in their Sunday best that Lea had laid out. She watched Pol climb into the wagon. How short his pants and shirt-sleeves were. He was growing so quickly. Already eleven, he would soon hit his growth spurt. Then how would she keep up with his clothing?

The day promised to be a scorcher. "Too bad the weather's turning hot again," said Lea.

"I know. It's been so nice and cool," said Nap.

Lea stared up at the clear, blue sky that showed no signs of change. How she missed the beautiful castles and images that had once filled her gaze before the drought. *Endless blue means endless heat.* Who could believe she'd learned to hate the cerulean colour she'd once loved?

When they arrived at the church, the children jumped down from the wagon and were herded inside. Lea enjoyed the respite of the cool breeze as she entered. The caretaker had remembered to open all the windows ahead of time. Seeing Cécile sitting near the front of the church, Lea moved the children in beside her. But there was something different about her friend that day. She seemed a little prettier, a little cheerier…a little plumper.

"Are you in a family way?" Lea whispered.

Cécile cupped her hand to Lea's ear. "Yes, I am!"

"How's Claude taking the news?"

"I've never seen him more excited about anything."

"I'm so glad."

Père Fortier smiled as he welcomed the congregation. They sang hymns and recited the Kyrie and Gloria. After the readings, he began his sermon. His words gave them hope as he prayed for the drought to end and for the rains to return, asking the Lord to have mercy on His servants of the prairies.

When they rose to accept communion, Lilian followed. How proud Lea was that her girl had received the holy sacrament. And soon it would be Claire's turn. Well…in a few years, anyway. But didn't time fly?

After mass, they joined the congregation for a simple lunch in the hall across the street. The children gobbled down their sandwiches and cookies before playing while the adults took their time enjoying conversing with friends.

"When are you due?" asked Lea.

"In December," Cécile replied. "It's been really difficult with Claude's gambling problem, but no one has money anymore, so he's been staying home and building furniture in the barn."

"That sounds like the start of a good business," said Lea.

"I hope so."

"It's so sad about all these hobos," Lea said. "I heard one fell from the train and died last week. They buried his body in the churchyard. But no one knows who he was, so they can't even send word to his family."

Cécile shook her head. "I know. Such poverty."

"Do you want the baby clothes your mother lent us?" Lea asked, a familiar pain jabbing her heart at the memory of the twins and Roger.

"Sure!"

"Good. I'll drop by some time during the week then."

"That would be great. Then we could have a good visit."

The crowd thinning, Lea caught Nap's wave from the corner of her eye. She turned and gave Cécile a hug, then joined the family on their way home.

They had only been on the road for about ten minutes when Pol pointed to the horizon in the distance. "What's that?"

"What?" Lea asked.

"Over there."

A mysterious cloud moved toward them. Lea gasped. "Oh, no, not another dust storm. We'd better head back to the church. We'll never make it home in time." She'd had enough of the last one, digging up their garden to rescue what they could. But this was different. She squinted. "That's not dust. What is it?"

"I don't know," said Nap.

It overtook them fast. Within minutes, insect bodies pounded them. Lea clutched Baby Denis to her bosom, covering his head as best she could with his blanket. Claire screamed and buried her head in Lea's side.

"Quick! Get down and cover your faces."

The children ducked into the wagon, their knees tucked in, and their arms covering their heads.

"What are they?" shouted Lilian.

"They're grasshoppers!" said Pol. "Millions of them!"

Frantic, the horses broke into a gallop, blinded by the insects.

"Hold on," said Nap.

The horses stampeded, racing recklessly, unseeing.

"Watch out! The horses are going off the road!" cried Lea.

Nap gave the reins a sharp tug, steering them to the right. They followed his lead, turning a little too sharply. The wagon tipped to one side. Nap yanked the reins in the other direction, and the wagon landed back on an even keel with an abrupt thud.

The horses continued to gallop out of control, their eyes slits, until the cloud grew thinner. They slowed to a canter, and then a trot, shaking their heads, their hides twitching and tails swatting at their rumps as they snorted over and over.

Lea and the children slowly raised their heads.

Then Lilian screamed and jumped onto the seat. "They're everywhere in the wagon!"

Nap halted the horses, then handed the reins to Lea. He leapt into the back where he swatted and stamped at the insects, wincing as they crunched under his feet, their yellow blood spattering the wood.

Lea threw her arms around the girls, consoling them as they sobbed. "It's okay. They're just grasshoppers, that's all. They're not poisonous."

"But they're in my clothes!" shouted Pol, pulling off his shirt and swatting at himself.

"In mine too!" screamed Lilian.

Lea undid the buttons of Lilian's dress and jiggled the garment until all the grasshoppers slid out. She did the same with Claire. Checking, Denis, she was relieved to see she'd been able to protect him from the bugs.

"Let's go home," she said.

Nap shook the reins, but as they neared the farm, Lea's spirit sunk lower and lower. "It's all gone!" she said. "Everything! They ate the little bit of wheat there was."

"It's like the plague in the Bible," said Pol. "Like the locusts."

Nap stared in disbelief, then did a hurried sign of the cross.

They traveled onward, the horses settling, until they came to the two hills that marked the entrance of the farm. Lea felt empty as she stared at their wheat fields where only stubble now lay, but when they got to within view of her garden, she burst into tears.

"Is there no end to this?" she asked. Handing Denis to Nap, she jumped down from the wagon and ran to where the plants had been growing. She bent down and dug her fingers through the dirt, feeling for the stems of what had been a flourishing garden. "I can't take anymore of this!" She raised her voice. "Why do we even go to church? Why?" She threw her face into her hands and cried, the dirt from the patch mixing with her tears. "God doesn't care!"

"Lea!" shouted Nap. "Stop it!"

"How are we supposed to feed our family now?" She was hysterical.

"Maman!" shouted Pol. "Stop crying. We'll find a way."

Lea threw herself down on the ground and sobbed. When her tears had nearly spent themselves, she looked up to see her children cowering inside the wagon, terrified. Forcing herself to regain control for their sake, she wiped her muddied eyes, then walked to the wagon and helped them down.

When the children seemed calmer, she turned to Nap and hissed, "Now will you get relief from the government?"

Nap nodded, his lips trembling as a small tear rolled down his cheek.

Chapter Twenty-Five
Relief and Catastrophe

Nap ate his breakfast in silence the next morning as though something weighed on his mind, barely answering the good-natured questions of his children. After eating only a portion of his meal, he left the table and put on his coat and boots. He strode to the barn and came out a short while later mounted on Prince, his hat tipped forward. But instead of spurring the animal into a trot as he usually did, he walked the gelding at a slow pace. A few hours later, he returned, his face etched in a frustration so deep it was impossible to contain. Lea knew immediately what had happened—he'd been to town to apply for relief.

"Watch Claire and Denis," she said to Lilian. Hurrying out the door, she met Nap as he led the horse into the barn. "What happened?" she asked, out of breath.

Napoleon stopped and shook his head. "They were so unfair."

Lea gave an anxious glance back at the house. "What do you mean unfair?"

"They didn't think we were poor enough," he said, placing the horse in its stall.

"Not poor enough? Did you tell them our crop was destroyed by grasshoppers?"

Napoleon nodded.

"And that we have nothing, absolutely nothing to feed the livestock?"

He nodded again.

"Then what?" Her voice rose to a frantic pitch.

Napoleon hesitated before speaking. "They said our children were too well-dressed."

"What? But I'm making their clothes from sacks, for heaven's sake!"

"I know." He looked defeated. "But apparently the guy saw you in town on Sunday with the kids when you had them all dressed up for church and decided we couldn't possibly be that badly off."

"So aren't they giving us anything?"

Napoleon sighed, his shoulders slumping. "Twelve measly dollars a month."

Lea's upper lip rose. "Twelve? How are we supposed to feed a family of six plus our livestock with just that?"

"Well," he said, "the twelve dollars is for groceries…for us...but we're not allowed to spend it on anything else."

"But what about the animals?"

"They said we could get feed from the government, but that eventually, we have to pay it back."

Lea let out a sarcastic huff. "And just how are we going to do that?"

Nap reached for her hand and held it firm in his grip. "I don't know, but it's a start. At least we'll have food for the family." His eyes begged her to agree.

"But what about winter clothes? Pol's growing like a weed."

He glanced away. "We'll have to apply to the Red Cross again."

Lea's voice softened. "Well, that's not so bad."

"I guess not." He shrugged. "And I thought…" Napoleon paused, "that perhaps you could teach me how to repair shoes like your father did. That way we could keep patching our shoes and boots."

Lea let out a resigned chuckle. "If that's what it takes."

Nap's eyes darted to the house and back. "But in the meantime, I don't want the children to know about this."

Lea hesitated before answering. "Okay."

"I mean *ever!* I don't want them *ever* to know we had to apply for relief as long as they live."

Lea held his gaze before answering, "I promise," uncertain how she'd keep the information from ten-year-old Pol's sharp eyes.

It was humiliating the next day when Lea took the wagon to Erwin's store where she handed the slip of paper from the government that informed the manager, Mr. Eickenberry, of their shame. But he filled out the order as though it were any other, his face expressionless. A few days later, when Nap came in looking for nails, Mr. Eikenberry wrote 'beans' on the receipt, since government officials regularly checked to be sure only food was bought with the money.

When Nap brought the nails home, he announced to Lea that it was time they extended their house.

"How?" she asked. "We have no money for lumber."

"The lean-to," he said. "It's not filled with wheat, so we might as well make our bedroom out of it. I can take some of the lumber off the barn if I need to."

Lea smiled at the idea—a place to call her own in their overcrowded cabin! Well, hers and Nap's, anyway. Like when they lived at the Gilberts'. Oh, how she relished the sweet memories of long ago.

For the next few days, Nap kept busy constructing the new room. First, he cut out a rectangle for the door and used the wood to build the frame that surrounded the opening. For the flooring, he laid down the leftover battleship linoleum he'd used when he'd built the cabin.

Lea grew excited about the project and added to it. Using leftover paint, she coated the entire floor of the house grey, then dipped a sponge into a different colour to form designs. But she didn't stop there. She soaked old gunnysacks she'd found in the barn in glue she'd made from flour and water and applied them to the bottom half of the walls. Then she got Nap to nail a one-and-a-half inch strip of wood horizontally to cover the edges of the sacks and help fasten them to the wall.

The day she finished, she stood back, admiring her work with satisfaction. "That looks so much better. More like a home than a shack. And especially with our new bedroom!"

"I'm sorry. I know I promised you a much bigger house," he said, slipping his arm around her waist. "But it's better than nothing, right?"

Lea broke into a whimsical smile. "Do you know what I'd rather have than a big house?"

"No what?"

"An outhouse. I'm so tired of the bucket. It stinks, and Pol doesn't want to empty it anymore."

Napoleon threw his head back in laughter. "Now, that I can do."

"How?"

"I have my ways."

For the next few days, Nap dug black clay from a hole near the slough. He mixed it with straw and water, stomping it with his bare feet, his pant legs rolled up. When it was the right consistency, he shoveled it into a bucket and carried it to the hole he'd already dug in the ground, then began to build his wall.

"Papa's playing in the mud," said Claire. "Can I play in the mud too?"

"No, Claire," said Lea. "You know we don't have enough water to give you a bath." She thought of how they had to re-use water over and over, first scrubbing the dishes, washing the children, and then the floor.

"What's he doing?" asked Lilian.

"He's building us an outhouse so we won't have to smell that stinky bucket anymore."

"But won't his wall fall over?" asked Pol.

"Where there's a will, there's a way," she said, casting him a mischievous glance.

At thirty inches from the ground, Napoleon added the toilet seat, then continued the construction of his wall, his family watching with great curiosity. When the structure was tall enough, he allowed it a few days to dry before adding a wooden roof and door made from barn lumber. Then he patched the hole in the barn using the same gumbo mix.

The day it was finally ready for use was celebrated as a great event. Nap ceremoniously tossed the hated bucket into the barn, and asked, "Who wants to be the first to try out the new outhouse?"

"Me!" shouted Lilian and Pol at the same time.

"No, me," said Claire.

Nap's gaze swept over his family before he spoke. "Okay, since this is such an important occasion, I choose Maman!"

Lea let out an exuberant laugh. "All right, then." She handed Denis to Nap.

Stepping inside, she closed the door and latched it. An old Eaton's Catalogue lay beside the seat, a substitute for the toilet paper they couldn't afford.

"I feel like a queen," she called after she'd sat down, relieved the seat didn't crumble beneath her.

Giggles from outside met her words.

When she was done, she opened the door to enthusiastic stares.

"Well?" asked Pol.

"What an experience!" said Lea.

"My turn," said Pol, running in before anyone else had the chance.

"No, me!" Lilian reached the door just as it slammed in her face. "Hey!"

"You'll be next, Lilian. Then Papa, then…." Lea stopped when she saw her youngest daughter doing her business in the dirt instead. She sighed. "Oh, Claire."

When they'd all had a turn, Pol stood up beside the outhouse and announced, "Today is a great day for anyone who has to go to the bathroom on the de Montigny homestead. This timely structure was constructed by none other than the great Napoleon de Montigny. You've all heard of Napoleon Bonaparte, the great builder of the French Empire? Well, now there's Napoleon de Montigny, the great builder of outhouses." He turned and faced the new structure. "I christen it 'The Peehouse'."

Lea threw him a warning look. "Pol!"

"Well, it is," he said, turning pink.

"Never mind," said Lea. "We'll call it the outhouse."

"Aw, shucks," said Pol.

For days afterward, the children visited the new facilities every chance they had, convinced they were living in luxury though they were dirt poor—until the days grew colder and it wasn't so convenient anymore.

***

It was autumn when Lea stepped outside to bring dung into the house and noticed the telling crispness in the air. She knew that feel—snow—and that she needed to take the Pol and Lilian to the Red Cross to choose clothing for the winter.

They spent as little time as possible in the church basement, picking out used jackets, sweaters, and pants for the two children. Lea was careful to make sure their coats were a least a size larger than what they normally wore. Searching for boots, she found a pair for Lilian, but had to dig for quite some time before finding anything for Pol.

"How about these ones?" she asked him.

"No. Those are ladies' boots," he said. "I refuse to wear those."

"But there's nothing else that'll fit you. What are we going to do?" she asked, frustration threatening to rise.

"I don't know." He curled his lip up in rebellion.

"Maybe we could disguise them somehow. Add something to them," suggested Lea.

"Like what?"

"I don't know. We could change the soles. Just try them on, okay."

Pol let out a huff. "Okay."

He took them to the most obscure part of the basement, slipped his feet in, and gave her the nod, then left hurriedly, leaving Lea to retrieve the boots herself. She found him later, cowering behind the church when she came out with the other children.

When they got home, Lea shoved the clothes away in the wardrobe, all except Pol's boots. Eyeing them, she calculated how she could disguise them. They really were rather dainty.

"Go get me your old boots," she said.

"Okay." Pol opened the closet door and dug inside until he found them and handed them to her.

"Let's see," said Lea, measuring the bottoms one against the other. "We could take the soles off of this pair and glue them onto the other ones. That would give them a more rugged look."

Pol nodded, appearing terribly worried. "Okay."

"And then we could change the colour to brown."

He gave another reluctant nod.

Lea got to work, first removing the soles from the old boots, then gluing them to the new ones. She added straps from the worn pair to the tops of the other. It was difficult work pushing the needle into the thin leather without her father's equipment, but she persevered. Next, she took out the brown shoe polish and shone them, but when she stood back, she noted the black was still visible underneath. Maintaining a positive stance, she waved Pol over.

"Well? What do you think? Here, try them on so I can see what they look like."

His face miserable, Pol bent down and laced them up.

Lea did everything she could to hide the dissatisfaction of her work. It was obvious they were completely refurbished, but she couldn't let Pol know her true feelings, so she faked a smile. "They look great! No one will ever guess."

Pol let out a despondent sigh. "Yes, they will."

"Can you fix my boots too?" asked Lilian.

"No, sweetie," said Lea, again maintaining the same false grin. "Yours are just fine. Besides, I have to make supper."

The next day, Pol came home in a snit, throwing the hated boots into the closet.

"What happened?" asked Lea.

"It didn't fool them in the least. I kept my pant legs down as low as possible, but when I sat in class at my stupid orange desk, my pant legs rose. And that's when one of the older boys shouted, 'Oh, my God! Hey, everyone, Pol's got girl's boots.' And the whole class started to laugh."

"What did you do?" asked Lea.

"Well, I was gonna punch someone, but then I remembered I wasn't supposed to. And I didn't have to because the teacher yelled at them anyhow."

"Well at least he did that," said Lea, relieved someone had stuck up for her son.

"And what about you?" she asked, turning to Lilian. "Did anyone laugh at your boots?"

"No," said Lea. "Another girl has the same kind. Now all the girls want them."

Lea gave her eyes a giant roll and slapped her forehead in disbelief.

Chapter Twenty-Six
The Bull

It was a cold November day when a visitor wandered onto their property. Frost lay thick on the ground, and the air had a bite to it.

"We have company," said Pol, staring out the window.

"Who?" asked Lea, stirring a pot of hot oatmeal.

"The neighbour's bull—the really mean one."

"Oh, no." Lea pushed the porridge to the back burner and hurried to the window. She knew how dangerous males of the species could be, charging humans who dared pass through their territory, even when it *wasn't* theirs. "Maybe he's just hanging out hoping to have a rendez-vous with Rose. Perhaps he wants to take her dancing in town."

Lilian giggled from her place at the table.

"Nap, go chase him away," Lea said.

"Sure, as soon as I have my oatmeal." He ladled some of the mush into a bowl.

"No, go now. The kids need to go to school soon, and we can't go out there with that bull hanging around."

Nap glanced at the clock on the shelf. "There's plenty of time," he said. "Let me eat my breakfast first."

Lea and the children stared out the window, watching as the bull wandered near the barn. He let out a loud moo. When Rose didn't respond, he mooed again, impatient.

"You won't get a date acting like that," said Lea. "Try being a little more subtle."

The children laughed.

The bull lifted his head and sniffed the air, then bellowed some more.

"Rose doesn't seem too interested," said Pol.

"She's always been picky," said Lea.

Spying the outhouse, the bull wandered over, sniffed the air, and circled it.

"Guess he smelled what's down the hole," said Pol.

"Or maybe he needs to go to the bathroom," said Lilian.

"I hope not," said Pol. "There aren't enough pages left in the catalogue for *his* big behind."

They broke into another fit of laughter.

"It may be he's just curious," said Lea. "He wants to know what that little barn is."

Without warning, the bull turned his backside to the outhouse and began rubbing it.

"Hey, look," said Lilian, pointing a finger, "he's scratching his butt."

Nap jumped up, leaving his unfinished oatmeal on the table. "That's not a good thing.

I'd better get out there." He threw on his boots and coat and flung the door open.

"Quick!" screeched Lea.

Nap raced outside, waving frantic arms as he ran. "Get out of here, you stupid animal!"

Startled, the bull turned and faced him.

"I said, get out of here." Nap picked up a rock and threw it, striking the bull in the ribs.

A ferocious roar ripped from its throat.

Nap threw another rock, striking its chest.

Screaming with rage, the animal backed away—right into the outhouse. The small structure collapsed, toppling onto the ground.

"No!" screamed Nap.

Furious, the bull lowered his head and pawed the ground.

Nap flung another rock.

When the stone struck its chest again, the animal aimed its horns and charged.

"Help!" Nap turned on his heels and raced to the corral, the bull in hot pursuit.

"Go, Papa!" shouted Pol.

"Quick!" Lea screamed.

Grabbing the top rung of the fence, Nap hurled himself into the corral just in time. "Ha! You missed me!" he shouted.

The bull huffed at Nap, enraged. They stood, regarding each other, man and beast. Then the bull turned and wandered away as though a human wasn't worth his while. Nap waited until it had moved farther down the road before simpering back to the barn, glancing over his shoulder to be sure he hadn't been followed.

When he came out again, Lea saw the hated bucket dangling from his fingers.

"Oh, no!" Lilian pinched her nose.

"I'm not emptying it," said Pol.

"Guess we'll be living with this until the ground thaws again," Nap said when he came in.

"Oh, well," said Lea. "We've been living with it all these years. What's one more?"

But as the nights grew longer and the days shorter with fewer trips to the barn, Lea wasn't so sure she could handle the bucket until the spring. Longing for their old cabin at the Gilberts' and its convenient outhouse, she thought of Cécile. She knew her friend was due in December, but she hadn't seen her in church for a while. *She must be too uncomfortable to ride in their Bennett Buggy.*

Christmas was approaching and with it, the preparations. Lea snuck out to the barn with Nap each night to help him build toys for the children. She'd hold the wood while he sanded it, always fascinated by his vision and how a toy could arise from a barrel slat. When they'd finished working on the gifts for the evening, they'd bury them under some straw until the next time they were able to steal away.

Baby Denis seemed to grow at an alarming rate—so different from Claire. While she had been so fragile, he was robust.

"Only a few more months," Lea said, "and you'll be walking everywhere. Then what'll we do with you?"

Denis gurgled back in what seemed defiance. He was nearly eight months old and as strong as an ox.

One day, as she prepared the bread dough, she turned to find her son standing in the crib. Startled, she cried, "Already?"

"Good boy!" said Lilian. She reached into his bed, lifted him up, and put him down on the ground. "I'm going to give him a walking lesson." Taking his hands, she held him in an upright position, pushing one foot forward, then the next.

"Breakfast!" Lea called a few minutes later.

"Coming," Lilian said, dropping Denis' hands and skipping to the table.

Lea gasped when she saw Lilian let go. The image of the boy falling backward and hitting his head flashed in her mind. But instead, her eyes rounded and her mouth dropped open. Denis hadn't even so much as landed on his bottom. Instead, he took three unexpected steps forward.

"Denis can walk!" shouted Pol.

"But he's only eight months old!" Lea said.

"Papa!" shouted Lilian. "Come and see."

Nap dashed from the bedroom and stopped, a grin stretched across his face. He scooped up the baby, laughing. "Why, you're just a wonder boy!"

Within days, Denis was toddling about as well as any one-year-old, getting his hands into everything, including the stove.

Terrified, Lea kept him in the crib for his own safety, taking him out only when there was someone to watch him. She couldn't wait to show Cécile how strong her boy was, wishing they had a telephone, but she'd have to wait until Sunday when, hopefully, she'd see her in church.

It was particularly cold the week before Christmas. The temperature dropped to minus forty, and the winds blew with great ferocity. But Lea wouldn't miss Christmas Eve mass for the world, so happy she was to share her news about her boy with Cécile. After bundling up the children, she placed the younger ones in the bottom of the cutter where the heated rocks lay, holding Denis between her legs to protect him from burning his hands. Then she covered them up with the blanket.

When Pol climbed aboard, heading to his usual spot, Nap grabbed his arm and handed him the reins. "Here," he said, "you're going on twelve. How about if you drive us to church today?"

Pol smiled with pride as he took the straps, sitting high on the seat, despite the extreme cold. His voice filled with confidence, he began conversing as though he were an adult. "It's hard to believe tomorrow's Christmas! I wonder what Bonhomme Noël will bring the children." He threw Nap a knowing look.

"I guess we'll have to wait and see," Nap replied, returning the gesture with a sidelong glance.

Suddenly, Lea was filled with Christmas spirit. Her heart soaring, she broke into song.

Les anges dans nos campagnes
Ont entonné l'hymne des cieux;
Et l'écho de nos montagnes
Redit ce chant mélodieux.

The children joined in too. When they got to the Gloria, Lea sang the harmony line, her voice rising higher than the others. When they'd finished that song, they sang another and another until they reached the church.

Lea descended from the cutter with Denis in her arms while Pol led the horses to the post where he tied them under Nap's directions. Lilian followed Lea, holding Claire's hand.

When they stepped inside the church, Lea knew there was something wrong despite the cheerful Christmas decorations—the large wreath with its four candles displayed near the front of the church and the crèche that awaited the Baby Jesus. The Christmas spirit she'd reveled in only a few moments before disappeared. Heads were bowed and expressions grave. Someone was sobbing. Searching the nave, her heart nearly stopped when she saw Mr. and Madame Gilbert seated in the front row, their heads bent and shoulders shaking.

"Stay here!" she ordered her children as she rushed to the front pew.

"But Maman," called Lilian.

"Just do as I say."

She hurried as fast as her legs could carry her, Denis bouncing in her arms. When she reached the Gilberts, she squeezed into their seat. "What happened?"

Madame Gilbert raised her eyes. Her face was soaked with tears. "She died." She broke into a fresh fit of sobbing.

"Who? Cécile's baby?" asked Lea, breaking into a cold sweat.

Mr. Gilbert shook his head. "Both. They couldn't get the baby out. There was no doctor. And now we've lost all our children." He laid his arm over Madame Gilbert's shoulders, and together they cried bitter tears.

Lea felt a wave of nausea overcome her. Retching, her hand flew to her mouth. Cécile was dead? But how could that be? She'd been so healthy. "Where's Claude?" she asked.

"He didn't come. He's beside himself with grief," said Mr. Gilbert.

A hand rested on Lea's shoulder. It was Nap's. His face dropped when he heard the news.

The rest of the mass was a blur. Lea sat with her four children, numb, as she listened to the priest describe what a terrible loss Cécile's life was to the community, and how she and the baby girl she had carried had surely gone to Heaven.

The trip home was quiet, the sound of the cutter gliding through the snow to the padded clip clop of the horse's hooves and an occasional cough erupting from one of the children.

The next morning, Lea and Nap went through the motions of Christmas, giving forced smiles and uttering false words of joy as the children marveled at the wooden toys and food Bonhomme Noël had brought. When Nap loaded up the cutter, his face long, they set out to celebrate Christmas with the relatives in Ponteix. But Lea went only in body.

She felt hollow when they were welcomed into Levi and Emma's home. She picked at the food that was given her and sat alone in the corner as the family danced to the music of the uncles' fiddles and banjo.

After a time, she felt someone sit down beside her. It was Levi. "What's the matter?" he asked.

"Oh, nothing." Lea tried to feign enjoyment, but when Levi pushed her further, tears welled up in her eyes and she broke down, telling him about the death of her best friend.

"Come with me," he said, his voice gentle.

Lea obediently followed her father-in-law to the back of the house where he took her in his arms as she cried.

"It's so difficult, you know, living out there all alone, trapped inside the house, our family growing, no money."

"I know." Levi regarded her with compassion. "It's difficult for us to watch you suffer too. None of us have ever known that kind of poverty." He paused a moment before continuing. "But Lea, I think I have a solution for you."

"A solution?"

"Yes, but you might not like it."

"What?" Lea tilted her head. "I'm listening."

"Perhaps what you need is fewer children."

"Fewer children!" She thought out the possibilities, then gasped. "No orphanage is good enough for them."

He let out a wry chuckle. "Not an orphanage, Lea. Why don't you let Pol and Lilian live with us? We have plenty of room, and there's a convent close by where they could go to school. They teach French. And there are a lot of things for them to do. There's a skating rink, a ballpark, and they'd have so many cousins to play with."

Lea digested his words before answering. "But I could never abandon my children."

"You wouldn't be abandoning them," he said, his voice kind. "They'd just be…on loan… until you get back on your feet. You've been through a lot."

Lea allowed the idea to take hold, but was immediately wracked with guilt. But how much easier life would be. Hadn't she been the one to convince Nap there was no shame in accepting help? She let out a sigh. "Let me think on it."

"All right," said Levi, taking her arm and leading her back into the living room where jokes flew about to enthusiastic laughter.

When the music ended and they retired for the night, Lea brought up the idea to Napoleon.

She heard his breath catch in the dark before he answered. "Lea, I know you're upset about Cécile's death and all, but can you really give up your children like that even if it's only for a few months?"

"Other people do it," she said. "And if they stay on the farm over the winter, there's a good chance they'll miss a lot of school."

"True," said Nap.

"It's not really like charity," she said. "They're family."

"Well, let's talk it over with the children first and see how they feel about it."

A few days later, she announced the news to Pol and Lilian.

Lilian's eyes rounded with fear, but Pol welcomed the news.

"Stay with Memère and Pepère? I'd love to!"

"Yes, but only until the summer," she said. "And then we'll come back and get you."

"But I don't want to stay here," said Lilian. "I want to go home with you."

"I know, Lilian, but—"

"Don't worry. I'll look after you," said Pol, laying an arm over his sister's shoulder. "And just think. We'll get to play with all the cousins. And we'll have real desks." He eyed Nap apologetically. "It'll be fun."

"Well, okay," said Lilian.

And so it was, that Napoleon and Lea returned home after the holidays, a family of four.

Chapter Twenty-Seven
Pol Rebels

Lea frowned when Napoleon handed her the letter from the convent in Ponteix. More than a year had passed since Pol and Lilian began attending the parochial school. A nervous tingle ran down her spine. Why would they be writing to her? She took the letter from her husband, tore it open, and began reading.

Dear Madame de Montigny,

It is with great concern that I write this letter to you regarding your son Pol. Though he is indeed an intelligent child, he is also very difficult. He spends much of his day disrupting the class by talking and passing notes to girls, and he never does his homework. So far, he hasn't achieved grades higher than in the seventies. Not a good average for a boy who was the star student in his previous school.

The other day, he was reprimanded for refusing to settle down and was sent to me for the strap. When I pulled it out, he burst into tears and begged me not to strike him, promising to improve his behavior. He seemed truly apologetic, so I allowed him to return to class. However, in the ensuing

306

days, he has resumed his previous conduct.
I strongly suggest you speak to your son or
we shall have to expel him.
Sincerely,
Mother Superior

Lea drew in a sharp breath. The nerve! Pol had always been the sort of boy a mother would be proud of, and his teachers had always spoken highly of him! She lay the letter down and began pacing.

"What's wrong?" asked Nap.

Lea thrust the letter to him.

His eyes narrowed, then rounded as he read. When he finished, he gave her an incredulous stare.

"What'll we do?" she asked, exasperated. "It takes three hours to travel to Ponteix, and I can't just drop everything to run and discipline him."

Nap's lips pressed into a thin line. "We'll have to write to him immediately warning him to behave or else."

"But what if it's the nuns?" she asked. "What if his teacher simply has no control over the class?"

"The nuns?"

"Yes. Or maybe even your parents. They're probably letting him run wild." Lea resumed her pacing.

Napoleon shook his head. "I doubt it. And even so, school only lasts another couple of months. Once we get him home, we can straighten him out. In the meantime, I think we should send him a letter."

"Let's!" With purpose, Lea stormed to the cabinet and took out paper and a pen, but as she thought out her words, a feeling of dread overcame her. Suppose he became so out of control, there was no turning back. Suppose the damage was irreparable? Her grip around the fountain pen tightened. She had to be firm, at least until she found out what was really going on.

> *Dear Pol,*
>
> *We just received a letter from Mother Superior informing us that you've been misbehaving at school. She says you've been disruptive, have been passing notes to girls, and refuse to do your homework! Pol, I can't begin to tell you how horrified I am! My son who was accelerated a grade and who has always been well-behaved?*

Lea's distress increased as she wrote. He was so far away. How could she possibly make him see the error in his ways? Sweat formed on her brow as she stopped and contemplated her next sentence, tapping the fountain pen on the table. Maybe she needed to scare him. She gave the pen a shake and continued writing.

> *If you don't mend your ways, I fear you will end up like the men who ride the railways unable to find work—a bum, a*

hobo. Is that what you want? Or perhaps you'll become a criminal and end up on the gallows.

A tear rolled down her cheek, her own words frightening her.

Pol, I insist you turn over a new leaf now before it's too late. You have two months left of school. Make them good ones.
Maman

She handed the letter to Nap to read. When he had finished, he added his own words.

Pol,
I can't tell you how disappointed and worried I am for you, my son. If you don't change, you could end up in Hell for eternity. Do you know how long eternity is? Well, let me tell you. You know how a diamond is the hardest thing in the universe? Now, imagine that every thousand years, an eagle rubs its wing on that diamond. Eventually it will wear out, right? Well, eternity is longer than that! So buckle down if you don't want to end up shoveling coal in Hell!
Papa

He placed the letter in an envelope, sealed it, and laid it on the table. "I'll take it tomorrow when I go to town."

For the rest of the day, Lea's emotions ran high. Her feelings fluctuated between anger and fear, sometimes blaming, other times feeling guilt at having abandoned her son. But then she'd reassure herself it couldn't possibly be as a result of her neglect because Lilian had remained true and they hadn't received any letters regarding her behavior…at least not yet.

Spring passed with the usual rituals of plowing and planting, Lea and Nap crossing their fingers that the drought had finally ended. Each day, she gazed out at the seedlings, saying a prayer for their survival.

At the end of May, they were distracted from their worries when news rocked the town.

"Did you hear?" Madame Bourlon leaned over and whispered in Lea's ear just as mass was about to begin.

"No, what?" Lea glanced back to see if Père Fortier and his acolytes were ready to begin the processional. They stood poised and ready.

"There were five identical baby girls born this past week in Ontario. Five! Can you imagine? And they all survived!" Her whispers were so loud, several people turned and stared.

"You mean quintuplets?" asked Lea, throwing another glance again at Père Fortier.

"Yes. It's never happened before anywhere in the world!"

The organ began playing a hymn while the congregation joined in song.

"Where did you hear this?" asked Lea.

"I saw it in the paper," said Madame Bourlon.

"That's amaz—"

The priest passed by, flashing them a disapproving glare.

"I'll show you a picture of them after mass," whispered Madame Bourlon.

"Okay."

When the priest had ended the service and completed the recessional, several women crowded around Madame Bourlon as she pulled out the newspaper clipping.

"Here they are," she said.

The women buzzed with excitement.

"They're so identical!" exclaimed Lea.

"Aren't they, though? And look, their names are—Annette, Emilie, Yvonne, Cécile, and Marie."

"The poor mother," groaned a woman who had twelve children. "I wonder how she'll fare with all those crying babies."

"I don't know," said Madame Bourlon, "but I heard she has five older children too."

"Perhaps the government will step in to help them," said another lady. "After all, this is the Depression, right?"

"I'd sure want help if I had that many kids," said Madame Bourlon.

The ladies broke into laughter.

Lea began saving clippings of the quintuplets for Lilian, certain her oldest daughter would be captivated by the story too. News such as this almost erased the report they'd read in January about how Hitler had banned Jews from becoming members of the German Labor Front making it impossible for them to find work in the private sector. What kind of man was he—such anger and hatred? Her muscles tensed at the thought of Germany declaring war and how it would affect her family in Belgium.

***

Lea was relieved when Nap loaded the family into the wagon for the three-hour trip to Ponteix at the end of the school year. She was certain Pol's misbehavior would diminish with his homecoming and that her worries were soon to be over.

She saw Pol and Lilian waiting on the porch as they drove up to the house. Lilian bounced up and down, her hands gripping the railing while Pol feigned boredom

How he's grown!

When they pulled up, Lilian ran to greet them. "Maman!" she cried, throwing herself in Lea's arms.

Lea held her daughter, Claire and Denis close behind.

"Wow! Look how big Denis has gotten!" exclaimed Lilian, letting go of Lea to pick up her brother. "He's got so much hair now too."

"That's right," said Nap. "He's not bald like he used to be."

"Papa!" Lilian wrapped her arms around his waist.

"My little girl. You're nine years old now. I can't believe it."

"And you weren't here for my birthday. But Memère made a cake and said we'd celebrate it today."

"A cake? Oh, boy! I can't wait. I'll do anything for a piece of *her* cake. Can I have yours too?"

"No!" Lilian giggled.

Lea approached Pol at the bottom of the stairs. When he said hello, his voice was scratchy and had dropped an octave. His face had lengthened and grown angular. She gave an inward smile at the mustache that now graced his upper lip.

Opening her arms, she expected him to fall into an embrace as he'd always done, but instead, he stood limp, his hands dangling by his sides as she engulfed him. "Too old for hugs now, are we?" she asked, letting go.

Pol scowled.

"What? You've outgrown your Maman?"

Pol gave an impatient sigh, reached out, and gave her a grudging squeeze.

After a meal and a visit with the cousins, Nap hauled out Pol and Lilian's belongings and loaded them onto the wagon. Pol remained quiet, ignoring the younger children, but most of all his parents.

"He'll be fine," whispered Nap. "We'll have our old boy back when we get home."

But it wasn't to be. Pol *had* changed, not only on the outside, but also on the inside.

"I hate it here!" he complained, throwing himself on the couch, a week later. "There's nothing to do, and it's so hot!"

Lea felt her jaw tighten and a headache beginning. "Why don't you go pull up weeds in the garden?"

"I hate pulling up weeds! It's boring!"

"Well, someone has to," said Lea, shaking her dusting cloth with a little more vigour than usual. "Otherwise, how will we eat this winter?"

"I don't care because I'll be in Ponteix!" he said, clenching his fists.

"That is if we let you go back."

Pol's eyes widened. "What do you mean if you let me go back?"

"Living in Ponteix has made you rude. Do you seriously think we'll let you continue in this way? Now go pick weeds."

Pol let out a rebellious huff. "Why does it always have to be me? Claire's old enough now. She's five. Besides, you already send me out to herd the animals every morning. That's more than enough."

Lea's jaws clenched tighter. "Pol, I can't do it all alone. I already cook, clean, make butter, wash and mend clothes, haul water, heat it, milk the cow, and do the stooking! I'm only one person, and I need help!"

"I don't care! I'm not your slave!" He stormed out of the house, slamming the door behind him.

Anger filled Lea, anger she couldn't rid herself of. She spent the rest of the day harbouring feelings of hostility that grew by the hour. How could she reach him? Better yet, how could she force him to behave? Didn't he understand the dire straits they were in?

Day after day, Pol continued in the same manner, pushing Lea's frustration deeper and deeper. Feeling exhausted and exasperated, she began making idle threats, repeating their previous warning that he'd surely end up in prison or on the gallows if he didn't mend his ways, or worse yet, that he'd end up in Hell. But as her impatience grew, she added another threat—that they'd kick him out if he didn't pull his own weight.

Then, one very brutish day, hot enough to melt butter, the situation came to a head when she asked him to push the handle of the washing machine for twenty minutes.

His face had turned a vibrant red, and he shouted, "Not again! I hate doing that! Get Lilian to do it!"

"She's not strong enough, Pol. It takes a young man to do this."

"But you're not a man and you do it," he said, his voice filled with sarcasm.

Lea tried a different tactic. "But I'm a grownup. I'm much stronger. Besides, I have to milk the cow. Please, Pol."

"No!" He crossed his arms.

Anger burned within her at her son's impudence. How dare he? Did he not know that every cell in her body screamed fatigue and had been for years? Deep rage rose to the surface threatening to boil over. "Pol, do it now, or else!"

"Or else what?" He taunted.

"Just do it!" she ordered through gritted teeth.

"No!"

Lea lost control, her anger seething. "Then it's high time you leave!"

Pol's eyes grew. "What?"

"I said, leave…now!" She pointed a forceful finger in the direction of the door.

Pol's lip trembled. "But…."

"Now!" She took two hard steps forward.

"But where can I go?" he asked, his teenaged bravado melting into uncertainty.

"You can join the men riding the rails for all I care."

"But I don't want to."

"Go!" She grabbed him by the shoulders and shoved him out the door.

A whimper escaped his throat as he was pushed. Falling to his hands and knees, he turned and looked back, his eyes imploring. "Please, Maman. Don't send me away. I'll do whatever you want. Please!"

316

"No! I've had enough of you!"

"Maman, non!" said Lilian.

"Pol!" Claire cried after her brother.

"Where's Papa?" Lilian asked Claire.

"In the fields. I saw him go there this morning."

Lea watched the distance between Pol and her grow.

"Maman!" wailed Denis.

Lea fought hard between her rage and her feelings of futility as the figure of her son grew smaller, the distance between them increasing. She couldn't lose control. She had to win. She had him exactly where she wanted. Then guilt descended on her. This was her son—her first surviving child. She'd already lost three babies. What was she doing sending him away? The image of the newborn boy she'd once held and cherished flashed in her mind.

The children's cries had grown more hysterical. Tears streamed down their faces.

"All right!" she snapped. "You can come back!"

Pol stopped in his tracks and turned. "What?" he shouted.

"I said come back."

Pol hesitated as though in disbelief, then ran all the way to the house, throwing himself in his mother's arms. "I'm sorry, Maman. Please forgive me."

"I forgive you. But you need to help around here, okay?"

"I will, I promise."

When Nap returned home, Lilian raced out the door to meet him. His brow was knit with concern as he listened to his daughter's words before coming in. Dinner was silent that night as they ate their cold ham and potato salad. Not a word was uttered other than to ask someone to pass this or that item. The evening was just as quiet.

Nap waited until they'd retired to their room and extinguished the lantern before asking, "Lea, what's wrong with you these days?"

She burst into tears. "I don't know. I'm just so unhappy. Cécile's gone, and now Pol is so rebellious all the time. He doesn't want to do anything to help around the house."

"But that's part of growing up," he said. "Remember how you were at that age?"

Lea nodded, wiping her tears. "I know. But I'm so tired, and I don't know why."

She heard a slight chuckle.

"I think I know why," Nap ventured.

"Why?"

"I've noticed you've put on a bit of weight lately. Could it be you're with child?"

Lea's breath caught. Pregnant? Again? She did a quick calculation on her fingers to determine how many weeks had passed since her last cycle. It was true. She was overdue for her monthly visit.

"And if I am?" she asked, gauging his reaction to her words. When he didn't answer right away, her muscles tensed. "You're not happy about it, are you?"

"I didn't say that."

"No, but you didn't answer."

"If God wants to give us another child, then so be it."

***

The summer continued, its smothering heat scorching the earth. Even the shade provided little relief for the family. Nap set up a two-lid potbellied stove to cook outside, thereby keeping the house cooler. But the intensity of the heat at night was still unbearable, their night clothes clinging to their sweaty bodies, making it difficult to sleep. Lea often lay for hours before drifting off into fretful dreams only to awaken early when Nap rose to tend the livestock.

The dust storms returned, clouds of dirt swirling and slamming against the windows, burying their crops and keeping them prisoners in their own home for days.

After one of these storms, Lea and the children busied themselves cleaning everything in the house. Even Denis swirled a cloth about on the coffee table.

"I'm helping," he said with a wide grin as his rag fluffed up the dust.

"Good boy, Denis," said Lilian.

Lea clucked her tongue with exasperation at how thick the grit that entered the house was and how it sifted through the tiny cracks in the window. She hated how it made them all cough for days afterward.

"Here, let me show you how," said Pol. "You have to press down hard."

"Like this?" asked Denis.

"Yeah."

Lea flashed Pol an appreciative smile though Denis' dusting was anything but adequate. At least Pol was trying.

The clip clopping of horse hooves caught her attention.

"Who could that be?" Lea asked.

A tall man dismounted his horse, leading it by the reins to the house. Lea dropped her cloth and rushed out the door.

It was Claude.

Lea gasped at how thin he'd grown. He looked haggard, dark circles beneath his eyes. It was as though he'd aged twenty years. "Claude!" she said. "We haven't seen you in church for so long. Where have you been?"

He looked away for a moment before his hollow eyes met hers. "I haven't been well."

"What's happened?" she asked.

His hands trembled as he spoke. "I can't stand it anymore." He shook his head disparagingly. "With Cécile gone…and my baby girl." He clenched his fists and bowed his head in agony. "There's nothing for me anymore. The farm…it was all for her…and now she's gone." He melted into shameless

320

tears, falling into her arms like a child, his head resting on her shoulders.

"Oh, Claude." Lea wrapped her arms around his heaving body.

"I treated her so bad." His voice shook. "She was so good to me, and I kept leaving her every night to drink and gamble in town."

Lea listened to his words as she held the man who'd caused so much hurt to her friend. She forgave him that very moment. "Yes, but you've changed, Claude. You got the homestead and you turned over a new leaf."

"But it was too late. It's my punishment. She was too good for me and now I've lost her." He broke into a fresh round of sobs.

"No, Claude. That's not true," she said, her voice tender.

"Yes, it is." His crying grew more hysterical. "It's all my fault! She could have married a better man and had a better pregnancy. It was because she had to work so hard…because of me."

"But it's not your fault the baby was breech. That could happen to anyone."

"No!" He released her and sank to the hot ground below, his crying worsening.

Fear gripped her. She knew the man was in grave danger of a breakdown. "Claude," she said, "there are other women out there. You can find a new girl…and start again."

"And what do I have to give? Barren fields that won't grow crops? I tell you, I just can't stand it anymore."

Lea knelt down beside him in the dirt. "We're all in the same boat, you know. We just all need to hold on a while longer. I know I have days where I feel I can't handle it anymore as well. You're not the only one. The whole world is in the same plight."

The door of the house swung open.

"Maman," called Claire, poking her face out, her eyes wide with terror. "What's wrong?"

"Nothing," she said, desperate to preserve her child's innocence. "Mr. Claude hurt himself. That's all. It's just like you when you scraped your finger." She turned to Claude, pasting a fake smile on her face. "Right?"

Claude nodded, pulled out a hankie, and blew his nose. "Yes."

"Go back inside and wait for me, okay? Finish the dusting and then afterward we can make some cookies."

"Okay." Claire reluctantly shut the door.

Claude rose. "I'm sorry," he said, tucking his handkerchief back in his pocket. "You need to get to your family. You're so lucky to have one, you know."

"You're right," said Lea, relieved he seemed to have regained control of himself. "Come by again, okay? You're always welcome here."

He nodded, wiped his eyes once more, mounted his horse, and rode away.

Lea watched him leave, shaken, yet somehow stronger for the exchange. He was correct. She *was* lucky. Luckier than many folks

322

in these parts—she wasn't alone at all. She had her four children, an adoring husband, a farm, and a family back in Belgium. Compared to many people, that was a lot.

Chapter Twenty-Eight
Quintuplets and Twins

In September, the family traveled back to Ponteix to deliver Pol and Lilian to their school. Pol's behavior had improved, and he had promised to try harder if allowed to return to the convent. They'd acquiesced. Besides, it was the perfect opportunity for Lea to have Dr. Lupien examine her at the hospital.

When the doctor saw her in the waiting room, his face brightened. "Ah, Leopoldine! How are you doing?" He swept his hand to one side, an invitation to enter. "I see you are expecting again."

"Yes." She let out a deep sigh.

"And how far along are you? Six months?"

Lea blushed. "No. It's only been four."

The line between his brows creased. "Perhaps you're further along than you think. Let's have a look. I'll give you a few minutes to undress." He left the room.

Lea removed her clothes and folded them into a neat pile. She put on the blue gown and tied the knot.

A few minutes later, Dr. Lupien gave a quick knock on the door, then entered. "Okay, let's check your weight first."

Lea stepped on the scale while he adjusted it.

"Oh, my, you have put on quite a bit of weight for only four months."

Lea gave an embarrassed smile. "I've been really hungry."

Leading her to the examining table, he held an arm out to assist her as she stepped up the stair. When she was sitting comfortably, he pulled out his sphygmomanometer, wrapped the cuff around her arm, and pumped in air, his eyes focused on the two dials. "Ninety over sixty!" he said, releasing the valve. "Not bad. Good, low pulse rate too." Lowering her down onto her back, he measured her belly, then placed the tips of his stethoscope into his ears. "Let's see if we can hear a heartbeat." He shifted the diaphragm to various parts of her abdomen, listening, then shook his head. "No heartbeat yet which tells me you're still in the early stages."

"So do you think I'm carrying twins?"

"Well, you've had them before, so it's possible."

Hope and dread stirred within her. "Maybe it's God's way of giving me a second chance. Perhaps these ones will survive—especially now that we have such good medical care."

His smile was modest. "Oh, you're too kind. Have you thought of any names yet?"

"I don't know," she replied. "Twin names can be kind of tricky. You can end up with something really bad if you're not careful." She paused and thought. "Like Kenny and Jenny, or Mary and Harry, or London and Paris."

They shared a laugh.

"I met a family once that named their boys Saskatchewan and Manitoba," said Dr. Lupien.

"Oh, dear."

"I guess we'll know the day they're born, hmm?" He tilted his head, his expression grown serious. "And how are you doing otherwise?"

Lea sighed. "About as well as can be expected. You know how things are—everyone's dirt poor."

He gave an understanding nod.

"Some people have lost nearly everything—like a friend of ours." She recounted Claude's story, the timbre of her voice growing husky as the telling unfolded.

Dr. Lupien's expression saddened at her words. "I hear many tales like that. Terrible. But keep an eye on him, okay?"

"What do mean?" Lea asked.

"Check on him regularly to make sure he's all right."

"Why?"

"He'll need a great deal of support to get through this. In time, you might want to introduce him to some nice girls."

Lea felt uneasy at his words. "There aren't any, though. Not with this drought. Except for those of us who are stuck here. And most of us are married with kids."

"You never know, though. Keep your eyes open. It's important he doesn't stay cooped up by himself. He needs to be around people."

Dr. Lupien reached over and felt her ankles. "No swelling. That's good." He stretched out a hand and helped her up. "I guess we're all done. Everything looks just fine. You may dress now."

"Thank you, Dr. Lupien." Her eyes momentarily dropped to the ground. "Regarding payment," she said. "I brought some ham. Would that suffice?"

"That's more than enough." He waved her concerns away. "As you said, these are hard times. So long as I can feed my family, I'm fine."

"You're so generous," she said.

"No, not really. It's all part of being a doctor."

"Somehow, I doubt that."

As September came to a close, Lea kept up with the news of the Dionne quintuplets to distract her mind from the drought and the usual failure of the crops. Following their story religiously gave her a temporary sense of relief and assuaged her guilt at farming out her two oldest children to their grandparents since the Dionnes seemed worse off.

"Can you imagine?" she said with indignation as she read the paper. "The Dionnes were going to loan their babies to the Chicago World's Fair and put them on exhibit like animals in a zoo."

"That's troubling, all right," agreed Nap, his eyes peering over the sports section.

"But now they've built what they call a hospital under the care of a Dr. Dafoe. And they're going to let tourists in to observe them from behind a screen."

He lowered the newspaper and frowned. "Why aren't the parents looking after them?"

"They've been deemed unfit!"

"Unfit? Poor children," said Nap, "to be treated like a sideshow."

Lea reached for the scissors and cut out the article. When she was done, she pasted it on an empty page in the scrapbook she'd been keeping for Lilian.

Autumn passed quickly, the canning of what food they were able to save, the making of buffalo berry wine, the butchering of the pig, as well as the knitting projects that kept Lea busy. Claire, now five, had become quite the little mother, looking after her younger brother, Denis, and keeping him well-occupied. The little girl had also taken to collecting the eggs from the chicken coop in the morning, only dropping the basket once.

When the holidays neared, Lea was only too pleased to return to Ponteix where her children surely awaited her anxiously.

The trip was tiring, her belly large and uncomfortable, but at least the cutter moved gracefully through the snow, the normal potholes in the road smoothed out by winter storms. With two months left in her pregnancy, her clothes strained at her growing girth. She longed to be rid of the extra weight, yet she knew she'd be more exhausted than ever once the baby was born.

Christmas changed that year in Ponteix despite the attendance of the various relatives, the music, and the usual spread of food. Nap's brother, who lived next door, had strung electrical wires between the two houses, connecting his radio to a loudspeaker in Levi and Emma's house. Though they celebrated the holidays with the same fervour as before, their festivities were sobered by the news that the Italian government had invaded Abyssinia under the Fascist ruler, Mussolini. Lea worried about Palma's husband since he now traveled from Italy to Belgium with his work.

**

After the holidays, her due date approaching, Lea returned once more to Ponteix, her bags packed. She took great comfort knowing Dr. Lupien would be close by when the time came for her to deliver the baby. How lucky she was to have in-laws who'd allow her to stay with them. But when what felt like a never ending journey of discomfort came to a halt, they arrived to find a notice pinned to Levi and Emma's door.

"Quarantine!" Lea exclaimed.

Close behind her on the stairs, Nap frowned as he read the sign. Exchanging an uncertain look, they hesitated, then Lea knocked lightly.

Emma answered. "Oh, so good to see you." She pulled Lea inside by the hand while Nap followed. "I was wondering when you'd arrive."

"What's happened?" Lea asked. "Why is there a quarantine?"

"Pol and Lilian both came down with the mumps a few days ago," said Emma, standing back a short distance. "It's been going around the town."

Lea gasped, her eyes enlarging. "Are they okay?"

"Oh, yes. They've got cheeks like a chipmunk, but they're fine. Dr. Lupien checks on them regularly."

"Perhaps we shouldn't stay then." Lea looked back at Denis and Claire who still waited in the cutter.

"Oh, don't worry about the younger kids," said Emma. "Pol and Lilian are locked up in their room all day. We bring them food, then dip our hands in the disinfectant that the doctor left beside their door. The little ones probably won't catch it. And even if they did, Dr. Lupien says it's better to catch the disease as a child rather than as an adult."

"But what about all of you? Are you allowed to come and go as you please?"

"No. Only Levi has permission to go to town. We're all stuck here until the quarantine is lifted. What about you two? Have you had the mumps already?"

Lea exchanged a glance with Nap. He nodded. "Yes, we both have," she said.

"Then you should be okay. The kids will be out in a few days."

Lea had no choice but to stay. She couldn't risk giving birth to her children with a midwife as they had with Claire.

The sign remained on the door as Lilian and Pol's symptoms changed to a hacking cough that left them gasping for breath. Terrified, Nap called for Dr. Lupien again.

"It's the whooping cough." The doctor gave his diagnosis while rubbing his hands with disinfectant as he came down the stairs. "There's a lot of it going around. I'll go home and make up a syrup for them. It tastes awful, but it should do the trick."

Lea's heart quickened each time she heard the children's wheezing coughs and desperate attempts to catch their breath, particularly since *ma tante* Lumina's little girl, Agnes, had already been claimed by the virus.

Lea went into labour on February twenty-first. As predicted, she did indeed have twins.

"A boy and a girl!" exclaimed Nap. "Talk about luck!"

"I guess I got my second chance," said Lea, smiling. "We lost Emma and Palma, but this time we'll keep them alive, right?" She nodded toward Dr. Lupien.

He nodded back.

"But what shall we name them?" asked Nap.

"Why don't we ask Pol and Lilian?" Lea's thoughts roved to the closed door upstairs in the house. "It'll give them something to do."

The kids set to work on choosing names. When they presented their list to Nap, he read them aloud to the others. "Napoleon and Josephine?"

Lea shook her head.

"Marc Antony and Cleopatra?"

Another vigorous shake of the head.

"Romeo and Juliet?" Napoleon let out a guffaw. "George and Georgette?"

Lea's face lit up. "That's nice. What do you think? Especially since King George recently died."

"Agreed."

***

It was in early July that Lea made a trip to the General Store in Val Marie with her usual list in hand, a twin on each hip, Claire and Denis close beside her. When she handed the order to Mr. Eikenberry, he set about gathering the items while the children gazed at the candy with eager eyes.

"Hot weather, eh?" Mr. Eikenberry said.

"Yes."

"I'm hoping the grasshoppers will leave us alone this year," he said as he took down some baking soda.

"Me too," said Lea.

"Maman," said Claire. "Can you buy some licorice, please?"

"Licorice?" she said, absently.

"Yico-wish," repeated Denis.

Lea grabbed two sticks to add to the order.

"Yeah, and hopefully we won't be hit by dust storms either." The grocer grabbed more items off the shelf.

"Mm-hmm."

Mr. Eikenberry bagged the order. When he'd placed the last of the purchases inside, he handed the candy to the children. His forehead creased. "So, have you been having problems with rats lately?"

"Rats?" Lea tilted her head in amusement. "I haven't seen any rats for a long time. Gophers, maybe."

"Hunh!" said Mr. Eikenberry. "It's a curious thing. Claude was here the other day. Picked up some strychnine claiming he was having a problem with rats. It was the only thing he bought. Didn't even buy his normal groceries."

Lea's eyes shot open. "Strychnine? Are you sure?"

"Yeah."

"How long ago was this?"

"A couple of days ago. Why?"

Lea's blood ran cold, remembering Dr. Lupien's words of warning. She threw her money down without waiting for the change and dashed out the door. "Gotta go!"

"Well, here, at least let me help you with your order," said Mr. Eikenberry, hurrying after her, his arms weighed down with bags. "And what about your change?"

"Give it to me next time," she shouted back.

He barely had time to throw the groceries in the back before Lea had loaded the kids and whipped the horse into a gallop. "Hold on tight," she ordered.

"Why are we going so fast?" asked Claire.

"Because we're late," replied Lea, her voice trembling.

"Late for what?"

"Papa wants you home for lunch," she lied.

"But we just had breakfast."

"Never mind."

They raced over the dusty road, the wheels bouncing over potholes and rocks, threatening to topple them.

"Maman, you're going too fast!" shrieked Claire. "You might break a wheel."

"Just hold on tight," she said, her heart beating wildly.

Why couldn't I have invited him for dinner? She chastised herself. *He was probably so lonely. But no, I was too busy with the twins and couldn't be bothered. And I didn't want the kids to see him crying again. I had to protect them.* She clucked her tongue with regret. *We could have asked him to come by after church. Anything would have helped. Please, God. Make him be safe.*

When Lea saw the two hills that marked the entrance to their farm, she took a sharp turn, nearly driving the wagon off the dirt road. As they climbed the hill, she slowed until they arrived at the cabin, then jumped down, taking the babies and groceries inside the house, Claire and Denis close behind.

"Lilian." Her voice was shrill. "Watch the kids. I have to go somewhere."

"Where?" Lilian leapt up.

"Never mind. Just watch them."

"But Maman!"

Lea ran to the wagon, turned the horses around, and gave the reins a wild shake. The horses galloped the entire length to Claude's farm, clouds of dust billowing behind them.

All was still when she arrived at the house. A lone cow mooed from the barn and chickens pecked the ground in search of food.

Filled with dread, Lea tied the horses, climbed the stairs, and knocked on the door, awaiting the telling sound of footsteps. When none came, she called, "Claude?" There was no answer. "Claude! Open up!" She knocked harder.

Heart pounding, she hurried to the barn, hoping with all her might that he'd come sauntering around the corner complaining about rats.

"Claude?" she called. The cow lowed again. Finding her way to its stall, goose bumps formed on her arms. *No one's milked her.*

Making a quick exit of the barn, she scoured the farm. *Where is he?* The chickens trailed after her. Could it be Claude was in the henhouse, injured? She hurried to the door of the small structure and called again. "Claude?" When there was no answer, she pulled it open. The dust inside made her sneeze, but all was quiet.

Maybe he's in the house.

Lea returned to the front porch, her mouth dry and her hands trembling. She turned the doorknob. It wasn't locked. As she pushed the door open, a horrible stench assaulted her nose. She hesitated, her blood rushing to her ears, so loud she could hear her own pulse. An intense need to flee gripped her.

No. I need to be brave. Her legs trembled as she took tentative steps into the living room. Beer bottles littered the coffee table, and the cushions of the couch were strewn about. A vase lay smashed on the floor next to one of the pillows. Lea wandered into the kitchen. A pot of cold oatmeal sat on the stove, and beside it, an open box of strychnine. Lea's breath came in short gulps at the implication. *Where is he?* Gathering up her courage, she moved to the bedroom. The bed lay empty, the quilt shifted over as though something had slid down off of it. Lea reluctantly walked to the other side of the bed, then let out a shrill scream. Claude lay dead on the floor, his head and legs arched back in an impossible position, his teeth gritted together in anguish, his eyes staring into nothingness.

Lea's breath came in gasps. "Oh, Claude, why did you have to do this? Oh, Claude." She shook her head from side to side, feeling faint. She backed away, slammed the door, leapt onto the wagon, and lashed the horses into a gallop again, this time steering them straight to the RCMP detachment.

When she arrived at the police station, she told her story through anguished sobs while the constable wrote down her words.

Two days later, the town congregated for Claude's funeral. Lea sat with the Gilberts, holding their limp hands, trying to be strong for them. But her actions were all a lie. Her strength had ebbed away from within her soul to nothingness.

She turned and stared at the congregation, the white church, the surrounding prairie, the never ending skies…and felt betrayed. There was no magic here—the dead prairie that failed them year after year, that starved their livestock, that stole her babies. There was nothing. Absolutely nothing! Lea bowed her head, despair threatening to swallow her.

As the months passed, an idea began to haunt her. At first, it was just an unwelcome thought, but it grew. She found herself throwing glances at her children and wondering how would they fare without her. Could Lilian look after the twins? Or perhaps the relatives could take them as they had Pol and Lilian. Could Nap handle his young family on his own? Surely the convent was obligated to house orphans.

She drifted through the motions of everyday life as though nothing were real, giving dull smiles when her children sought her approval, laughing hollow laughs at Nap's humour, feeding and changing the twins, doing the usual fruitless chores that would never amount to anything—ever. Then one agonizing day, when the coldness of winter trapped them inside, the truth came to her—it was all futile. There *was* no hope. Wasn't that why Claude had taken his own life? She became more listless each day.

"Papa," said Lilian, drawing close to her father's ear one day, "there's something wrong with Maman."

"It's okay," said Nap, watching Lea with wary eyes. "But watch out for her, okay?"

"Okay," said Lilian, exchanging worried glances with Pol.

One evening, in early summer, darkness triumphed over Lea's mind like a black knight whose merciless sword had cut through her being. Rising from her chair, she shuffled to the door, and began walking. She walked to the pasture, lifted the latch, and opened the gate. Stepping through, she continued to the end of the enclosure. Then she climbed the fence and trudged on, farther and farther from the home she'd tried so hard to create, to the outlying fields, the fields she and Nap had toiled over, cleared of rocks, plowed, planted, only to watch their crops die each year. She walked to the edge of their homestead until she arrived at the

Devlin's coulee where they'd hauled water every summer in their feeble attempts at saving the wheat. By some miracle, the water was still deep.

Lea sat for a time on the rocky shore, mesmerized by the ripples on the water, amazed that something as simple as this liquid was the cause of all their difficulties. For want of water, their crops failed. For want of water, dust storms buried their land. For want of water, they risked starvation. For want of water, her dreams had been stolen.

Lowering herself to her knees, she braced her hands against the ground. "I'm sorry, Nap." Then she shoved her head into the murky liquid.

Mud and brown water clouded her vision. The water slapped above her, muted. *All I have to do is take one breath—one breath, and then it'll all be over.* She closed her eyes…and breathed in.

Chapter Twenty-Nine
The Lady

Lea drifted in a sea of quiet, free of thought, unburdened of sorrow—just floating. A dazzling light in the distance lured her. She glided toward its promise of peace and tranquility. As she moved, it grew more brilliant. Her eyes instinctively narrowed as awareness slowly reclaimed her. Suddenly, she felt hard ground beneath her—not the dirt she was accustomed to, but something else—tiles. White tiles. Her eyes moved a little farther to where pearl-coloured fabric stretched across the floor. Curious, she reached out and fingered it—satin? It'd been years since she'd felt the silky touch of such a fabric. Not since before the war in Belgium. Her eyes traced the folds of the cloth. They rose like tall pillars of shimmering light that led to a glowing visage—a lady's face, beautiful though etched with lines from a life hard-lived, furrowed deep within her ivory skin.

"Maman!" Lea whispered. She glanced about her, realizing she was anywhere but on the farm. "But how?" Then she remembered. She'd taken her last, fatal breath.

Maman's eyes brimmed with tears. She regarded Lea, her brows tipped, questioning. *Why?*

A wave of guilt swept over Lea until she recalled her reason. "I just can't do it anymore." Her voice was a mere wisp.

Her mother's head tilted to one side. *What's happened?*

A tear slid down Lea's cheek. "It's a place of death, Maman. So much death. And I can never escape. Ever. Except…"

Maman shook her head, then took her by the hand.

Lea was whisked to a brick road that ran past the house of her youth. She was ten, racing, laughter bubbling from within her as she threw a glance over her shoulder at her sisters— Mathilde and Palma! "I'll get home first" she called, letting out a breathless giggle. "And the last strawberry tart will be mine."

"No, you won't," Palma shouted. "I will. You'll have to eat the stale bread." Palma reached swift fingers and grabbed Lea's dress, slowing her down as they giggled helplessly.

Just as quickly, her memories shifted to the dining room of their simple home. Papa sat in his usual spot at the head of the table. The grandfather clock gave a steady, reassuring tick. She looked around at her siblings—François, Camille, Mathilde, and Palma—innocent of the perils of war, free of worries, recounting humorous stories of their day at school. How simple life was then, before the Great War, the Great Drought, before the Great Depression. *Great! Ha! Why do they call them great? They aren't great! They're abysmal. A test of endurance.* An endurance Lea had no more of.

Gently pulled back, her eyes met her mother's again. "I remember," said Lea. "We had good times, but that was so long ago."

Maman offered her hand. When Lea took it, she raised her to standing position, still towering, still radiant.

A gentle wind swept them away. Lea closed her eyes and allowed it to carry her. When she opened them again, they soared over the homestead. How vast it was. Acres and acres of cleared land. They'd done so much work, she and Nap. Removing the sod, clearing rocks, year after year. In the distance, she saw the house, a mere speck compared to the land—small, crowded, wet laundry hanging everywhere. And then she saw him—her one true love, the soldier she'd given her heart to, the father of her children. Forlorn, yet not bitter. Always hopeful. Always optimistic. A spark within ignited, thawing her heart. Could she really leave him to all this alone? How torn he'd be when he discovered her body floating in the coulee.

A pretty, dark-haired child ran toward him. He bent on one knee, placing something in her hands, his grin wide.

"Papa," the little girl cried, her eyes lighting up. "A baby bird!"

"Oui," he said. "I found the nest this morning in a stook. You'll have to take care of it and feed it."

"Oh, Papa! I will, I will!" The child ran to her older sister. A boy of the same age joined them. There was something familiar about them. Lea understood. It was George and Georgette, older now. But who was the little one? Georgette reached down and took the nest from the child. Together, they brought the bird into the house, their faces filled with purpose as Nap watched from afar. Realization gripped Lea. *The child! She hasn't been born yet.*

Panic filled her. Had her actions stolen Nap's little girl from him?

Her mind cleared of the vision, and again, she found herself standing before the lady, the firm tiles beneath her feet.

Maman's lips were pressed together, her eyebrows raised. When she spoke, her words were gentle. "Choose life."

Choose life? Lea repeated the words. *Choose life.* Looking past her mother, Lea saw fields and fields of golden wheat and white clouds that spread long arms over scintillating blue. *Angels of hope.* Peace filled her, and she knew then that their problems would soon be over.

"But will I be happy?" she asked.

Maman nodded. *I promise.*

Arms seized Lea by the waist, jolting her.

"No!" Pol's voice screamed from afar.

The dream vanished. Her body was shoved forward, head down. A spasm of coughing overtook her. Throwing up water, she gasped, then fought to breathe only to cough again and again.

"What were you doing?" Tears rolled down Pol's cheeks.

Lea hacked up more water while he beat her back.

"Were you trying to kill yourself? Like Mr. Claude?"

Lea avoided his gaze, knowing full well he'd see the guilt that swam in her eyes.

When the fit of coughing passed, she sat up, and took her half-grown boy into her arms as he sobbed. "It's okay, Pol. I'm here. And I'm not going anywhere. Mr. Claude was wrong to take his own life." She brushed her fingers through his hair, his tears falling on her shoulders. "Everything's going to be all right."

They sat for a long time at the edge of the water, Lea's wet hair dripping down her dress, Pol's shirt dampened. When his tears finally dispelled, she rose and took him by the hand and lead him across the brown fields.

"You know what?" she told her son.

"No, what?" he asked, his voice still trembling.

"I'm going to have another baby."

"When?" asked Pol, his brow creased.

"I'm not sure. And you know what else?"

"No, what?"

"It's going to be a little girl."

"How do you know?" Pol threw her an inquiring glance.

She flashed him a smile. "Sometimes a woman just does."

"Oui, Maman."

"And Pol." She stopped and grabbed him by the shoulders. "Promise me you'll never tell your father what you just saw."

Pol hesitated before answering. "Okay, I promise."

Lea gave his hand a squeeze, her eyes roving over the earth she knew would produce a bumper crop in just over a year. She gazed up at the blue sky, at small fluffy clouds drifting across the cerulean splendour. Prairie skies. They *were* beautiful even if they didn't always produce rain. Lea let out a sigh, then whispered, *Merci, Maman.*

***

A month later, Nap returned from town, a wide smile pasted on his face.

Lea met him at the door. "What happened?"

Napoleon grabbed her and hoisted her up in the air. "I've got work!"

Lea's mouth dropped and her eyes widened. "What kind of work?"

"They're building a dam ten miles north of town, and they need carpenters to make the forms. That means we'll have an income again."

"Oh, Nap, that's so wonderful!" Lea cried, throwing her arms around him.

Lilian and Pol came out to greet their dad, each with a twin in their arms. They smiled when they heard the news.

"Maybe we'll get a new house now," said Pol, "in town."

Lea let go of Nap. "Don't be so impatient, Pol. Just a little at a time."

"Well, you never know." Napoleon winked. "Oh, and by the way, this came for you today." He handed her a letter posted from Belgium. Lea took the letter and opened it.

My dearest Leopoldine,

It is with great sadness that I must inform you of Maman's passing. She died in the wee hours of the morning on June thirtieth. She'd caught a cold that quickly changed to pneumonia. We tried poultices and steam, but nothing worked, not even the medicine the doctor brought for her. It was terrible watching the life ebb from her. François, Camille, Mathilde, Papa, and I were by her side those last few days, holding her hand as she slipped away. She kept asking for you, saying she wanted to see you one last time. We tried in vain to tell her it was impossible as you lived far across the Atlantic Ocean on a homestead in Saskatchewan, but she was too delirious to understand.

Then, on the thirtieth, her eyes grew distant as though she saw something far,

far away. Perhaps the afterlife? She stayed that way for a time, and then she whispered the most peculiar thing. "Choose life," before taking her final breath. I don't know what she meant by that.

We buried her two days later in the Chatlineau churchyard in her satin wedding dress as she requested. When her tombstone is erected, I'll send you a photo.

Maman's death was probably a blessing in disguise as I believe she was growing feeble of mind. A few years ago, she told me the strangest tale. She said that while sewing, one evening, she heard your voice. Thinking you had arrived home and wanted to surprise her, she immediately ran to the window and looked down to the streets below. Of course, you weren't there, so she returned to her stitching only to hear your voice again a moment later. She said she turned about the room, but saw nothing. I guess she never got over your leaving.

As far as our family goes, things have gotten serious here in Belgium with the threat of Hitler. I'm certain our fair nation will soon be at war again. I know I've been saying it for years, but emigrating to Canada looks like a real possibility, especially since Dino was recently attacked by a thief who attempted to slit his throat. He insists he has no idea who the man was, but I suspect it has something to do with this business of driving back and forth from

Italy to Belgium. He's always been so secretive about that. Who knows what will happen. I dream of the day you and I will see one another face to face again.
Meilleurs voeux,
Palma

Lea folded the letter, her gaze meeting Nap's. "It's from Palma. She says Maman passed away."

Nap's face fell.

"It's okay," Lea said. "It was her time."

Chapter Thirty
Yolande

Yolande was born on a cold, frosty day in November in the town of Bracken. Dr. Lupien had warned Lea ahead of time that he'd be absent and that she shouldn't try to give birth with a midwife because of her age. Anything could happen at thirty-six, and Bracken was the nearest town with a hospital.

Lea gazed at the baby girl she held in her arms. Soft, silky, dark hair and fine features—a definite resemblance to the vision Maman had shared with her. The birth had been difficult, but she had been rewarded with a wonderful child who after only a few months was already sleeping through most of the night.

The twins, however, were another story altogether, climbing everywhere they weren't supposed to, grabbing things from the others with a haughty "mine", having temper tantrums when they didn't get their own way, throwing food on the floor. Lea sighed. Two babies, triple the trouble. It would have been so much easier had she only had one, but she wouldn't have it any other way. She was going to make the most of it. Besides, she had the older kids to help out now.

The crop had failed again, and the grasshoppers had been worse than ever, but Nap's income of thirty-five cents an hour enabled them to buy what food they needed at the general store though they still had to accept relief from the government to feed the livestock.

Then one day, great news came to the family when Nap announced the government was compensating a whole three hundred and fifty dollars to farmers who built an irrigation dam on their land.

"Perhaps you could enlarge our coulee to meet the government standards," said Lea.

"That's what I intend to do," he said. "And it'll double as a bit of a swimming hole in the summertime for us too—a break from the heat."

"Oh, boy, a giant pool," said Claire, her voice enthusiastic. "And we could all learn to swim. Even the babies."

"No." Lea gave her head a vigorous shake. "You don't want them to drown."

"No." Several voices echoed her words.

"Life is far too precious," said Lea.

When Nap began building the dam, Pol, now fifteen, stayed to help him more often than attending school. Unfortunately, they'd lost two more horses when one of them broke into the wheat storage and eaten his fill. Pol had taken the kids to school in Val Marie, but on the way back, the horse collapsed and died, its belly bloated. Belle, the other horse, passed away shortly afterward, leaving Nap no option but to recapture the slightly wild King and Queen.

After several attempts, he was able to break them, but not until they spooked and stampeded, one horse jumping the fence while the other dug in its heels, splitting the wagon in two. Nap repaired the cart as best he could with what scraps of wood he could find and continued to train the horses. When they were finally broken, the work on their dam began in earnest. Nap hired a neighbour, a Mr. Laturnes to help excavate it, adding *his* two horses to make a team of four. Together they ploughed the existing coulee, digging it deeper and wider than ever before. When it was the desired length and width, Pol helped his father to rip-rap the water side. Taking the walls of rocks Nap and Lea had cleared away over the years, they lined the bottom to prevent seepage. The work seemed to suit Pol well. It was good use of his time since he wasn't very school-minded anymore.

But the greatest surprise of all happened the following summer on an afternoon when Lea thought she'd drop in on some new people in town. She'd heard a woman from France had moved to Val Marie along with the other families who'd come to work the irrigation project. And since it had been a particularly frustrating morning with cranky babies and plenty of crying, she packed up all seven kids in the wagon and drove them to town.

It was a hot day, the kind that tormented them each summer. The sun was merciless, forcing trickles of sweat down their foreheads, but the threat of the heat didn't worry Lea this year. The wheat had been planted and was growing well. The spring had been wet, and the rains had continued. She knew they'd finally get that bumper crop they'd dreamed of for nine years.

When she arrived at the small house on the edge of town, several children played in the yard, their clothes mismatched and patched, their feet bare. She counted them—ten in total. The cabin they lived in was tiny and dilapidated, in need of a coat of paint and a new roof. Lea clucked her tongue in sympathy. Then she spied a pile of lumber that lay hidden within its shade. Was this going to be used for repairs?

Pol jumped down off the wagon first, followed by Lilian and Claire. Lea handed them each a twin. After helping Denis, she lowered herself, gathered Yolande in her arms, and walked up the path to the house.

A plump, blond woman with her own baby hanging on her hip answered the door. Lea frowned. There was something familiar about her. "Hello," Lea said. "I heard you were new in town and thought I'd drop by to introduce my family and bring some cookies."

Several children stopped and stared, the word "cookies" repeated over and over while they licked their lips in anticipation.

The woman gave her a very curious look. "Lea? Is that you?"

"Yes…." Lea drew out the word as though it were a question.

The woman's face lit up. "Why, you haven't changed a bit. You're just as skinny as you ever were." When Lea gave her a blank stare, she asked, "Don't you recognize me? I know I've put on a few pounds, but…"

"No…I don't." Lea searched the woman's features for a clue, feeling helpless.

"It's me, Marie-Ève. Don't you remember? We traveled across the Atlantic together, and then to Quebec City by train."

Lea's chin dropped. Nearly losing her grip on Yolande, she threw her arms around her long lost friend. "Marie-Ève? I can't believe it! What are you doing here in Saskatchewan?"

The blond woman let out a boisterous laugh. "It's a long story," she said. "Come inside and I'll tell you all about it."

"Oh, no. Why don't we just sit outside where there's a nice breeze? It's too hot to go inside today."

"Good idea." Marie-Ève said, turning back.

The two ladies sat on the steps, their babies still clinging, the cookies laid out on a plate between them only to disappear into appreciative mouths within a few minutes.

"So what have you been doing all these years?" Lea grabbed the last sweet before it vanished.

Marie-Ève took a bite of *her* cookie, then began her story. "Well, if you recall, we started out in Quebec City."

"Yes, I remember. And you hoped to spend your wedding night at Château Frontenac. Did you?" Lea asked.

The woman laughed. "No. But we did stay at a nice little inn. It was quite romantic."

"Oh, good." Lea took another nibble of her cookie.

"Anyway, things went well and Guy had plenty of work as a carpenter. I felt like I was back home in France...except for my family. But that soon changed because of Guy's huge clan."

Lee smiled since she knew what was coming.

"Such warm people," Marie-Ève said. "Such a *joie de vivre*. I just loved them, and I soon felt safe again despite all that happened during the war."

"I know what you mean. My experience was similar. When I met Nap's family in Wide View, I felt like I'd found a new family too."

"That's good." Marie-Ève's face changed. "But then we fell on hard times like everyone else. By that time, we had six kids and no way to support them other than the garden in our back yard."

Lea nodded, understanding all too well.

"So Guy traveled the rails back and forth across Canada looking for work. Sometimes he'd get a job for a few months, send money home, and then he'd move on, going from one province to the next. Oh, how I'd worry about him every time he left. I'd heard stories about fights in the camps and how men were beat up and left to die. And just as I began to despair, he'd show up at the door. Of course, you can guess what happened every time he'd come home."

Lea's eyebrows raised, questioning. "What?"

"Another baby."

The two women covered their mouths as they erupted into knowing giggles.

"But it must have been tough bringing up so many children on your own," said Lea.

"Well, yes and no. There were plenty of cousins who gave us clothes. Sometimes they weren't always in the best shape, but it's amazing what one can do with a thread and needle and a patch here and there. And Guy's sister lived close by, so we had lots of help from her. And, of course, as the other kids grew older, they helped too."

"So how did you end up here?" asked Lea.

"On one of Guy's trips, he stopped in Swift Current where he joined some men in a hobo camp. And as they ate their beans around the fire, he heard one of them say the government was building an irrigation project near Val Marie. The men were pretty excited and several of them planned to set out the next morning. Guy knew he had to get a jump on them, so he rose in the middle of the night and walked all the way here."

Lea's eyes widened. "He walked?"

"Of course. There was no train to Val Marie. What else could he do?" She shrugged. "And when he finally arrived, there was already a long lineup for the jobs. Anyway, to make a long story short, he was the last one hired. And since it was an ongoing job, he sent for all of us."

"But that must have been expensive, bringing you all here—eleven children!" Lea said.

"Twelve…." Marie-Ève winked. "There's another one on the way."

Lea gasped. "Oh, my!"

"I kept saving a little bit in a jar each month. It wasn't much, but after a while it added up. No one knew about it except Guy and me. So what about you, Lea? We always wondered what happened to you. Remember how we tried to exchange addresses just as the train was leaving? And neither Guy nor I could find a piece of paper to write on?"

Lea nodded and let out a sigh. "It was hard, to say the least." She recounted the story of how they'd worked for the Gilberts before acquiring their own homestead, about the hardships of clearing the land, and of the hopelessness of the drought. Her voice lowered to a whisper when she relayed what happened to Emma, Palma and Roger, wiping helpless tears as she spoke.

Marie-Ève dabbed her eyes too as she listened. Taking Lea's hand in hers, she squeezed it. "You poor thing. But everything turned out for the best, *hein*? You had six children and now this beautiful little girl."

Lea gazed down at her baby and ran her fingers through her hair, admiring her cherubic face. "Yes, my little Yolande. I had her in November." She tipped her head toward Pol. "That's my oldest one over there," she said. "His name's Pol. He's fifteen. He's helping Napoleon finish the dam."

"You're building a dam?" asked Marie-Ève. "But I thought Nap was working on the irrigation project with Guy?"

"Yes, he is," Lea explained. "He's building the dam after work and on weekends."

"On weekends!" said Marie-Ève. "But doesn't he ever get time off?"

"Not much. But he doesn't care. Not when the government's offering three hundred and fifty dollars for it. He'll do anything to get a hold of that kind of money."

"Wow! Three hundred and fifty dollars! That's a fortune!"

"It sure is, and it's awfully welcome after years and years of living off our garden…and the government." Lea's face reddened at her confession.

"It's okay, Lea," said Marie-Ève. "We've all had to accept help one way or another."

"I know. It's just that Nap is so proud. He doesn't want anyone to know."

Marie-Ève placed an arm over her friend's shoulder. "Lea," she said, her voice earnest, "Don't be so hard on yourself. The Depression has been difficult for everyone. *I* think you've done quite well."

Lea nodded. Could it be true they'd succeeded despite everything?

When Lea left Val Marie that day, her heart soared. Perhaps she'd lost Cécile, but now she'd found Marie-Ève, and she knew they'd pick up their friendship where it left off.

One day, Pol ran to the house, a letter in his hand. "Maman!" he shouted. "It's from the Government of Canada!"

Lea abandoned the bread she'd been kneading and raced to meet him. Could it already be the cheque they'd awaited? After all, the government officials had already given their mark of approval, impressed by the work Nap had done. "Let's see." Grabbing the envelope from him, she frowned. "Why has it already been opened?"

"I'm sorry, Maman," Pol said. "I couldn't wait. I had to look."

Lea took the contents out and read it. She let out a whoop.

"What is it?" Lilian jumped up from the floor where she was having a pretend tea party with the younger children. The others turned, their eyes wide with excitement.

"It's the cheque from the government!" She waved it in the air. "Three hundred and fifty dollars!"

"Three hundred and fifty dollars?" repeated Lilian.

358

"Yes!" Lea cried. "Three hundred and fifty dollars!"

The cheque passed from Lilian to Claire, then back to Lea again.

"I wanna see it too," said Denis.

"Okay." Lea held it down to his level until the boy seemed satisfied.

"What are we going to do with all that money?" asked Claire.

"I don't know, but let's surprise Papa tonight."

"Yeah!" said Denis.

When Nap returned that evening from the irrigation project, a beautifully decorated store-bought cake graced the table. "What's the occasion?" he asked. "Another baby? It says Congratulations. Congratulations?" He eyed each one in turn, searching for a clue.

Lilian's finger flew to her lips, a warning for the younger children to keep quiet, but Denis leapt forward.

"We got the money, Papa!" he shouted as he jumped in his father's arms.

"Denis!" cried Lilian.

"What money?" Napoleon asked.

"The three hundred and fifty dollars," said Claire. "It came in the mail!"

"Blabbermouths!" Lilian took the cheque from its spot on the cabinet and handed it to her dad.

Nap's eyes rounded as he read it. He broke into a wide grin.

"So what are we gonna do with it?" asked Lilian.

"I know exactly what we'll do. We'll build the new house, the one I've been promising all these years." He slipped his arm around Lea's waist and kissed her.

"A new house! Yay!" shouted Claire.

"Yay!" The younger children copied her.

The family sat down to dinner, chattering about the details of the new home now that providence had smiled upon them.

"We'll build it in town," said Napoleon, poking a piece of potato with his fork. "That way no one will ever have to miss school again because of the snow."

"But what about the farm?" asked Lea.

Nap laid down his fork and finished chewing before speaking. "I know a fellow who's looking to rent land. He says he'll plant and harvest the wheat. I could offer him two-thirds of the crop in payment and keep a third for us."

"That sounds fair," said Lea.

"And perhaps Pol could help me build the house since he's not too keen on school anymore."

Pol gave a sheepish smile. "Okay."

A few days later, Nap surprised them again when he gathered the children around him and announced, "I bought a lot in town behind the school today."

The family broke into excited chatter.

"But that's not all. I also bought a small house that we'll move to the site. We can live in it while we build the new one."

The kids nearly burst with excitement.

"Pol, how'd you feel about starting the basement tomorrow…instead of going to school?"

"Sure," said Pol, smiling.

Within a week, they'd prepared the small cabin to be moved. Nap and Pol built the formations for the foundation using rocks encased in cement. When they were ready, they transported the temporary dwelling onto the land, moved in, then began planning the rest of the structure. Nap bought a second shack, dismantling it for the lumber. Each day, he and Pol took the wood to the site where they stored it until needed.

When the time came to extend the small house they lived in, Lea set up a tent beside the cabin where they spent the summer months until it was ready.

The new house was the envy of everyone in town. Painted white, it had two front windows, and was decorated with scalloped shingles. Inside, were three bedrooms—one for the girls, one for the boys, and one for Lea and Nap. The living room was large enough to host plenty of company, though it would be difficult to hide Nap's buffalo berry wine from the RCMP now that they were living in Val Marie. But best of all, the kitchen had a pump so they wouldn't need to fetch water from the well.

Lea lovingly painted the walls and stenciled them with images of roses. She made curtains for each of the windows with flour sack fabric—pink and blue blossoms for the girls; cowboys and horses for the boys; and for her own room, men and women dancing beneath umbrellas. But the best part about the new house was the outdoor facilities. At last, she could throw away the hated bucket! What a luxury! Lea felt as though she were back in Belgium. She couldn't wait until Nap built the small barn in the back for King and Queen.

One night, as they sat outside, watching the children play, Napoleon took her hand in his and asked, "Are you happy now, my love?"

"You mean because of the house?" asked Lea. "Of course!"

"No, I mean the rest. I never did fulfill my promise to you," he said. "I promised you a successful farm, and now I've gone and rented it to someone else."

Lea's fingers closed around his. "You haven't broken your promise, mon homme," she said. "We can still see fields of wheat that stretch out as far as the eye can see. And the skies are still splendid. It's just we're not living on the farm anymore. And I'd much rather be here than in Europe with everything that's happening with Hitler."

She thought of the second-hand radio Nap had bought and how they'd listen to the news each night about how Hitler had stolen Austria, torn up the Treaty of Versailles, and redrawn the map of Europe. War was imminent at the hands of such a tyrant.

"And you don't mind if I support the family doing carpentry?"

"Of course not," she said. "You're very good at it, so why not?"

They sat in silence for a time, watching the children. Pol would soon be old enough to join the forces should Canada join the resistance against Hitler. And before long, Lilian would be dating. But the other kids would keep her busy for years to come. Yolande crawled up to her and pulled herself up, her little fingers clutching Lea's dress. Lea bent down and took the little girl in her arms.

Her thoughts traveled to the graveyard in Ponteix where the twins and Roger lay. A familiar hurt tugged at her heart. She'd had difficult times for certain—the solitude, the loss of children, the drought, the grasshoppers, the dust storms, Cécile's death, Claude's suicide. But in the end, she had a great deal to be thankful for—seven healthy children, a house, and a husband. She leaned back and watched the movement in the sky. Tall, blackened clouds promised rain.

"Dark castles of hope in the sky," she whispered.

"What did you say?" asked Napoleon.

"I said everything is perfect as pie." And with that, she reached over and kissed her husband's cheek.

The End

Epilogue

My grandparents, Leopoldine and Napoleon, never returned to farming. Napoleon continued to support the family in his chosen trade, carpentry. Eventually, they moved to Alberta, and then to Chilliwack, British Columbia, where they retired. Though Leopoldine did indeed thrust her head in the coulee in frustration that day, in actual fact, she didn't attempt suicide. Pol never told his father what he had witnessed. Leopoldine was thrilled beyond words when her sister Palma finally immigrated to Canada in 1959. She never saw the rest of her family again.

Dr. Onil Lupien was the first pioneer doctor in Ponteix, Saskatchewan. He worked tirelessly to look after the good people of his town. In 1943, he diagnosed his own throat cancer. During the last three years of his life, he continued to do his hospital rounds wheelchair bound. He died in 1946 and is buried in the Ponteix cemetery.

Pol joined the air force during WWII where he finished high school. He attended medical school at the University of Ottawa. He married Pierrette Joanisse and had four children. They settled in Chilliwack, B.C., where he practiced medicine for almost thirty years. Influenced by the example of Dr. Lupien, he was renowned for his compassion and devotion.

Lilian married Art Ring who ran a successful pig farm in Alberta until their retirement in Chilliwack. They had four children. She now resides in Brooks, Alberta.

Claire studied psychiatric nursing, but abandoned her studies to marry Clarence Hala, as was the fashion those days. They had four children. Suffering most of her life from ill health, Claire died at fifty-one from complications of leukemia. She is sorely missed to this day.

Denis studied geography at UBC. Always lured by the mountains, he never lost his childhood affinity for climbing. He starred in a Calgary documentary about mountaineering, and his photograph appeared in several magazines. He lives in Chilliwack.

George joined the air force and later became a building contractor in the Fraser Valley. He married Beverly Novak and had four children.

Georgette married Ed Evans after living and working on her own in Alberta. They settled in Cache Creek, B.C., where he worked as a carpenter for the school board. They had five children.

Yolande married John Chambers after a brief courtship of two weeks. They owned their own appliance business in Chilliwack. They had four children and are still happily married to this day.

Emma, Palma, and Roger lie buried in the Ponteix cemetery. Carrying the loss of these three children to the grave, Leopoldine and Napoleon were never able to speak of them, their emotions too overwhelming. So moved was I by this story that I traveled to Ponteix to lay roses on their grave.

Other Suzanne de Montigny books published by BWL Publishing:

A Town Bewitched
(winner of the Dante Rossetti Award
for Best Coming of Age Novel)
The Legacy (Shadow of the Unicorn,
Book 1)
The Deception (Shadow of the
Unicorn, Book 2)
The Revenge (Shadow of the Unicorn,
Book 3)—Coming soon

Suzanne de Montigny loved writing stories as a child, creating her first novella at the age of twelve. She has kept it on her shelf between her textbooks and novels all her life. As an adult, she pursued a career in music education, teaching school for twenty years. It was there she discovered she had a knack for storytelling. When her father passed away in 2006, she developed an overpowering urge to begin writing again. She has received awards for her "Shadow of the Unicorn" series and her young teen novel, *A Town Bewitched.*

She lives in Burnaby, B.C. with the four loves of her life, her husband, her two boys, and Buddy the bichon frisé.

Please visit Suzanne's website at:

You can also find her at:

And you can follow her on Twitter at:
https://twitter.com/sfierymountain

And last but not least, here is her blog:
http://suzannesthoughtsfortheday.blogspot.c
a

Bibliography

Amadeo, Kimberly. "Worst Stock Market Crash in U.S. History." *The Balance*. The Balance, 20 Feb. 2016. Web. 21 Feb. 2017. <https://www.thebalance.com/stock-market-crash-of-1929-causes-effects-and-facts-3305891>.

Bailey, Patricia G., Janice Dickin, and Erin James-Abra. "Influenza (Flu)." *The Canadian Encyclopedia*. The Canadian Encyclopedia, 29 Sept. 2009. Web. 13 Oct. 2016. <http://www.thecanadianencyclopedia.ca/en/article/influenza/>.

Berton, Pierre. "Dionne Quintuplets." *The Canadian Encyclopedia*. The Canadian Encyclopedia, 04 Mar. 2013. Web. 03 May 2017. <http://www.thecanadianencyclopedia.ca/en/article/dionne-quintuplets/>.

Brennan, J. William. "Regina." *The Canadian Encyclopedia*. The Canadian Encyclopedia, 23 Sept. 2012. Web. -5 Oct. 2016. <http://www.thecanadianencyclopedia.ca/en/article/regina/>.

Cafasso, Jacquelyn. "Body Lice Infestation." *Healthline*. Healthline Media, 15 Oct. 2015. Web. 15 July 2017. <http://www.healthline.com/health/body-lice>.

Canada, Library And Archives. "Land Grants of Western Canada, 1870-1930." *Library and Archives Canada*. Library and Archives Canada,

25 May 2017. Web. 06 Apr. 2017.
<https://www.bac-
lac.gc.ca/eng/discover/land/land-grants-western-
canada-1870-1930/Pages/land-grants-western-
canada.aspx>.

De Montigny, Joseph Leo Pol. *My Story*. Chilliwack,
B.C.: Published by the Author, 2006. Print.

Dyck, Bruce. "Dirty Thirties: Fact and Myth." *The
Western Producer*. The Western Producer, 28
July 2005. Web. 10 Jan. 2017.
<http://www.producer.com/2005/07/dirty-
thirties-fact-and-myth/>.

English, John R. "R.B. Bennett." *The Canadian
Encyclopedia*. The Canadian Encyclopedia, 21
Feb. 2008. Web. 19 Nov. 2016.
<http://www.thecanadianencyclopedia.ca/en/arti
cle/richard-bedford-viscount-bennett/>.

Foot, Richard. "Battle of Vimy Ridge." *The
Canadian Encyclopedia*. The Canadian
Encyclopedia, 20 July 2006. Web. 15 July 2017.
<http://www.thecanadianencyclopedia.ca/en/arti
cle/vimy-ridge/>.

"How to Pluck a Chicken." *Raising Chickens*.
Raising Chickens, n.d. Web. 09 Aug. 2016.
<http://www.raising-chickens.org/pluck-a-
chicken.html>.

*Images+of+clothing+made+from+flour+sacks+in+
the+1930s - Google Search*. N.p., n.d. Web. 15
July 2017.
<https://www.google.ca/search?q=images%2Bo
f%2Bclothing%2Bmade%2Bfrom%2Bflour%2
Bsacks%2Bin%2Bthe%2B1930s&tbm=isch&tb
o=u&source=univ&sa=X&ved=0ahUKEwjemL

7zqfrTAhUK9GMKHTGUAFsQsAQIMg&biw
=1536&bih=704>.

Kernaghan, Lois. "Halifax Explosion." *The Canadian Encyclopedia*. Ed. Richard Foot. The Canadian Encyclopedia, 13 Jan. 2011. Web. 15 Aug. 2016.
<http://www.thecanadianencyclopedia.ca/en/article/halifax-explosion/>.

Lacoursieìre-Stringer, Rachel. "Dr. J.-Onil Lupien (1884-1946)." *Histoire De Ponteix = History of Ponteix*. Ponteix, Saskatchewan: Ponteix History Committee, 1981. 338-39. Print.

Lupien, Paul. *Doctor Joseph Onil Lupien: A Humanitarian Mission Fully Accomplished*. Quebec City, Q.C.: Published by the Author, n.d. Print.

"Meningitis Symptoms in Babies." *Meningitis Symptoms In Babies*. Meningitis Research Foundation, n.d. Web. 15 July 2017.
<http://www.meningitis.org/symptoms/babies/>.

Morton, Desmond. "First World War (WWI)." *The Canadian Encyclopedia*. Ed. Tabitha Marshall and Richard Foot. The Canadian Encyclopedia, 05 Aug. 2013. Web. 15 July 2017.
<http://www.thecanadianencyclopedia.ca/en/article/first-world-war-wwi/>.

Pertussis (Whooping Cough): Questions and Answers. St. Paul, MN: Immunize.org, n.d. PDF.

Struthers, James. "Great Depression." *The Canadian Encyclopedia*. Ed. Richard Foot. The Canadian Encyclopedia, 11 July 20132. Web. 14 Apr. 2017.

<http://www.thecanadianencyclopedia.ca/en/arti
cle/great-depression/>.
"Village of Val Marie." *Village of Val Marie*. N.p.,
Jan. 2017. Web. 23 Mar. 2017.
<https://valmarie.ca/>.

Manufactured by Amazon.ca
Bolton, ON

38511023R00205